Exit Interview

an a.k.a Jayne novel

Exit Interview

an a.k.a Jayne novel

Dana Cameron

Exit Interview: an a.k.a. Jayne novel

DCLE Publishing LLC

ISBN-13: 978-1-7371536-2-7

Cover Art by Errick Nunnally

Chapter One: Nicole Bradley

Three unlikely things have happened since breakfast, and the uneasy feeling I've had for days suddenly morphs into urgency.

Chase, Mr. Heath's number two, stopped by the good bakery. He usually just picks up coffee and whatever at the joint next door, but when he needs reassurance, he goes to the good bakery, which is fifteen minutes out of his way. I'm not even sure he knows he does that, but he should. We're supposed to pay attention to the little things, and that includes ourselves. Large and blond, his Midwestern Scandinavian heritage written all over his face. If I'd met him on the street, I'd assume he was also a bigot. Corn-fed and confident, a walking billboard for privilege. As it was, he is carefully polite and businesslike around me.

Lee is late, and the boss didn't say anything, because he was late, too. Mr. Heath—and it is always "Mr. Heath" with everyone, from the cleaning staff to senators; if he were married, his spouse would also call him "Mr. Heath"—is never late. He makes it a point of honor, demanding the same of us. He didn't even glare at Lee, didn't even glance up, possibly because Mr. Heath had already changed the meeting time and place twice, but I don't think so. Something's definitely up.

Heath usually has the aura, physique, and bonhomie of a retired football player meeting old friends: silver hair cut short, tanned, blazing blue eyes. Right now, he looks like someone who's in the process of dismantling a bomb. I've seen bombs defused before and...this looks just like it. That he shows how he's feeling is downright alarming.

And then there's the subject of the meeting, the elephant in the room, the thing so obvious that even the noob Whitehead can see it: Mr. Heath has declared the impossible, that one of our own has left the ranks, gone rogue. Even worse, I realize, maybe simply through the emotion he's trying to conceal from his voice, that he's talking about the one I call "Cave Girl," an officer who's loyal to a fault, direct as a missile strike and about as subtle as a drag queen during Mardi Gras. I mean, yes, she's superb at what she does, quiet and lethal, though I never understood her preoccupation with the direct physical assault. It's a matter of differences in philosophy, aesthetics, something that we've disagreed about since training when we got to know each other, and was further emphasized when I moved from fieldwork to the intelligence side of our business. That isn't the thing that's worrying.

It's not even that she, among all of us, even among the ones who are most like her, is so clearly Heath's favorite tool, fire and forget. The really strange thing is that she's adored him, worshiped him for so long. I can't imagine what must be going on that she'd turn on him.

In fact, it's so unlikely, I'm hard-pressed to believe that's what actually happened.

We're given our orders and dismissed. I get the usual surveillance and deep dive into her phone and computer use, but I know that's a laugh, because, well, Cave Girl is happier banging rocks together. While she doesn't entirely mistrust technology, she has a healthy respect for technological hygiene.

That's the funny thing, because when the Department was first established, it was meant to be all tech, all at a distance. Since Heath took over from the late Ms. King, there's more and more wet work, which I find unnecessary and distasteful. I understand the occasional need, of course, but it was always meant to be a last resort. Fewer of our fingerprints, more practical results: you take away the money, gear, maybe drop a few hints, anonymously, at a distance, to your target's foes, and voila. More disorganization in your crime and more disruption to your terror cells; less cost to the taxpayers. It's that elegance that appeals to me.

My unease about Rogers now reassures me: It's there for a reason, even if I don't understand why. And I want to understand, badly.

So because of that improbable morning, I don't hand Mr. Heath the resignation letter I've been pondering for the past three months. Not yet.

Things are just getting interesting again.

Chapter Two: Jayne Rogers

Several weeks earlier...

In an anonymous DC office building, largely abandoned for the night, my boss and I are celebrating. Drinks in his office; his usual two fingers of bourbon; a rare, scant quarter-inch for me. We're marking the end of a job; nothing special. I'd scored a very nice kill on an asshole who was funneling our weapons to the very people he was supposed to be fighting. There was also the fringe benefit of removing a major sex trafficker. Those who sell children deserve a long death, but I believe the shitheel in question knew nearly ten whole minutes of real pain and terror before I sent him to hell.

"Just about flawless, Jayne. Quiet, lots of return on the investment, and a nice, wet edge to follow up with the rebels." Mr. Heath hands me the glass.

"Thanks, sir." I hook the cane on the back of my chair and take the bourbon from him.

"Confusion to the enemy," he says, and we clink. "Good job."

I sit, warm with the praise. I like setting things right. "Confusion to the enemy."

Anyone could see the health, the power, the dedication coming off him in waves. Everything about the man is larger than life—the build of a varsity lineman, pioneer grit, and more brass than a bag of doorknobs—just looking at him, you know he loves the job.

But as soon as I'd walked into the room, I felt something was wrong. Like the headache when a low-pressure front moves in. Oppressive, unsettling. I wait for him to tell me what I need to know.

"Let's see the jaw."

I sip gingerly, then tilt my head up. "Docs said there'd be virtually no scar."

"Better not be. I put in a req for our best plastic surgeon." He nods, satisfied, as if I aced a test. "That was too close."

I nod as well. "I should have gotten out of there faster, but when I saw the car was gone, I had to improvise."

"Jayne, please, I wasn't bad-dogging you. You handled it perfectly, right down to 'borrowing' the police car. I just want you to take care of yourself. We can't afford to lose you, not now, not with our resources so stretched. Not with such big projects on the horizon. That's why I'm moving you."

"Sir?" His change of demeanor is even more shocking than this news. Anyone else would have said he looks as solid and upright as an oak. To me, Heath suddenly looks like death warmed over, a hundred years old, a shell of himself.

"Mr. Heath?" It's not for me to ask, if he's not telling, but I can't help myself. Something's badly wrong.

"Ah, nothing. Old age and cynicism."

It takes me by surprise, this admission. Something serious has taken the wind out of his sails.

I'm not sure what to do. It would have been wrong, somehow, for me to offer sympathy, an arm to lean on. If he isn't telling me, that's his business. He only tells me what I need to know.

"I'm taking you off the Kola case."

"But...*why*?" It's out before I can stop it. I'd been working with Kola for a while now, and I was doing well with him. We speak the same language.

Mr. Heath raises an eyebrow. "You'll leave in two days. You'll find the brief on your phone."

This feels like a demotion. But the job is what is important, and I go where I'm needed.

✳

Two weeks later, Parc La Fontaine in Montreal. It's a lovely place, even after dark, though it's noticeably colder than DC at night. At least it's stopped raining.

But everything is wrong.

Time for a gut check: Why do I know the asset won't be here? After so much careful work, our first official "date" went just fine, and he agreed to another. He was just a quiet guy from Novosibirsk, chatting up the off-shift waitress who happened to know someone who might be able to help with his problems.

How do I know he won't be here in the park? How do I know something else is brewing?

I run over the meeting again. It went well. He was nervous, to be expected, but eager. I was fun, understanding, inspiring confidence, just the sort of girl you'd want to have help you. Textbook casework, actually...

Oh hell.

It's never that easy.

The right thing to do is confirm what's happening and do something about it.

The smart thing is to withdraw to the shadows and wait until I can identify the source of my uneasiness. Don't show myself until I know what's wrong.

I wish I was smarter.

I haven't seen any surveillance since I entered the park. I don't see any now, but I know someone...wrong...is out there. The hairs prickle on the back of my neck, the adrenaline pumps.

I want to run. But I need to know what's going on. I free the knife from my arm sheath, and wait.

He comes from the left, the knife in his left hand. It's definitely not the shy guy who left Russia with a head full of information about loose nukes. He looks like a local, black hair and the three days' growth of a beard, he's built like a fireplug, not much bigger than me...

I step outside him, get the angle on him. I wonder why his bosses, if they knew *I'd* be here, didn't send more men.

It's the same reason I'm not going to scream. I have questions and the Service de Police de la Ville de Montreal will only get in the way.

Too quiet around here for gunfire. It'll look like a mugging if he can manage it.

We tacitly agree to keep it a private party.

He's quick, he knows what he's doing. He's businesslike about it. Professional.

I stumble when I realize: I know him.

Franklin. I've fought him before. Practice, in our gym.

He's a traitor? *Franklin* has turned? I'd always imagined him doing keg stands as a freshman, a jovial goofball exterior hiding a mind like a steel trap—

I'm thinking too much; I move instinctively. Hear his blade slash the air where my head had been.

He sweeps up again. I block the blade with my right arm. I scootch out of the way, sucking in my stomach. At the same time, I try a quick jab to the throat. It lands. He's always been surprised I've got the reach. He's a little slower to get the knife back up.

We're both cut. It's a *knife* fight.

What's going on here? He knows who he's fighting, he knows it's *me*.

I need answers, but to get them, first I need to survive.

I flick the blood on my hand into his eyes. He flinches and I try a tackle while he's going overhand. The tackle works, but he gets a foot behind my knee on his way down.

I'm on top of him now, working to keep him surprised.

We're tangled up, arms over our heads, each hanging onto the other's knife hand. We're pressed so close I can tell he had garlic with dinner, that he needs deodorant. I slam my knee hard into his groin. There's a chance he won't even notice if he's too hyped up.

I'm in luck. He grunts, his grip loosens. My knife is free, but I'm not strong enough to keep his hand caught forever. The fine gravel of the pathway is sticking to our mingled sweat and blood.

I press my advantage. "Why? What—?"

"...fucking traitor..."

"Bullshit."

"Heath doesn't bullshit."

Heath? *Heath* sent him? I'm so shocked, I lose focus.

His hand slips, just a little. I twist free, but lose my knife: too slick. He's recovering. He's stronger than me, and pissed off.

Why is he so angry at me?

He twists, I hang on. Through his teeth, breathing heavy, he says, "I asked for this job. The thought of you, selling us out—"

He's talking to distract me. It's working. Heath—the idea is so absurd, I don't know where to begin.

Focus. It's a struggle to talk and not lose my grip. "You're wrong. What the hell is going on—"

"You've always been the best liar—"

Now *I'm* pissed. Focus.

I can tell from the way he's tensing, I can see it in his eyes: He's going to roll us over. When he's on top, he'll cut my throat.

Change of plans. I'm not going to get to ask any more questions.

I lean forward. It's not enough to reach my blade, but it lets me keep my weight on his side while I reach inside my coat.

Every good waitress has a pen handy.

It glides through Franklin's eyeball, meets resistance, and then slides straight into his brain.

He stops thrashing in a moment. I drag him off the path, but I can't do much to cover it up. I'm exhausted. Time's wasting.

I toss him and find the number of the last caller on his cell. I hit the button, praying it's all a mistake.

"Is it done?"

I hang up. It's Chase's voice on the other end. If it's Chase, it also has to be Heath.

It has to be a mistake, a terrible misunderstanding...

Heath doesn't make mistakes.

My boss wants me out of the way.

Why? And what is he telling people? Whatever it is, it's awful and they believe it. Why do they believe it?

Mr. Heath has sent me to my own execution.

People—*my* people, my family of choice and shared experience—are afraid of me.

I take a deep breath. I'll only live if I can figure this out.

He took me off the Kola job. That was unexpected, sudden.

Has Kola told Heath lies about me? Is he pulling a double-cross of some kind?

I don't think so, but one way or the other, Kola has information. I need to see him, find out what he knows.

Heath may be after him, next.

As soon as I have the thought, I know I believe it.

It's Heath who wants me dead.

God*damn* it.

I have to move.

I want to sit. I'd like to cry. Training takes over. I wipe down the surfaces I've touched. I promise myself whatever I'm feeling now I will turn back on whoever is doing this to me one-hundred-thousandfold.

I get to the pen, and almost take it. It's a nice pen, silver, a present I received from Heath for my "graduation." Instead, I leave it and walk out of the park, trying not to limp.

Heath will understand when he sees the pen. I don't take gifts from traitors.

A few hours later, I reach a gas station near Autoroute 15. While I fill up the car and suck down some calories, I consider running. North and west takes me to the Route Transcanadienne, to safety and anonymity. No one would ever find me. South and east will eventually take me to US Interstate 87, which will lead me toward Washington and certain death.

I pay for the gas and pull out. Heath wants me out of the picture. If I knew the plan, when I unknowingly failed whatever test he set me, would I have gone along with it?

It doesn't matter. He's taken that choice away from me. He's declared war on me.

Now I have another choice. Not revenge, but—I need to know what he's doing. Decide if I need to stop him.

I barely pause as I take the route that will lead to Washington.

Chapter Three: Amy Lindstrom

"Amy." The bartender at Chez Guillaume leaned my way as he arranged his setup. "The guy at the end of the bar has been staring at you for the last hour."

I nodded, thanking him, but I couldn't afford distraction.

My attention was on a willowy woman in her late fifties, with elegantly coiffed white hair and the profile of a matron from the classical period. I was so sure she'd be alone; I'd hoped to speak to her today. With her husband unexpectedly present, my plans had to change.

When the man at the table turned to me, I didn't avert my gaze quickly enough. I cursed as he stood. He was coming over to me. I felt my stomach clench.

Some people may strike you as feline, some as canine. Anton Kola's dead eyes screamed "shark" to me. His round little head with its flap-away ears and garden gnome-quality nose would have been comical on anyone else's shoulders, but there was nothing humorous about him. His suit was expensive and bespoke, belying his early start in organized crime, hopscotching around Europe as opportunities arose, either to make money or take out the competition. The richer he got, the more he'd distanced himself from his old ties, preferring to focus on the arms trade. Much of it was legitimate, and the small percentage that wasn't, was, of course, the most lucrative.

I don't like bullies. I don't like people who profit from the misery of others. I especially don't like Anton Kola. He was responsible for the death of my brother-in-law, Tommy, and my broken leg. I still have nightmares about the car accident. I can still see and smell the wreckage, hear the terrible noises of a dear life ending.

Even if my hatred of him wasn't personal, his wealth keeps shaping the world as his private marketplace for years. His money enables any disgruntled party to acquire the power to destroy their enemies, real or imagined. The more these parties are able to make their influence known, the more governments and law enforcement clamor for military supplies, and Kola is happy to supply them, too.

Anton Kola provides the powers that be with the excuse that armed conflict—at every level of society—is not only necessary, but inevitable. That brute force is the only solution. He creates the problem and the solution, and the distraction that keeps those powers from imagining a different way to be, a different future.

He does it from several inconspicuous office buildings around the world, but more often from his many private estates. Perhaps no one on the street would recognize him, his name, or his power, but I've made myself obvious in investigating him.

I turned, again catching the stare of the bodyguard at the bar. He was glowering now; his boss was supposed to be left undisturbed. But there wasn't much he could do in a public place if they weren't actually going to throw me out.

I straightened and smiled. "Good afternoon, Mr. Kola."

"Ms. Lindstrom."

I saw his evaluation of my inexpensive and rumpled wardrobe and smirked at his distaste. Anything to get him off-balance. Smothering surprise and cold revulsion, I said, "I was wondering if we might have a word. There are some questions about—"

"I do not speak to reporters. I certainly will not speak to you. I've made it patently clear to you—and your family—on other occasions."

The room spun for a moment: He couldn't have just said that? But he did: He meant Tommy. I steeled myself, forcing myself into calm, forcing myself to pay attention to him.

"Now I'm telling you directly: Stop following my wife, my daughter. I will not tolerate this harassment of my family."

"There's no harassment," I said. "I certainly didn't expect to see you to-night. I happen to frequent the same restaurants they do, that's all."

"I doubt that very much. I want to be quite clear. Stay away from my wife, Miss Lindstrom. This is the last warning you'll receive."

"What happens if I'm at Naiad Spa for a sea-salt scrub the same time she is?"

"See to it you're not. It's now your responsibility to ensure you never meet my wife again. It would be too unfortunate if you did."

"You can't possibly be threatening me."

"Of course not. I have no need. But stay away from my wife. I promise you, you'll be happier."

He nodded, glanced at the guy at the bar, and returned to his wife's table. Mrs. Kola's bodyguard continued to stare at me as he reached for a phone, presumably to call the car. As the Kolas departed, I was treated to a profile view of Mrs. Kola. She didn't bother to acknowledge my presence. I might have been a dirty washrag on the bar counter, had Chez Guillaume allowed such things to exist.

I didn't blink as they walked by. The bodyguard wasn't so classy, for all he wore an excellent suit. It should have covered his shoulder holster beautifully, but he made a point of hitching back his jacket so I could see it. I could just make out the faint trace of a port-wine mark on his neck, nearly obscured by his collar.

I winked at him, betting I could make him break training. But Kola's staff, legitimate and less so, were the best. His boss had done all the speaking; there was nothing for him to say, and provocation be damned.

I looked down at the cocktail napkin I'd been toying with; it was wadded up and damp. If I was scared, it meant I was doing my job. I was on the right track.

Shortly after they left, Kola's car driving off reflected in the mirror behind the bar. The bottles largely obscured the image. Perhaps it was the bottles that reminded me suddenly of Grandpa Bolling.

Chapter Four: Jayne Rogers

Driving from Montreal has been a mercy, I realize as I reach the Beltway. Calming and mechanical, it has allowed me to me to act on my own behalf without thinking. But now, I have to plan.

I'm alone now. I need firepower, especially if I can't get support.

I hit a drive-through and caffeinate myself to just shy of hyperactivity. The coffee's burnt, tasteless, but it's high-test. I continue on, happily wary. A little paranoia can't hurt.

The news isn't good as I visit the first three of my hidey-holes outside the capital. I can tell, a mile away, they're being watched. It's either remarkably sloppy work by the Department or they've looped in a few of the other agencies, because they do look like Feds. The bad news is only two of these caches were Departmental; the third was my own private setup.

The fourth is farther out of the way, also my secret. I head out there, fingers crossed, a fallback plan brewing.

I don't see anyone.

I pass the turnoff road, do a wide circuit, check for anything that might suggest a trap.

Nothing.

I pull off the pavement, down the dirt road far enough to be hidden from the outside world. I check for recent tracks. Nothing. I do a three-point turn and park. I want to be heading in the right direction if I have to jam. I get out, unholster, check the gate. The padlock still looks as though it's fused to the gate with rust. No fresh metal, no pick marks.

I leave it and check the woods on either side of the gate. Nothing but deer tracks.

I wait. I listen.

Nothing.

I breathe deeply, smell nothing that shouldn't be out here, and start to walk in. I add very little to the sound of the wind rustling leaves and birdsong. There isn't a trail, really, but I find my way cleanly.

Three hundred feet down is the ruin of a house. Nothing but the cellar and chimney are left, and they're being reclaimed by two hundred years of weeds, tangles of briers, and, recently, a few bold saplings. Easy enough to stumble upon it and break an ankle. I pause, but see no sign anyone's been here. None of my watch snares tripped.

Another fifty paces and I'm there.

I'm drawing down on an old privy, in almost as bad shape as the house, but still standing.

I hear a movement inside. I find a fist-sized rock and throw it, southpaw, against the wall, hard as I can. A squirrel explodes out, rocketing into the underbrush, cussing me out all the way.

If the squirrel was inside, I doubt a human is in there.

Removing the board that looks as though it's keeping the privy safely nailed shut, I open the door, letting my eyes adjust to the gloom. All my banging should have sent any other critters scurrying. I have no desire to run into a black widow or a copperhead. Although I see plenty of bird shit and cobwebs, there's nothing to keep me from my business. Using my knife, I pry up one of the dusty floorboards made to look permanently filthy. Underneath, fitted into a niche so it's almost invisible, are savings against a rainy day in a compact black waterproof box. The box opens without a sound, and I claim my treasure: a pile of cash, a fake passport, virgin credit cards, a couple of burner phones, several boxes of ammo, two magazines, and another SIG Sauer, twin to the one in my hand. I take everything and replace the box and the boards. With luck, I'll live to replace this stash.

I leave as I came, no trace left of my exit. Pulling the car out to the pavement, I use pine boughs to blur my tire tracks on the dirt road. I toss the branch, dust off my hands, and head to the District.

On the way, I stop by Georgetown to check if Kola's left a message. I'm surprised to see a mark on his habitual spot. I pull over and use my phone to check the anonymous IRC we've established to communicate for a message.

He's concerned I've been removed from his case. He no longer trusts Heath and wants to meet me in person, ASAP.

That'll be difficult, but I have a cover that might work.

Chapter Five: Amy Lindstrom

Lindstrom, I tell myself, you're perfectly anonymous in your red-beaded gown. Camouflage in the wilds of Georgetown's social jungle. While I waited in line for valet service, I identified at least two Volvo station wagons I knew were ordinary chassis containing souped-up engines and definitely-not-factory-made bulletproof glass. I occasionally make a specialty of not fading into the woodwork. My Prius, for example, was a novelty among the Mercedes, Bentleys, and Rollers, and discreet town cars that weren't going to be entrusted to the valet service. There was one Rimac One—the ultimate in electric supercar chic—but even the Teslas were another stratosphere away from my poor, dinged up Toyota. But tonight, I needed my car, and I needed to blend in, so I unplugged my phone—squelching Halsey going up to the "Castle"—and crammed it into my too-small evening bag.

I had a tip ready and handed it over to the valet. I never miss a chance to tip; it's good for my job.

I handed my invitation to the assistant at the reception, who checked it against the list. I recognized her, and smiled. She glanced at the list again, double-checking, then smiled back.

On the other side of the most discreet body scanners I'd ever seen, Mrs. Emmaline Bolton was greeting her guests.

"Amy, dear." She left the greeting line, took my hands, and kissed my cheek. "So glad you could join us on such short notice."

"Thank you for having me." I was a little surprised that she hadn't waited for me to come to her.

"How *is* your mother? It's been ages."

Before I could formulate a response—clearly, she'd spoken with my mother recently because *I* was here—she continued. "Please, there's someone who's asked to meet you."

"Oh?"

"Mr. Anton Kola."

"Mrs. Bolton—?" I wanted to see him, badly, but he didn't want to see me—he'd made that clear at Chez Guillaume. How would I explain to my mother that I'd ruined her best friend's dinner by inspiring violence from Kola's bodyguards?

Kola looked up in that moment, and caught my eye. He raised his hand— he wasn't actually gesturing to me, was he?—and then began to cough. His wife put her hand on his arm and smiled reprovingly at him: Was he eating too fast again? That smile was replaced by a look of concern as her husband kept coughing, now clutching at his throat, then his chest. The men around them crowded in.

A shout, followed by the crash of breaking glass. A scuffle broke out. Anton Kola collapsed and left my sight.

Mrs. Bolton stopped, excused herself, and, without missing a beat, turned. Her assistant was already there, giving orders: headset on, cell phones in hand, 911 summoned. Mrs. B. wasn't one of Washington's most successful hostesses for nothing.

I didn't even have time to swear again before I saw something even worse. A flash of familiar red hair in my peripheral vision told me the competition was closer to Kola than me. I wasn't surprised to see Ted Burke, another reporter, closing in on Kola, and it gave me a prickle of irritation. How did he get invited to the event? I sped up instinctively, but with the growing crowd of bodies, I couldn't get any closer than about five feet.

"Mr. Kola!" I called, but it was already too late. The guards closed in around him, and guests were unceremoniously hustled out of the way. I could only watch helplessly as a couple of men in formal wear picked up the prostrate arms dealer and carried him out of the room. His wife, tears streaming down her ashen face, was supported by Mrs. Bolton, and they were followed out of the room by uniformed guards who bristled, barked into their cuffs, and made it all too clear no one was else was getting near Kola.

"Wow. That's not how I expected the evening to go," Burke said, sidling up to me.

"You didn't get anything from Kola?"

"No. I mean, I wasn't convinced I could get him to talk to me, but I had to try, a guy like that, right? And maybe I was lucky." His pale white skin was a little gray under the freckles. "Anton was scarfing down the apps like they were going out of style. He squashed that poor waiter when he fell. I might have been seriously hurt."

I recognized the brand of gallows humor all too familiar to reporters. "Yeah, that would have been tragic." We found our way out to the hall amid the excited buzz of the other guests. The party was officially over, as it usually is once the nominal guest of honor is carted off in an ambulance.

Why had Kola been gesturing to me, especially after our last encounter? We had reason to hate each other, even before that. But this was too much of a coincidence: the Kolas and me at the same party, the very night he died? I wanted to feel relief or satisfaction at his death, but seeing him carried out— drooling, bluish, and undignified—only provoked questions about what his demise might mean to the rest of the world. He was key in so many armed conflicts. Any number of people would have coveted his wealth and connections, not to mention his inventory. Too many coincidences, I thought. Too much out of the ordinary.

"Do you have a mint or something?" I said absently. My mouth tasted of copper, an adrenaline reaction.

"Yeah, uh, somewhere..." He pulled out a little tin and offered me one.

I took it and shrugged, easing the shoulder straps of my gown.

We both said aloud there was no point in waiting around. There'd be no news on what happened for at least an hour or two, and by that time, it would be all over the place, through other official channels. We'd missed our chance, is what we told each other, though both of us knew it was a lie.

"Hey, you want to grab a coffee or something? Maybe a drink? I mean, it's not every day I get to wear a dinner jacket. I don't know about you—maybe you go into the office like that." He smiled.

I snorted. I usually made the bare minimum of "professional" attire at work, and he'd seen me around enough to know it. I glanced at Burke; his jacket fit him well, which must have been a trick—he was tall and it would have been all too easy for an ill-fitting jacket to make his lanky frame look like a scarecrow.

"Can't. Gotta get back to work," I said. He probably wanted to pick my brain about Kola.

"Maybe another time."

"Sure. Gotta run." I found the loo, and once inside, I texted my editor to let him know what was up.

Damn it all.

As I stared into the mirror, I knew there was nothing I could have done differently but it was just such a waste of time and effort. I mean, I don't ever spend $300 on a haircut and style. I don't usually get manicures, and the last time I wore red beaded evening wear was...never. I was so close. I'd just have to find another way, that's all. But now, no one would get near Kola's wife, no one could get near his friends, no one would be able to get within a mile of his doctors. I ticked off the list of possibilities. If there are less than six degrees of separation between you and anyone else on earth, Kola seemed to be more socially remote than most.

I'd been right on the edge of two minutes any other reporter would have given eyeteeth for. And he had to go and choke on a canapé. Suddenly I realized I had another option.

The waiter had been right in the middle of things. Maybe he would be willing to talk about what he saw, if he hadn't been squashed beyond the capacity for speech.

I straightened my shoulders and got down to the work of salvaging the evening.

The crowd had thinned. Those few left were whispering in scandalized tones. Some were worried, some were delighted—new gossip is a valuable commodity in a town where the social currency is information—and some were just wondering where to finish the night, now that they were all dressed up and suddenly free for the evening. I noticed that those who might have the most cause to be concerned about the evening's events were nowhere to be seen.

I moved across the room and people started to notice me in a way they hadn't earlier in the evening.

"Amy, do you know what's happened?" an elderly senator in a tux asked. It was Senator Bowen, who'd been near Kola when he collapsed.

"As soon as I do, you'll see it in the paper," I said, craning to find Jean-Yves. If anyone knew anything, he would. "What have you heard?"

"That Kola had a heart attack and he's been taken to the hospital. I don't know which one. No one knows anything, he just keeled over. Did you—?"

I spotted Jean-Yves by the service entrance. "Nothing. I didn't see a thing," I said as I made a beeline across the floor.

The caterer was surrounded by his staff. "Go, all of you." He waved them away. "Tomorrow, I will see you at the usual hour—non—an hour earlier."

The wait staff left quickly but silently; professional demeanor was especially important when the guest of honor had toppled over.

"Ah, Madame Amy!" He threw his hands up. We air-kissed, once, twice. Then he noticed my dress. "How beautiful you look tonight! Extraordinary! And that color!" He stepped around me, the better to see. "You should dress so every evening. You are perfection itself."

"Merci, Jean-Yves. Tell me what happened. You see everything."

"I saw nothing. Kola, yes, he was off his diet, but tonight, he ate, he enjoyed himself."

I shook my head. "There has to be something else." Mrs. Bolton had arranged top-notch security, and Jean-Yves' own reputation was impeccable. "Who was near him? I couldn't see much through the crowd."

"No, it is a rarity to see him outside his home, very strange."

But that's twice I've seen him, recently, I thought.

He closed his eyes, envisioning the scene. "There was his wife. Always so carefully dressed, so aristocratic, despite coming from industry. There was Senator Bowen, I think. And the software billionaire, Charles Neal. Then our hostess, Mrs. Bolton, joined them. She is why you are here, no? Frankly, I am surprised to see you. So many people, Madame Amy, do not like what you do."

"Mrs. Bolton's a friend of my mother's," I said slowly, "but I was very surprised to get her invitation." When I heard about the dinner, I'd immediately called Mother and begged her to wheedle me an invite. She'd firmly refused, but the invitation had arrived all the same. And yet Mrs. B. had acted as if she hadn't heard from my mother in ages.

Time to change the subject. "What about the waiter?"

"Ah, the little brunette, Marie. The poor thing, ouf, she was nearly crushed when he fell over. She went to the hospital as well."

I tried to reconstruct the scene in my head. "Had she been serving him?"

"Not at that time. She had been circulating, just as I like, very discreet, very courteous, and was going back to get a bottle of wine." Reminded by that, Jean-Yves found an unopened bottle and did what was necessary to pour himself a glass. He offered me a drink as well, and I accepted to keep him company. "He had just stopped her when he collapsed. Her back is probably broken, poor thing. I shudder to think what the insurance will be."

"What hospital did Kola and—what was her name, Marie?—go to?

"I'm sure they took them to GU Medical Center. They would not take him to Walter Reed, would they?"

I smiled. "Jean-Yves, you're superb."

We air-kissed again and I left the shambles of the party behind.

Chapter Six: Nicole Bradley

I'm knocking at Heath's door the moment he opens it.

"Kola's dead." I know this before most people who weren't at the party. In fact, I know he's dead before most who *were* there.

He nods. "Just heard."

I don't know how he knows, but it doesn't matter. "I checked with a source at the hospital; they said it was a heart attack, but..." I shrug. With what's been happening, it's too much of a coincidence. "Who do we have on the scene?"

A short, bark of a laugh. "Jayne Rogers...she was identified there."

He hasn't answered my question. He looks ten years older.

If he'd said his mother had done it, I couldn't have been more shocked. "What? I thought she was in the wind? Why would she come back here? Why would she be anywhere near Kola?"

"I believe she was there to kill him." His last words are just a whisper. He's rocked, and worse, he's showing it. That makes me nervous, a man who prides himself on composure and being rock solid.

"You can't know that." He looks at me and I shrug again. "I know, but I find it highly improbable that she would..." The truth is, it's been a couple of years since I've seen Rogers in person. We are *not* BFFs. "Who wants Kola dead? Who wants what he has?"

"Perhaps she's working for his competitors, other dealers. Maybe she's thinking bigger than her pension."

"What would she do with even a portion of Kola's stockpile? She can't think to take it to the market; she knows we'd be on her in a hot minute."

Either he's collected himself or he's putting up a good front. It was clear that Rogers was a particular pet of his. Well, I say "pet"—she's more like a favorite raptor. There's more of the usual authority in his voice. "The upside is that she's made herself known, and in a most spectacular fashion. This will make it easier to find her now. Let the team know that I'd like to see everyone in ten."

"Of course," I say. I mean, I know his admin has gone home for the day, but just because I work best behind a keyboard doesn't mean it's my job to sub in. And I don't think it's because of my Black skin, at least not this time. At my job, I'm surrounded by a rainbow of white, from mayo to whey. Still, it's just another clue as to how bad this is.

I reach out and let everyone know about the meeting and then spend the next eight minutes thinking furiously. None of this feels right, and while I have no way to prove that something's up, I need to dig in more.

I mean, Rogers is a lunkhead, bordering on a Luddite, but she is loyal to a fault. Or was...

Loyal to a fault. Interesting that expression comes to mind right now. If there was anyone I might have pegged for this kind of move, it's not Rogers. That in itself is telling.

Chapter Seven: Amy Lindstrom

I checked social media, added another alert for "Kola" with "hospital" and "dead," and left a hastily scribbled note with Mrs. Bolton's assistant before I drove to Georgetown University Medical Center. First stop, naturally, was to make inquiries about Kola. No one was answering questions, not even mine. I could ask my questions at the press conference they told me was already scheduled. That meant Kola was dead. I asked about the other person who'd been brought in, the waiter, Marie, and got nothing but blank looks. That lit up my interest. It was a quiet night at the hospital, and the only admittance had been Kola. I thanked the doctors and the nurses, all of whom knew me, and got busy. When I can't find someone, it means they don't want to be found for a reason. And that makes me want to find them all the more. That Pulitzer on my home desk ain't for nothing.

I went back down and around to the area in front of the ambulance bay and found two guys having a cigarette with three nurses. These were my peeps. I put a little extra wiggle into my walk, vamping it up in my outfit, and got a laugh from the nurses. The paramedics also took notice, but they didn't know me as well as the nurses did, and went wide-eyed at my finery.

"Jesus, Amy, I almost didn't recognize you!"

"Nice backyard you got there, Lindstrom! Shake it, baby!"

A shimmying sashay brought me the rest of the way over.

"Thanks, Lainey. And that's officially all the action I'll get tonight." I pulled out a crumpled package of Camels from my bag. "Waste of a good dress."

"I wouldn't say that," one of the paramedics said. He gulped.

"Careful, Jay. She's only wearing it because she's working." The nurses nudged each other and smirked.

"Where do you work?" Jay asked.

"*The Washington Item*," I said.

His eyes lit up. I wasn't a call girl or a nobody. "So you're a journalist?"

"Journalists are what out-of-work newspapermen call themselves. I'm a reporter."

"You know we can't tell you anything," Lainey said abruptly. The other nurses nodded solemnly in agreement. I dug out a cigarette and when I couldn't immediately locate my matches, Kerry lit it for me.

I nodded my thanks. "Yeah, I know. Kola's DOA. There'll be a press conference in an hour." I was guessing, but it was a good guess. SOP.

"We can't tell you anything," Lainey repeated, but she nodded all the same.

"It's okay, I've got a call in; someone else will come in to cover it. I just told the caterer I'd see if I could find out what happened to his waiter, that's all."

"What's he look like?" Jay's partner asked.

"She." I wracked my memory. It had all happened so fast. "White, five-five, brown and brown. Medium build, youngish—mid-twenties, maybe? I can't be sure. I don't remember any makeup, nothing fancy, anyway. I thought she was a guy, at first. Hard to tell, with the monkey suit."

Jay got excited. "That was your girl, Toos. The runner."

The paramedic with a name badge that said "Toussaint" nodded slowly. "Her pulse was racing when we took her out, but by the time we got done with a neurological, it was back down to normal." He frowned as he remembered. "Actually, her BP was really low and I was afraid she was going into shock or something. She said she worked out, that it was normally low. As soon as we pulled into the bay here—" He jerked his head over his shoulder, down toward the ambulance dock. "—she took off. I checked the supplies. She didn't clip anything. But I thought she was taller than five-five." He paused. Toos was good looking and I found myself wishing that he'd take my vitals. "She had a tie-dye T-shirt on, under the serving suit."

"Maybe Phish?" Lainey said. "Maybe an upcycled tee?"

"I thought she had blue eyes," Jay piped up.

Toos snorted. "No, Jay, she had green eyes." He turned to me and gave me this sexy little shrug and half smile. Woof. "A lot of catering places pay under the table," he explained. "Maybe she just wanted to keep a low profile."

I nodded, though Jean-Yves couldn't afford to do anything under the table, not with his visibility. "That's probably it," I said. "Any idea where she headed?"

Toos shook his head. "Sorry, I didn't see. Too busy."

I nodded again. There were lots of places she could have gone once she cleared the bay. "Thanks anyway. I'll just tell Jean-Yves to check the till and look for a new waiter." I ground out the rest of my cigarette. "You guys take it easy."

"Sure will. It's been quiet, tonight, except for this," Lainey said.

I left my card with Toos—just in case he should hear anything more about our girl, I said, though I think Lainey knew better—and winked at Jay, who turned six shades redder than my dress, before I walked out to the street.

I turned left, thinking furiously. Not the parking lot. Her car would be back wherever she'd met Jean-Yves for work. My money was on her heading back toward campus, where there were lots of people, shops, bars. That's where I'd go if I were trying to get lost.

My feet ached. I thought, suck it up, girl. This is hot, this could be what Tommy was hoping you'd find. He went through a lot more and was still stonewalled at every turn. You owe it to him, all the information about Kola he sent your way.

Tommy had conducted research for the UN's Committees on Sanctions. I did my damnedest to get it out in front of the world. He'd been one of my best, one of my only, friends. I liked him too much to dream of sleeping with him. When something about his earnestness and integrity lit sparks with my

Dana Cameron 29

otherwise decidedly un-sparky sister, I was shocked and happy for them. He died just about two years ago, and while my leg has healed, the terrible memories of the crash remained. And I missed him like hell.

Stop whining about your tootsies, Lindstrom. Get it in gear.

But Jean-Yves hadn't said Marie was a student, so I was betting against the dorms. There was no way I could follow her across campus and expect to find her; she had too much of a lead on me. Resigned, I got back in the Prius. I couldn't go home yet, not without narrowing it down, having a look around. A gesture, if nothing else.

I wound my way through the beautifully maintained streets of Georgetown, each house a fashionable jewel costing upwards of five million. Nothing. Then going down Prospect Street, I caught a glimpse of a tie-dyed shirt glowing weirdly under the streetlamps and knew I had my girl. Fate smiled on me: I pulled into a recently vacated parking space. Fate crapped on me: She was going down the Exorcist Stairs, about a hundred shallow, steep stone stairs that led down to M Street. At least I knew which way she was going.

I followed as quickly as I could, all too aware of the echo of my heels on the stairs, the sweat saturating my beautiful dress. I tried to ignore the nagging suspicion I was about to lose her to the restaurants and clubs. When I got to the bottom, out of breath and my hair starting to loosen out of its twist, I saw her enter the bar down the street.

It took a moment to follow; I was drawing more attention now. There was a bouncer at the door and he looked at me askance. But he didn't ask to see my ID, which was disappointing. He smiled when I told him I had a question, and the smile went away when it wasn't about him. Then he recognized me from that infamous picture that went with the article that had made my career, and he perked up a bit. I was completely willing to trade on my identity, and he was more cooperative after that.

Yes, a short, dark, chunky woman in the tie-dye had gone in, just a short time ago—

So far, I thought, not one person has given me the same description of Marie.

—right before the featured DJ started. And yes, since I was only going to stay as long as it took me to find her, I didn't have to pay the cover. The space in the doorway suddenly dwindled; I realized I actually was paying as I squeezed past him, leaving a bead or two behind as souvenirs.

The thumping I'd heard from the speakers outside the bar became a compressive pounding, like CPR, as I entered. All eyes were on the DJ as auto-tuned vocals poured from the speakers, so my red gown didn't attract as much attention as I feared. All eyes save mine—and hers, I realized. I saw my waiter, standing by the bar, a beer clutched in one hand, looking around nervously. It was too dark to take a picture from this distance, and when she saw me, she put the beer down and scuttled with rat-like speed and agility through the crowd toward the restrooms. I followed, shedding more beads and stomping on a few insteps as I tried to follow.

With one final dig of my elbow into the firm and patrician abs of a McDonough MBA, I made it to the bathrooms. There was a line outside of the ladies' room and a chorus of protests followed me as I shoved my way through, but it's amazing what clamping one hand over your mouth, the other against your stomach, and rolling your eyes will do for you in bypassing a line. No luck tonight, though.

There was no such line outside the men's room, and a whole lot less protest as I barged in. There were offers of sex, concert tickets, coke, sex, molly, sex, exam papers, and sex. She wasn't in there either.

That left the fire exit, and no one noticed when I opened the door, tripped the alarm, and was back out in the night air.

The only choice was to follow the alley, reeking with the most foul stench imaginable—layers of piss, rotten eggs, and stale beer vomit—out to the rear of the building.

At the end of the alley, I had two choices, neither good. One was to go back to M Street, but if she'd gone there she was probably lost to me, at least for the moment. The other was to follow the alley that led into a small open construction area behind a defunct and silent restaurant. Someone was building an addition.

Marie was nowhere to be seen. The yard was empty, a temporary site tool shed closed up tightly. There was, however, an open padlock on the door at the back of the new addition to the building.

I reached for it when I felt cold metal on the back of my warm neck.

"Do as I say and you won't get hurt," a voice said, low and serious.

Chapter Eight: Amy Lindstrom

I couldn't tell if it was Marie. In the shadows of the alley, I was in no position to ask questions, not with that gun muzzle warming itself against me. My mouth was dry, my heart pounding.

"Okay." Maybe it was just a mugging—*just* a mugging—I would get through this—

"Give me your bag."

I handed it over, my hand shaking, still not sure who I was dealing with. I wanted to know.

"Put your hands up, take three steps backward, then stop."

"Okay." My pepper spray was in my crammed bag—shame on me for not having it in my hand. I'd have to try something else. I didn't like my odds against a gun, you don't *ever* take them for granted. But I couldn't do *nothing*...

I was taking the second step back when a hand seized my neck and shoved me to the right. I braced to slam against the closed door, but it opened, and I fell down. I hit the floor, landing hard on my side and wrist. The door shut behind me. I rolled over to my back, one foot tangled in my dress, but the other up in the air, ready to launch a kick at the first thing that came near me. Thank God for slit skirts.

It was too dark to see anything. Suddenly, a bright light blinded me, and I was left with a residual picture of what I'd seen in peripheral vision: a basement, cardboard boxes scattered around me. The windows were barred and the cold concrete floor beneath me was gritty with debris. There was a smell of sawdust and machine oil.

Something moved to one side and I kicked. I didn't land it. I heard the sound of metal on metal. The gun was still very close to me.

"Who...who are you?" I said, trying to focus, trying not to shake.

"I ask the questions. Who are *you*?"

"Amy Lindstrom. I work for *The Washington Item*."

"Bush league." The voice was faintly annoyed, maybe female. Hard to tell, but that was the least of my worries. "I mean, who do you *work* for?"

Maybe this would tell me something. "I...I told yo—ow!"

I gasped. A sharp pain tore up my leg. I'd been kicked hard in the side of the knee.

"Don't screw with me, I don't have the time." The voice was soft, calm. "Who do you work for?"

I could barely draw breath, the pain was so intense. Even with my eyes closed, the flashlight was like daylight. I was way beyond even my depth, unable to see, unable to discern what this crazy person wanted. "I d-d-don't know w-w-what you mean!"

Another kick, this time, to my ankle on the same leg. I wasn't sure I'd ever be able to walk again, it hurt so badly.

"Try again," the voice said.

I took a deep breath, then another, trying to calm my stammer. "I'm a rep-reporter for the *Item*, I blog, I do pod-podcasts, I don't work for anyone else!" I was desperate not to be kicked again.

Two brief sentences in something that sounded like Russian followed.

"Huh?" The shock of the first kick resolved into a throbbing ache; tears coursed down my face. This was a nightmare. I had to focus, climb out of the fear and pain.

I tried to take a deep breath. I couldn't control anything but myself, and I was determined to do that. "Look, I don't know what you want, but you m-m-must have me confused with someone else. I don't know what you're s-ss-say-ing, I write for the *Item*. I mean, you can look at today's paper, it has an article with my byline." My notoriety might get me out of this. "And in my bag—"

"Enough. You know what I can do. That's just basic physics and anatomy. You don't want me to do anything clever, right?"

I saw a gleam of metal reflecting light and tried not to imagine what that meant. I took another deep breath and summoned what I could of my skills at negotiation. "I don't want anything but to give you the answers you want. I work for the *Item,* that's all." Another deep breath, not too long a pause. "In-depth projects on international affairs and military big business. I don't know what it is you want, but if you tell me, I will help you."

"I know you—shh!"

The light suddenly went out. The doorway was blocked off; whoever it was had closed the door silently. I heard a scrape of something heavy being dragged. Just as I'd gathered my wits enough to realize this might be a chance to escape, a strong hand clamped over my mouth. Cold metal against my throat. This time it felt sharp.

If I moved, I'd get my throat cut.

Quieter than a gun, I reasoned. I wished I could turn off my brain.

"If you make a noise, you'll die." The words seemed to be spoken inside my head. "If you're quiet, there's a chance we'll both survive. Whatever you think of me right now, the people following me are sixty times worse. And they don't want anything from you."

The implication being I had something she—he? they?—wanted, and that was keeping me alive. I clutched onto that hope, slender as it was.

"Nod once if you understand."

I nodded as slightly as I could, feeling the grip on my mouth tighten even as I did so. Then I heard the faint noise. Someone was upstairs in the abandoned restaurant.

I saw the familiar flash of blue lights through the barred window. Just the thought that help might be so close made me jerk, almost enough to overcome my immobility. Suddenly, I felt the cold of the metal anew. A warm trickle I

Dana Cameron 35

knew wasn't sweat slid down into my cleavage. I willed myself to relax, but the tears continued, tracing the same path as the blood from the nick on my throat.

Voices came from outside. Answering questions the cops put to them, from the cadence of the conversation, but I couldn't hear anything clearly. I kept waiting for something to happen, for the inevitable scuffle, shouts, shots. Someone rattled the back door but it didn't open. My captor tensed up. I concentrated on trying to breathe, trying to take in everything I could. Then I recognized a noise from when my grandfather smoked his cigars—an old-fashioned Zippo lighter snapping open.

Help wasn't coming. Not if everyone outside was sharing smokes.

We waited. At this point, the only thing was fight as hard as I could, to shake loose as many clues from my killer as possible. I wasn't certain how well my fingerprints would show on the surfaces I'd tried to touch, but blood and hair was a different story. Whoever it was would pay for killing me. And if I had my way, she'd hurt, too.

"We're leaving now." The whisper was no more than a breath in my ear.

Hope sprang up inside me as the hand left my mouth. "We" and "leaving" the two most glorious words I'd ever heard.

"You can let me go. I don't even know who you are."

There was a pause, and I could feel my heart pounding, realizing my fate was hanging in the balance.

"We'll see."

Chapter Nine: Nicole Bradley

The office smells of late night. Burnt coffee, take-out grease, sweat. It's just one more reason I prefer to work outside of meatspace; the drab anonymity of this faceless building, constructed hastily, efficiently, and therefore unimaginatively, crushes my soul each time I walk through the door. I understand but don't accept the notion that there should be no distractions in the workspace. While I wear the forgettable suit of so many in DC, I make sure it's well tailored and that the fabric is lovely to the touch. I believe that beauty clears the mind and creates space for the imagination to work. We need more beauty and imagination in the world, but the Department won't be the source of it, alas.

See? The drabness *is* distracting. Back to work.

The new containment procedures are in place, courtesy of the ground teams, and I've activated every possible tracing device around Rogers. This requires thinking beyond the usual thing and getting into the head of the target. My imagination is one of my best assets and I add a few wildcards that might hit lucky. I expect that unless she's completely lost her mind, Rogers is desperate—we're closing in on her—and she may get sloppy and go where she's comfortable. It's not likely, given her record, but overly confident is as bad as overly cautious, especially where she's concerned.

At the meeting, I understand that she's not the only one who's running on nerves.

"Are you sure you wouldn't like me to take our team out?" Chase is getting impatient. He's a solid officer, eager, dedicated, probably trustworthy. "A number of them have made it clear they would like to be in on it, when we get Rogers." He crosses his arms. "For Franklin."

"We'll get her," Heath says. "We're going with the current plan until we have new information."

Chase hesitates. "I just don't like this. So close to..."

He pauses, and I know he's changing his words to conceal something from us. Interesting.

"So close to home," he finishes.

"Can't be helped, son."

Interesting. Heath is practically coddling Chase. To be fair, Chase almost never asks the same question twice and seldom disagrees with Heath. The boy's rattled.

Another call comes in: Amy Lindstrom has been asking questions about Kola. I pull up the reporter's full file. She has some tentative connections with Kola. Her renewed interest now, at his death, bears examination. Even more interesting. She probably didn't kill him, but she certainly had reason enough to want to in her past.

I let Heath know, and he grunts, acknowledging my information. Again, it's as if he already knows what I'm bringing him. "I don't like the presence of a reporter coincident with the reappearance of Jayne Rogers."

"It certainly adds another layer of unwanted scrutiny to a touchy situation, sir," I say. "Is there any chance that Rogers was trying to connect with her?"

The theory's out there, but to his credit, Heath considers it. "I can't see why. Why come back here, if she's going to expose us? I think it's much more a matter of the DC demographics at one of these parties than anything else. But keep an eye on Lindstrom, just the same. She's a curious case. Family's Old Dominion to the bone, but being practical, they married into outsider money before the Civil War."

Automatically everyone looks at me, the only Black person in the room. I keep my face passive; I'm used to it.

"Lindstrom is touchy, about her family's money, about their place in society, about her role as a reporter. So yeah, keep an eye on her."

I nod and return to my desk.

Later that evening, I head home. After the usual checks on my security, I try to quiet my unease cooking dinner. The precision of the kitchen and perfecting a meal is meditation to me. Even after a glass of wine, though, my brain is going a thousand miles an hour and I can't sleep. I know myself well enough to realize that I'm missing something, something I should be paying greater attention to.

Time to start digging.

Chapter Ten: Amy Lindstrom

"We'll see." The words echoed in my ears.

Something pressed against my neck. My hands flew up instinctively.

A quick flick on the knuckles and another hiss in my ear didn't reassure me, but the pressure didn't increase. Then, the noise of ripping fabric. "Knock it off. I'm just wiping off the blood. The cut's already closing."

I sat in the dark, gathering my wits and a scrap of courage: I'd made it this far. Any chance I got to escape wasn't going to last long or look likely. Keep breathing, keep calm...

"Why were you following me?"

Relief flooded through me. It *was* the waiter. "You were near Kola when he collapsed. I was trying to get a statement from him for my next piece. I thought you might have seen something."

The iron grip on the back of my neck tightened and I froze.

"You were looking for Kola—"

"I'm doing a series of articles on his part in the illegal arms trade. I was invited to the dinner by a friend of the family. My family."

"And now Kola's dead. Tell me about that."

I didn't have anything that wasn't public knowledge, which made it easy for me to appear cooperative. "They said he was DOA at the hospital. I don't know what the cause was. They're having the press conference now."

"How'd you do it?"

"How'd I do what? Follow you? I couldn't miss that stupid shirt of yours." Something struck me. "Wait a minute. You wore that on purpose, to...stand out. You wanted to see if anyone was following you. Did you kill him?"

"No." There was a pause, then, "Okay. We're going to leave. Stick close. You try anything, I'll gut you and let you bleed out in the alley."

I shivered in spite of myself. They're just words, Amy, just words so far. Keep looking for that opportunity. You're still alive.

"We're going to walk several blocks, get into a car. With any luck, we'll be safe. Do you understand?"

I nodded. I didn't want to run into whatever was scaring her. I wanted to avoid that so much it was like an ache. I didn't know if she was lying or not, but right now, she was a connection to Kola I couldn't ignore.

Plus, there was the gun. And the knife.

I heard another ripping sound and felt the punctuation of sequins and beads as the cloth ripped along them. The bottom half of my dress was torn away. Before panic could even register, I felt my head snap back and fingers comb through my hair. Hairpins scattered to the floor. Suddenly I was free again.

"Put this on."

A bundle of cloth was pressed into my hands. From the feel of the weave outside and the cool satin inside, it was the caterer's jacket. I shrugged my way into it and felt the lining seam give; my bust and shoulders were a lot broader than hers. The exterior seams held, but the sleeves were ridiculously short. I realized she was disguising us.

"It's not a beauty pageant." Her voice seemed to answer my thoughts. It was briefly muffled. She must be changing, too. "Let's go."

She took my right arm, holding it in such a way that my hand was bent toward the inside of my wrist. Anyone looking at us would think she was hanging on to me, affectionately or drunkenly, but she could have snapped my wrist instantly. I could feel taut muscles in her shoulders and arms. She paused once, to check outside, then fresh air hit me as if I were Lazarus stepping out of his tomb. I hope to never smell that particular combination of dust, construction debris, and rat shit ever again.

We headed out the back of the construction lot, down toward the White-hurst Freeway, as fast as my battered feet could move.

We avoided the lights like cockroaches scurrying under the fridge, but I could tell Marie would have no trouble keeping this pace all night for as long as she needed to. Her legs must have been a good six inches shorter than mine—she really was pretty short—but she found a stride that had me hustling to keep up. To be fair, her feet weren't blistered from running around in heels all night and her legs weren't bruised from some maniac's kicks. That's when I realized the explosive pain was only a memory, my leg and ankle moving just fine. Something to keep in mind. She'd known exactly what she was doing.

Marie, if Jean-Yves had her real name, which I doubted, was what I remembered: eminently forgettable. Shortish, white skin, darkish hair, unremarkable in every way. Though I'd had the impression she was medium to heavyset in build, this was perhaps disguised by the oversized man's sweatshirt she now wore and the messenger bag slung over her shoulder. She was as quiet and quick as a guilty cat and focused like few people I'd ever seen. She held onto my arm, her grip never loosening, but she didn't pay any other attention to me once I'd stopped trying to drag my feet. All her attention was on finding her way, perhaps losing my way, and looking out for anyone who might be following us. Good luck to them, I thought.

We arrived at a parked car, a Tercel that looked like it hadn't seen a car wash since it left the dealer's lot about twenty years ago. "Shit heap" was far too kind a description. Twenty minutes of driving around in circles, doubling back, and retracing our steps brought us to a rundown neighborhood. Here we hustled into an apartment building, pausing only long enough for Marie to unlock the door and close it quietly behind us.

There was a box in the foyer. The return address was a pharmaceutical company. She picked it up and brought it with her.

We climbed two flights of stairs perfumed with boiled cabbage and sickly sweet talcum powder. Marie dropped the package in the doorway of apartment 3C. We entered 3D.

As soon as she shut the door and turned on a light, I skidded to a heap on the floor, shuddering with exhaustion and pain, ready but too afraid to give into my panic entirely. She grabbed a couple of bottles of water from the counter. She tossed one to me; I fumbled catching it. It grazed my fingertips at the last moment then rolled under the sofa. She almost frowned, then went back and got another bottle. It would have been easier for her to just get down and reach under, but such a move would have left her vulnerable to me had I the strength or the wit to attack. I was drained, but still keeping my eyes open for a way to get out of this.

I was also damned curious.

"Not even going to open that box you stole?" Sass, Lindstrom? Sometimes I surprise myself.

"Mrs. Nowacki is seventy-four. She's home and locked up long before dark. She watches *Wheel of Fortune* with her dinner, then a couple of gossip shows, then a repeat of *Wheel* right before she goes to bed at 9:30. She gets her medicines via UPS and they come late around here. She likes me to pick up any packages that come for her. Sometimes I walk her dog when her arthritis kicks up."

Her explanation shocked me. Not so much that she might have been a good neighbor, but the fact she bothered at all. "Oh."

"Drink your water."

I couldn't help myself. I tore open the bottle and began gulping the drink.

"No, no!" This was the first time I'd seen her show any emotion. Interesting. "You're going to throw up if you drink that fast."

"Sorry, I've never done this before."

"Never drunk water?"

"Never been kidnapped."

"Oh." There was the ghost of a smile, or maybe just the impression of movement. "Well, it's not hard. Trust me."

With that, she took the water away from me, pulled a chair over, and sat, observing me as I remained huddled on the floor. It took a minute to work the buckles loose from the first of my wrecked shoes. It felt like heaven to get it off my throbbing, bleeding foot. She took a slow drag off her own water, and the sweat running down my clammy back reminded me of just how thirsty I was. I tried not to watch her drink.

Instead, as I worked on the second shoe, I tried to catalog what she really looked like. Definitely white, with medium brown, shoulder-length hair with split ends that needed trimming. Brown eyes, probably; she looked fatigued in the poor lighting. There were smudges under her eyes. My mother would have said that her thick eyebrows needed some attention, too. Her mouth was wide, with narrow lips. She was small, and with the right clothes, I would have said she was a slender build, but now I knew she was athletically built, well-muscled. She wasn't breathing hard, either. She was in better shape than me, despite my regular time at the gym.

"Who are you?" I asked after a moment. It was as much my reporter's instinct as it was a distraction as I memorized her features. "Who do you work for? Not Jean-Yves."

"No, *you* tell me all about *yourself*. And Kola. Until I'm happy."

"I told you. You can look in the paper there. Page three." Thank God I had an article in the paper. I didn't always, not when I was working on a project.

"'House Debates Use of Military Subcontractors' by Amy Lindstrom, Washington Item Staff Writer.' Impressive. But there's no picture." She took another sip of water and I licked my lips.

I hesitated, then said, "My bag. May I...?"

She reexamined the beaded purse, bulging like a small football. The clasp sprung open as soon as she touched it. "Really pack it in there, don't you?"

It took a couple shakes before she could unwedge everything. Phone, keys, tiny wallet. She examined them all minutely, then put them aside. "Pepper spray? You're more likely to get it in your own face." She set the spray aside, picked up a small matte black tube, and examined it closely.

"It's just a lipstick," I said.

"Expensive." She put the tube down. "What am I looking for?"

"In the wallet. There's an article." I swallowed, this time not from thirst or fear. "It has my picture."

"You carry a picture of yourself around with you?" Faint amusement, as she picked up the creased and blurred piece of newsprint, and carefully unfolded it.

"I carry it for other reasons," I said. It was the article about Tommy's death and his work.

She read the head the article to herself, glanced at me, then refolded it and replaced it in the wallet. She repacked the rest of my stuff, more efficiently than I had. "Huh. Thomas Thornton. Your brother-in-law, right? He was the one at the UN, the one you were in the accident with?"

I swallowed, and tried not to think about the crash. "The Council for Sanctioning. His specialty was studying the movement of illegal arms around the world. He'd pass me things if I could use them, and I'd give him—and his projects—exposure. Name and shame the most flagrant violators, that's all they can do. He'd point me toward some of the bigger offenders and I'd do research, see if there was a reason Washington wasn't going after them. Shine the light on them all."

"And that lead you to Kola? Tell me what you know about him."

"Like I said…" I breathed a little easier with the article put away. "…I wanted to interview him. There've been some curious things going on with his business lately, and I figured—"

"You figured he'd tell you all about it." She nodded. "Of course, one of the most secretive and dangerous men on earth would be likely to tell you everything if you asked him nicely. Try again."

"I never *expected* him to tell me anything," I said. Her sarcasm angered me, like I didn't know how to do my job. "I was going to ask about how his daughter was doing—she just had a baby. A first grandbaby—a grandson—was bound to elicit a response. I figured that would be the first step and then I could look into other things from there."

"What's your interest in him?" She took a sip of water. "I mean, recently."

That was too casual; that was where *she* was interested. Could she have killed him? I hadn't seen anything, I was too far away, but in front of all those people… I needed a minute to think. "Can…may I have some water please?"

She hesitated and then passed the bottle back to me. I restrained myself to drink a little, slowly.

"Thank you."

"You're welcome."

Again, a surprise. I filed it away for later. "I've been following the arms trade for a while, and lately something's going on." I took another small sip.

"Tell me," she said.

I nodded tiredly and abruptly the water was gone. I looked up, confused.

Her face was blank, not warm enough to be called stony. "I wasn't being conversational. Tell me about the 'curious' stuff. Tell me what you know."

I almost cried out with frustration, but took a deep breath. "I wasn't holding out on you. Jesus, don't you ever cut anyone slack?"

"Why would I?"

"Well, you don't have to be such an asshole about it." I sighed heavily. "Okay, you know how these things work, right? That with the right permits, an end-user certificate, you can buy anything from handguns to SCUDs to MANPADS to tanks. And, to the horror of nearly everyone else in the world, selling these things, again with the correct paperwork, is perfectly legal. It's when you start selling them to countries—or individuals—under UN embargo that you're illegal. Mr. X says he's selling a load of timber to a country, but it's tons, literally tons, of rifles. Mr. Y claims he's shipping grain when it's a missile. And because it's illegal, they generally use cryptocurrency, sometimes gold or gems, cash, anything portable and valuable and untraceable. The deals are often made in depths of the dark web, but the real-world smuggling routes are the same ones used for drugs and antiquities. The illicit arms trade is intertwined with these, as well. Thing is, the UN can't do anything about it. They have no jurisdiction, no right to enforce their embargoes. The best that can happen is that Interpol 'red-flags' the most notorious dealers and then governments go after them on other charges."

I took a breath. "These people cause and sustain every war in the world. They supply both sides, and when a country's in ruins, they supply the gangs and warlords who spring up after." I was getting angry, and I caught myself. "But you probably know about this, if you're interested in Kola."

"Don't assume anything about me. You can skip the mechanics, though."

Through the thin walls, a clock chimed the tinny three-quarter hour. No clock towers or church bells nearby... Surely it couldn't be only 8:45? A lot had happened in the past couple of hours.

Talking about what I knew helped. "I've noticed some definite disruptions in the usual patterns. I think something's up. A lot of people who wouldn't ordinarily been seen together are meeting. I've checked with a couple of sources and they've been noticing the same things. No one knows why."

"For example?"

"Fishbourne, Mittlehopf, and Ben-Saiah were all seen arriving in Zurich," I said, naming three of the biggest arms dealers in Europe and North Africa. "And while no one actually saw Toshiyama there, he's not been seen in Tokyo for three days."

Marie nodded, so I could tell she understood the significance of my words. "How do *you* know all this?"

There was no reason for me not to tell her; most of what I knew was available to anyone who cared to look or ask. "Partly, I pay attention to what their wives and mistresses are doing. Their schedules are built around their husbands' plans. I talk to servants, drivers, shop assistants, sometimes the kids' teachers or nannies. I'm pretty good at asking the right questions in the right character— none of them are going to speak to a reporter, of course. Their kids talk a lot at clubs, when everyone's had a few and the boys are showing off how tough they are." I frowned. "It's not impossible. The world they occupy is rarefied, beyond elite, but not impenetrable. It's only…indirect. Has to be. You don't want to annoy your parents if they're so blasé about violence that they arm terrorists."

She nodded, slowly. "Social hacking is one of the easiest forms of getting information. Most low-level hacks are likely to be through the wetware, not software."

"Wetware?"

"Brains. Or meatsacks. People."

Charming. "When unusual things start happening with that crowd, you know something big is up. I was just starting to follow up on it, when I received my invite to the dinner. Kola…he had recently warned me to stay away from him, his wife, but I wanted to see what he looked like, if he was nervous, confident, scared, whatever."

"Back up. How'd you get invited? You said you know Mrs. Bolton?"

"She's been a friend of my mother's since before the Deluge."

"So? Why you, a reporter, at this shindig?"

"I begged Mother to wangle me an invitation, and she refused. Then the invitation showed up anyway, and, well, I wasn't going to ask too many questions. The only thing is, Mrs. Bolton sounded like she hadn't talked to my mother. And she'd said *he'd* asked to meet *me*."

My kidnapper watched me a minute, her head cocked. "So, you saw him. What did you think?"

"I didn't see him for long," I said in a hurry. "I'd just come in, was working my way over when he fell. But he seemed good." I struggled to remember my impression. "Too good. Maybe a little wired."

"And that's why you followed me?"

I nodded. "You were the only one near him who wasn't part of his coterie."

The clock next door chimed the hour; a dog barked for nearly thirty seconds. When it stopped, Marie looked up in consternation. "Come on. We're going."

"What?" Every fiber in my exhausted being protested.

"Move or we both die. Now!"

Chapter Eleven: Jayne Rogers

As soon as I realize someone followed us to the apartment, I pick up Amy Lindstrom's bag and mine and shove her to the window.

"What? Oh, no way!" Amy balks when she sees the window and the fire escape, really digging her heels in. "Oh God, no. There's no way—"

"Out." We have no time. Someone is next door, on to us.

The window slides open easily. I've worked hard to keep it looking like it was painted shut, like everything else in this old building. Amy still isn't moving, so I lay the wrist lock on her and shove her out. She stumbles out onto the flaking metal fire escape and it sways under her weight. She hugs the bricks, goose-fleshed, eyes closed. She's more afraid of heights than she is of me and that makes this hard.

We don't have time.

"Humans shouldn't really be allowed to move around at this height. It isn't natural," she says, her voice going higher. She's clinging to the wall like it's every one of the Avengers.

"Gotta go now," I say.

She doesn't move, can't do anything but moan and hang onto the wall. For her, the height is worse than whatever is chasing us from the room.

There's no time for advanced psychology. I squeeze past her, the ancient fire escape shuddering under the added weight. It's only through supreme self-control she doesn't scream. If her fingers were a little stronger, she'd drill straight into the greasy, sooty brick. I climb around her and lower the ladder. So far, so good. There's no other noise but her hyperventilating and the traffic below.

"Okay, Amy ...Amy?" I speak right into her ear. She's shaking even worse than in the cellar. "You've got to listen to me. We have to leave now. We have only a few minutes, maybe. Keep your eyes closed. I'll get you off this, okay? I'll be with you. I won't let you fall."

"Just...just go. Leave me." She looks like she's gonna puke.

I can't quite suppress a grin. "I'll lose my merit badge if I leave you up here."

"Fuck. Fuck. Fuck, I can't."

"Yes, of course you can."

"Oh, shit. Fuck you. Fucking goddamned fucking freak."

She's melting down. I have to distract her.

"Yep, that's fine, but we've got to move." I swing onto the ladder, which sways under me, but I know precisely how much weight it will bear. "Keep your eyes closed. Step one step to your right. Put your hand out. Little farther. Good, take the rung. Scooch over a little more, good. Other hand. Now step out. Just step sideways onto the rung. Don't think about anything but my voice. Don't open your eyes."

She does as I say, desperate to be off the rickety little platform. The rusty metal flakes away under her bare feet, and she almost slips, bursting into a fresh, cold sweat.

I talk slow, low, reassuring, before she can freeze up. "Good. Think about the world a little differently, okay? Pretend you're at the gym. I know you go to the gym, right? Sure you do, you're in great shape. Pretend you're on the stair-climber. Step down, step down—no, don't stop, keep going! Keep going. It's all just steps, one to another."

"Easy for you."

"Yeah, well, I could do without the view I have. Doesn't that thong drive you up the wall?"

That shocks her so much, we're almost to the bottom of the second floor before she realizes we've been climbing down the whole time.

I do some emotional calculations as we reach the sidewalk. I put my hand on her shoulder to bring her back to the fact we need to keep moving. She sags a little. It's strange how much a little bit of humanity, simple contact, can mean. Then she gets mad. I'm the reason she needs a pat on the back. But her anger works for me, too. I grab her upper arm and we're off.

She steps on something jagged. "Fuck!"

"Not much farther." I point to the Tercel. "Right here." I shove her in. The child locks keep her in the car so I can get into the driver's seat.

"Buckle up," I tell her, as I shut my door.

She glares. I stomp on it.

The outside of the car gives no indication what's under the hood.

I tear around the corner, riding up on a curb.

"Fuck! What the fuck are you trying to do?" she screams. "Why did we leave? Please, just let me out!"

I jerk the wheel and narrowly miss a rat the size of a beagle tearing at a seagull's carcass. "*Wheel of Fortune.*"

"What?"

"The show didn't come on. It was nine o'clock. Mrs. Nowacki didn't turn the TV on."

"Well, did you ever think she might be dead? We could go back and check—"

"The dog stopped barking." I try not to let my anger show at this unnecessary murder.

"What?"

"If she was dead, then she didn't feed Maxie," I say. "That Westie doesn't stop barking until it's fed. The show didn't come on, but the dog stopped barking. They're both dead. Someone was getting ready to drop in on us."

"Jesus Christ."

I take another sudden turn down an alley not meant to be a byway and glance in the rearview. "Crap. They're here."

I hear screeching brakes coming from behind and know it's for us. A black sedan flashes past the far end of the alleyway we've just exited. A motorcycle skids down the alley, following us.

The motorcycle knocks over trash cans but keeps coming. I hear more brakes. A second car is coming down the street. The motorcycle follows so close to the second car the motorcyclist skids, nearly dumps out. Two vehicles right on our tail. At least one more somewhere ahead.

These guys aren't the cops. "Something's wrong."

"No shit!"

This isn't Heath's style. Who made me at the party?

We're heading into the green-lawned suburbs with their compact but pricey homes.

"Who are those people? What did you *do*?"

I concentrate on the road ahead. "I think they're Anton Kola's men."

"Why they would be after us? Kola threatened me, but...oh. They think *you* killed him?"

She's quick, I'll give her that. "We need help. We need to get off the street. And I need to think." I look at her, wondering. I sort through a CD sleeve attached to the back of the visor and slide a disc into the player.

Amy wants to believe the ancient tech is a secret weapon, by the looks of her. She wants me to save us. Then—

"This is a one-way street!"

We *are* traveling the wrong way. "Yep." I almost tell her to keep it down, but...

...but the black car finds us, blocking the road up ahead. The other car and the motorcycle not far behind. There are no side streets. Our options have officially run out.

I'm concentrating harder than before, if that's possible, and speeding up. I hit the play button.

Loud EDM from the nineties pours from the speakers in the back.

Amy's full-on losing it at this point. "What is this?"

"The Prodigy." As if that answers her question. "I work better with music."

I slam on the brakes and turn into the driveway of one of the elegant little houses lining the road. We run out of driveway all too soon and are shortly traversing small parks and smaller backyards. One of them had a built-up terrace.

The Tercel grabs air.

Amy can't close her eyes, so she digs her fingers even deeper into the seat. "Oh, God, oh shit, oh—"

We land, bouncing sharply. The car's suspension is barely up to the job: My teeth clack together, and Amy's head hits the side window. She's holding it together, though, by sheer will, and I make a note that she's tougher than she looks. Raking metallic scrapes and thuds as we clear trash cans and a chain-link fence surrounding a pool. We're so close I smell the chlorine. We mow through a flock of antique plaster flamingos before we reach another street.

I'm trying to draw attention to us. I want us to be around as many people as possible who're armed and legally sworn to uphold the law. Preferably, fans of Amy's writing. Ordinarily, I'd avoid the cops like the plague, but right now, I need their attention. My odds are reasonably good I won't get shot.

The motorcycle hasn't slowed. I have no idea where the cars are and expect them every moment.

The speakers are pounding so hard, the windshield is pumping, and any kidney stones we might have are rapidly dissolving. I open the window. Music blares out into sleepy suburban Arlington.

At last. Sirens began to wail close by. They're for us.

We don't have much time now. "There's something in the glove I want you to get for me," I shout over the music. "Can you do that?"

Amy nods, probably hoping it's a grenade or a nuke.

A shot cracks the rear windshield. I feel safety glass shatter and spray across my neck. Amy screams and tries to cover her head. Not much time, now...

"In the glove compartment is a bottle," I yell over the music, the bullets, Amy's hollering. "I need you to get it out for me. Do it now."

She pulls out a pint of liquor. "Are you crazy? A Molotov cocktail won't stop them! You've only got the one bottle!"

"Take a big swallow," I tell her.

"What!"

"Just drink some. Now."

I turn up the music to eleventy-seven, ear-bleed territory. She does as I ask; she has no other choice. We hit a bump. Amy sloshes cheap rum all over herself.

"Now what?"

She's still hoping there's a plan. And there is. Barely. "Give it to me."

She does, and I take a good swig from the bottle, spilling some on myself.

"Shit! What are you doing? That won't help!"

"Yes, it will." I roll down the window and get ready. Timing is everything now.

"There's no one close enough behind us for you to hit!"

I don't throw the bottle behind us. The motorcycle's there, and now the two sedans are in the street ahead of us.

Another moment and I throw the bottle to the side, hard as I can.

Right into the parking lot of the Cherrydale Police Department.

Chapter Twelve: Nicole Bradley

The Bolton party erupts with new information for me. Of course, I pass everything off to Mr. Heath, but since I don't know *how* we know that Rogers was there, I start a little side project for myself. I don't bring anything to Heath that I can't back up. He's never asked for speculation—not from me, anyway—so I don't offer it.

What I'm most curious about: Why was Rogers there? Who alerted Heath to the fact that she was there? I recognized none of our people at the event, but perhaps Heath had someone on the household staff. And the dinner itself is just...odd. What does Emmaline Bolton have to do with Anton Kola? There's no particular reason an investigative reporter should be there, either, but something about it gets my antennae twitching. I do some background on the reporter and something starts to slide into place. More connections, not terribly distant, start to emerge.

I cast a look at the clothing and jewels of the guests; although I'm naturally curious and critical about how they dress, noticing a new piece of jewelry or a too-often worn gown can also be useful intelligence. To my astonishment, I notice that Amy Lindstrom actually made an effort to get beyond her "I'm a serious reporter and I dress poorly to prove it" attitude. I file that away for later.

"Bradley, what do you have?"

I told him what I'd found from preliminary research: phone calls, food orders, the guest list. I found the way Rogers got in, via the catering gig. "Marie Tremblay" was an old identity of Rogers, and she either assumed that we wouldn't notice or remember, which struck me as odd. Why use a confirmed Department cover? "I'll check out her hire date with the caterers," I told him.

"She's running, so she's getting sloppy." Heath nodded. "The caterer?"

"Impeccable reputation for twenty years, known for their ability to work around private and government security. The owner wouldn't hire anyone he wasn't one hundred percent with, and Emmaline Bolton would never take risks. I doubt that's it."

"Check anyway," he said, as if I hadn't already.

"Certainly. Do you know why she was there, Mr. Heath?"

"Since we believe she was the one who killed Anton Kola, we need to figure out who might have put her up to it. Or worse, whether she has her own reasons. She has too high a clearance for this to be nothing."

Back at my desk, I begin asking myself the questions I wanted to ask Heath.

The last thing Rogers was working on before Montreal was the Kola case. Why one of the most powerful men in the world chooses to abandon that position? I cannot say, other than it's the privilege of wealth and whiteness to believe that your own decisions and wishes are paramount and largely without consequence to you.

I know Kola supplied Heath with a lot of our gear, but it can't just be his retirement causing Heath's distrust of Rogers. He's not the only dealer in town, only the largest, with the most comprehensive stock. Why did Kola suddenly suspect Rogers was untrustworthy? Or had he?

I also want to have a look at the records of the Bureau du coroner in Montreal. While it's always been a courtesy for our Canadian counterparts to alter the report for whatever story we need for the Department, I'm always curious to see what the difference is between the first report and the last "official" report. Context is all.

I cruise around their server and find timed backups of the report. I look at the first one and feel my eyes widen.

Oh, this is interesting. There was no mention of the type of pen she stuck through Franklin's eye in the official report, the one we all read. I recognize the model: I have one myself, somewhere. Heath hands them out after training graduation. Nice, anonymous, handy. You can get them at any stationery store, popular for first communion or high school graduation presents. But Cave Girl, she carried that thing around with her always, a talisman. I used to tease her about it, and she'd blush or tell me to fuck off or whatever, but we knew the truth. She treasured that pen because it had come from Heath.

In any other situation, I wouldn't have thought a Department operative stabbing someone through the eye anything personal or passionate. I mean, it's a case of closest weapon, closest target, isn't it? It speaks volumes to me that she *left* that pen in his eye. Her message to Heath.

Oooooh, she's mad at him.

But why? I need to find out whether she's going off the rails because she's been corrupted or because, perhaps, somehow the Department has.

Something very bad is going on.

Chapter Thirteen: Amy Lindstrom

"Shit! What are you doing?" I screamed again. I was getting good at it, with all this practice. I threw my hands over my head. "Who are they?"

The sirens I'd heard in the distance caught up with us, and the police station was buzzing like a shattered wasps' nest. Squad cars flew across the puddle of rum and glass in the parking lot as if to greet their comrades on the street, whose flashing lights were visible behind us.

Marie slowed. The motorcycle zoomed past us. The sedan across the street did a text-book defensive U-turn and tore out. Its twin pulled out of the side street ahead of us, where it had been waiting, and similarly vanished.

Which just left me, Marie, and a whole world of very unhappy cops. Cops hoping for a quiet evening, but in whose ears the complaints of an outraged constituency were still ringing.

One squad car pulled out in front of us and joined two others forming a roadblock. Marie accelerated.

"Are you crazy?" I dug my hands into the upholstery, still hoping for an open casket at my funeral. "Slow down!"

She slammed on the brakes, throwing me forward before inertia shoved me back. We spun in a graceful series of sliding three-sixties, almost as if we were ice skating, and came to a stop just alongside the line of police cars. Three more pulled up behind us; two were from outside Cherrydale.

Marie said, "Now listen. You can tell the police anything you like, but I don't recommend the truth. You can do that, but you risk the black hats out there—dangerous men by any standard—thinking we're connected. That's something I'd avoid, if I were you. Tell them you don't know me—"

"I haven't the faintest fucking idea who you are!" My voice came out shrilly, beyond hope of control. I reached up to where my head ached and my hand came away bloody. The sight made me catch my breath. "My God, you killed Kola, and now you're going to kill me!"

"—call me Cherie, say that you thought you knew me from college, you were drunk, I offered you a ride home. I was drunker than you were. And, no, I didn't kill Kola."

Like she'd admit it to me. I took another hitching breath, trying to keep from puking. "And what are you going to say?"

"I'm going to tell them the same. Don't worry. They won't be interested in you. They'll just tell you to be a little more careful about your drinking companions." She grinned. If I'd had the strength, I would have hit her, wiped that stupid smile off her face.

The shouts from the cops were growing louder and louder. I worried that bullets would follow.

"What about you? You're just going to leave me?"

"The cops won't worry about me. The others don't know you were with me. I think." She unbuckled her safety belt, tossed me my handbag, and released the child lock on my door. "I believe you're exactly what you say you are. If I learn otherwise, I can always find you."

The cold words stung, after the friendly way she tried to reassure me about the police.

Without another look, without a will-you, nil-you, she opened the door. All the cops went on point. She rolled out of the car, skidding across the pavement as if her feet were on ball bearings, until she fell flat on her face. It was one of the most spectacular drunk acts I'd ever seen, but I didn't watch it long. I got out of the car, as carefully and nonthreateningly as I could, stumbling myself. It was no act; the adrenaline had drained away, leaving me with spaghetti legs and a head almost too heavy to hold up. Every part of me was bruised and aching, and my forehead was bleeding. I raised my hands, and when I was cuffed, the relief was so great I sagged against the officers who held me. Even their shouting was welcome after the noise in the car and the panic, and I was pitifully, shamefully grateful that I was a tall, blonde, white woman in these circumstances.

On the way into the station, I decided it was best to stick with the story Marie—or was it Cherie?—had suggested. I had no idea who was after her, but I wanted as much official and physical distance from the woman as possible. I was acutely aware that there were cell phones filming us as we were hauled in, citizens who'd either been complaining about our ruckus or who were there to pick up errant family or friends. For them, we were nothing more than the best kind of excitement: scandalous happenings that didn't involve them. I hated to think what this was going to lead to if someone recognized me on social media.

I put in a call to Jacob, my editor, but hung up after the fourth ring; there was no point going to his voicemail. And there was no way I was going to call my sister. She'd have to find someone to sit with Lucy and I just couldn't bring myself to impose my work on her again. So I called Ted Burke; there was a good chance he was still awake after the disastrous party, anyway. Then I sat back to cool my heels.

Scary Spice made her call too, and I heard everything she said. I just didn't understand any of it. She identified herself as Cherie and asked for Uncle Frank, telling an abbreviated version of our story, still in drunken tones: "Cops. Crashed the car, sorry. I dunno where we are, where am I? Cherrydale. Fine, fuck you." With that, she slammed the phone so hard it bounced off the hook and swung by the cord. The cops didn't like that and she might have gotten a few egg-sized lumps on the way back to the holding cell, but as soon as she got there, she passed out. I hoped they gave her an even dozen.

I think it was all an act. At one point, she didn't even seem to be breathing. I got scared and tried to wake her, but she just rolled over, snorted, and batted at me, and never got any more conscious than that. I spent the next three hours waiting for Burke, trying to figure out what the hell had just happened to me.

Marie/Cherie woke up before Burke came and didn't say anything, just sat there holding her head and moaning. At one point she rolled over to one side and had the heaves, which got us a lot of space from our not-unreasonably curious cellmates. The cops came for her in a pack, calling out her name: Cherie Deveau. This was strange. Everyone else who'd gotten out before us had just the one escort, a weather-beaten old grouch who looked as though she enjoyed her job. The cops—three guys, brass, all of them—didn't say anything more than her name, but their compressed lips and grim faces made me wonder why she was getting this kind of treatment. At that point Cherie, or whoever she was, dropped the drunk act and left as quickly as possible.

Didn't even say goodbye to me. Didn't even look back.

Bitch.

Ted Burke showed up, finally, looking rumpled, confused, and concerned. He was wearing sweats, his carroty hair was standing up on one side of his head, and by the sleepy, lost look on his face, it was obvious I'd woken him.

Once we were in his car, I said, "Thanks, I'll pay you back."

"Um, you gonna tell me what's going on? Last I heard, you were going back to work."

"I can't."

"What, there's no story here? Look at you!" His voice was hoarse with disbelief.

I looked down. My dress was torn to knee-length, I was wearing a jacket two sizes too small; I was spattered with blood, dripping with sweat, barefoot. There were cuts, bruises, and scrapes yet to be revealed.

"I really can't go into it." I sounded pathetic. I *was* pathetic. Because he was there for me at two in the morning in a suburban police station, I said, "Look, something happened tonight and it was bad. It's not a story, at least, not the one I thought it was, and you'll see for yourself in tomorrow's *Item* that I've got nothing at the moment. Even if I did, it's past the 9:00 p.m. deadline. I'm just hoping if I go to bed as soon as I get home, I'll forget as much of this as possible. I'm doing you a favor by not telling you anything. I'm pretty sure it wouldn't be healthy for either one of us."

Maybe he believed me. He was silent all the way back to Arlington. Only at the curb outside my condo's building, did he ask me again, "Amy, what happened tonight? You...you look like hell."

"Thanks."

"No, I mean...you know what I mean. Are you going to be okay on your own?"

"I always am. Thanks again."

I bolted before he could ask me again and was in the lobby in an instant.

Once out of the elevator, I double and triple-checked the locks and alarm for my condo. I took a shower, leaving my ruined masterpiece of a dress on the floor, and cleaned up my foot. As I glanced at the picture of my grandparents, I wondered if I'd ever learn to keep my nose where it belonged. Then, feeling pleased with how composed I was, I took a Valium and went to bed.

As soon as I closed my eyes, however, I began to see memories of the crash that killed Tommy, felt the panic being trapped in seat, lights, sirens...

I made it to the bathroom just in time to throw up. I brushed my teeth and took another shower, trying to pace my breaths. I waited until I was done shaking, then crawled back into bed.

Chapter Fourteen: Nicole Bradley

I'm sitting in the daily team meeting in Heath's office the day after Kola's murder. No one's happy. The other six team members in front of Heath's desk are frustrated and tired. I think of them as "The Boyz,"and somewhat interchangeable, at least in terms of their personalities and presentation—most in khakis and sports jackets. All are white, save for Lee, and all have the look of ex-high school athletes used to winning, the same macho attitude. All are newer to the Department, brought in since Heath took charge.

Cooper's got buzz cut blond hair and the intense gaze of a zealot. The new guy, Whitehead is young, a pale towhead, painfully eager to prove himself. Nash and Schmidt look enough like each other that they could be related, but they aren't. They have the same curly brown hair and varsity cheerleader smiles in round little faces. She wears glasses and is a foot shorter; Nash has grown a straggly beard for an undercover tech assignment. Lee is the youngest, Chinese-American, and his marksmanship is the envy of us all. Right now, he's wearing a hoodie, jeans, and a messenger bag for his present cover. Morris is the largest and built like a castle wall. He's dressed like an accountant at the moment, and I wonder where they found a suit to fit him.

"I don't need to tell you, Kola's people botched this," Heath says. "It would have been nice to have them do the job for us because they clearly suspected Rogers. But they didn't. Rogers has gone to ground. That's fine. She's one of us, so we know her tricks."

There's some angry muttering at this.

"None of that." Heath stands, and the muttering stops. "I don't want anything less than total respect for Jayne Rogers."

Sullen silence. They're jealous of his respect for her.

"You know what to expect. She's as good as any of you. Anything you can do—hand-to-hand, sniper ops, demolition, counterterrorism, insertion/extraction, intelligence—assume she's better. She's had the training, and she's put it to good use in her previous missions. We'll find her, we'll take care of her. It's our responsibility. We keep it in the family."

Consideration, then nods. They're agreeing because he's the boss, not because they agree or like it. They're out to take her head, every one of them. I find this predictably childish and alarming.

"We'll fix this. And then we'll move on. Okay?"

It's a rhetorical question.

"She may be excellent, she may, for whatever reason, have turned. But apart from that one decision, we know her better than anyone. This is a matter of time and patience."

"Why was she in Montreal?" Lee asks. "How does that connect to us?"

"It doesn't. It's possible that she was meeting with another arms dealer, possibly someone who ordered Kola's death. I sent Franklin to observe and...well, we know the rest."

"Is it possible it's not her?" I ask. Dangerous to stick my neck out now, but I'm on the cusp of a very, very big decision and I need information.

"What do you mean?" Heath asks.

"Are you sure it's not Franklin who's the turncoat? That he wasn't taking her out, so that he could get to Kola, but she ended up killing him? Who benefits from this?"

Heath considers it, but the others bristle. "Why are you such a fan of hers, suddenly, Bradley?" Schmidt asks. She's the only other woman in the room. "You used to hate each other."

"We didn't hate each other. I found her tedious." Again, my voice is almost empty of emotion; it helps conceal the fact that I find them tedious for many of the same reasons. "I'm trying to examine all the angles. Even the unpopular ones," I say. "Unless I'm missing a piece of the puzzle."

"You don't think that Kola's death, with Rogers present, isn't significant?"

"Oh, I do. I want to make sure that she wasn't there to try and protect him, and that she failed. She hasn't checked in because she knows what it looks like."

I see a few glances exchanged here.

"It was Kola himself who let me know he didn't trust her," Heath said, finally. "I pulled her from the case because she'd said a few things that raised red flags for him. And also I've just confirmed that she's killed several other officers, our own people: Alex Segura, Dan Malmon, Errick Nunnally, and Heather MacLeod."

There are gasps all around. I allow myself one, as well.

"So we finish the job, the way we wanted. We find her, we do it quick and clean, just like any other job. Get busy."

Dismissed, we return to our posts—in this case, I'm back at my computer. In addition to my other tasks, the first thing I need to do is confirm that Cave Girl is going off the rails. I still don't like what Heath's telling us and how it comes only a bit at a time. Even with the "need to know" nature of our organization, something doesn't smell right.

I'm searching when the answer comes to me mid-keystroke: He's trying to kill her off. Or he was trying to kill Franklin—no, Rogers herself told me what it was, when she left her beloved pen in Franklin's skull. Heath's lying to us, and if he's lying about offing his operatives...

The betrayal is colossal. A moment after I figure this out, a cannonball of lead and acid conceals in my stomach. Anger feeds off that, and I feel better.

A thought strikes me and it's a bleak kind of irony: Even if I wanted to extricate myself from this and retire, as I'd planned, I couldn't do it now. I'd just be painting a big target on my back. I'm going to have to stay in until I know I can vanish safely.

But I won't do that until I know what's what. I don't like waste, and I need to know that Franklin died for good reason, and why Heath may want us all dead.

I leave for the night. I have a lot of work to do, and bonus homework because, for nearly the first time, I don't believe a single word that Heath is saying.

I pull out one of my burners and text the only person I know I can trust.

"Need to talk," I type.

"My chatroom, tonight."

Chapter Fifteen: Jayne Rogers

I've used my one and only get-out-of-jail-free card. I'm pretty sure I've exhausted whatever good will "Uncle Frank" might have held for me and I don't want to overreach. I find a low-budget tourist hotel and sleep. I wake up far later than usual, with a mad bee in my bonnet. I need information. I need to see Heath.

He's smart enough not to keep regular routes to his usual haunts, including his cover at State, but he's also high enough up to have to keep certain appointments with Langley and, very occasionally, 1600.

It takes a few days, with the precautions I have to take, but I find Heath at the office, no surprise. One of our buildings is in a teeming business park. It's got its own separate exits and entrances, and the parking garage attendants are all our people. Even with my changed look, I don't dare go in there. But I need intel.

Options. A direct approach: Snag someone, get their ID, and go right through the front door. Bold but not unexpected, and they'll have changed the entry codes. I'm bound to be recognized.

I think about the privy in the woods and wonder if the same scenario will work here. With a big enough rock, could I flush all the vermin from the outhouse? Steal a car, park it next door, rig the battery. When it blows and everyone scurries outside, I can either pick off who I need or get in amidst the confusion.

It's not a bad idea, just too big for what I need, and I'm not ready for that yet. I need more information before they get really paranoid and close up tighter than a nun's nasty.

Going in now is a stupid idea. Premature, dangerous, underpowered, possibly motivated by anger.

On the other hand, I'm not known for being stupid, for acting prematurely or angrily. They wouldn't expect that of me, despite the hands-on approach.

I like it.

Carefully disguised with nine-to-fiver clothes and makeup, I wait until I estimate there'll be only a few of my former colleagues in the office, then rig a car battery. Actually, I rig a series of them, at intervals guaranteed to cause chaos and confusion.

Timing has to be exact. In an emergency, everyone has a job and a few will stay behind. I need to sneak in at the moment there'll be the most disturbance, the fewest people, the most information.

Boom.

Three of my former colleagues leave. Morris, in the lead, looks fit to be tied; he always had a short temper and the roid rage physique to go with it. Schmidt is hustling out, a file case tucked under her arm, looking remarkably like any other startled exec. Nash is in charge of investigating the disturbance—I go in the opposite direction from him, slipping in as the civilian denizens of the multistory office building start to panic and cause commotion.

The next battery blows, increasing the chaos. I need to get to work.

A straggler blocks my way. Lee thinks I'm a confused secretary, running the wrong way. Then something clicks for him: I'm not moving like a panicked civilian. Before he can react, I jab him once in the gut and twice in the nose. When his head is back, I step around and slide a headlock on him. I take his passcard as I set him down, unconscious.

The rest of my timing is good. I can't believe my luck as I touch the card to the reader and slip in. This floor, veal pens surrounded by a ring of offices, looks like some kind of Internet company, with logos and trademarks that could mean practically anything. They're doing everything by the drill. Heath's office door is open. I head in there, trying to concentrate through the noise of the fire alarms outside.

The new kid is at Heath's desk, cleaning house. It's Whitehead, someone Chase was bringing along. Chase was always eager to cultivate protégés and develop their loyalty to him. I've always thought of Whitehead as "Pinky," a bland, yellow Lab puppy of a guy, who must have something going on, or he wouldn't be pulled for the Department. I was never able to determine whether he did, or whether it was just blind adoration for Chase that singled him out.

He's quick, for one thing. As soon as he sees me, he shoves most of the striped burn bags into an incinerator that looks like a trashcan, drops the rest of it, and comes at me, drawing.

The gun's not an issue for long. I close in too fast.

Then he recognizes me.

He shoves me away, a new anger in his eyes, and grabs for a paperweight to bash my head in. "Fucking traitor, Rogers!"

"Heath's framing me!" I twist. He brings the paperweight down. It misses me, shatters, and probably hurts his hand badly. He's not feeling it.

"Bullshit!"

"He's lying."

He's too busy trying to break my grip, and break my neck if he can. His violence doesn't surprise me. I feel the same way about betrayal.

We don't have long. The other guys will be back. I can't take him with me. I can't interrogate him in a way that would work. I need to go, now. I let him shove me down onto the desk. When he follows too quickly, I help him continue over the desk. Before he can get up I back roll onto him, then slam his head into the floor until he stops.

He'll have a concussion. I don't kill him. I can't bring myself to do it. Yet. So far, he's only doing his job and he didn't manage to kill me. Leaving him alive might make the others wonder why he's not dead, when they know how easy it would have been for me. I'm not the sentimental type.

I clean house, and I clean the desk. A fat file still in a burn bag. I grab it. Everything else got torched when Pinky saw me.

I stoop and take his wallet, his ID badge, and his phone. Then I jam.

Hours later, I've covered enough ground to ensure I haven't been followed. There are several interesting things though when I hack into Whitehead's phone. He's looking for houses in Delaware, which makes no sense. He's too young to be thinking of moving so far from work.

One lovely thing in the file from the burnbag: a paper copy of Heath's schedule for the month. The schedule is nothing sensitive, but I put it aside, after noting one date, unmarked, is circled. I'll check that later.

Now I need to find Amy Lindstrom again. She's more involved in this than she believes. The other file I rescued from Heath's office has her name on it, and her whole history inside.

Chapter Sixteen: Nicole Bradley

Although Regina Jones took medical retirement after she was shot in the back, she and I stay in touch. We met during training; Rogers was her roommate, and as Gina and I shared an affinity for the technical side of intelligence, we spent hours at our keyboards together. The constant clatter of keyboards and our half-spoken, half-typed conversations drove Rogers crazy, which only made us redouble our efforts—it was fun to watch her fulminate.

Gina agrees that, given Rogers' past and her devotion to Heath, it's highly unlikely that she'd be corrupted by an outside party. We do some preliminary digging, and see a few odd things, too many coincidences, but nothing definitive. There's just no way Rogers could have done everything that Heath's accused her of without leaving a trace.

The one thing that's clear is Heath is lying about who killed his officers. Why would he lie, rather than putting us onto the trail of the real killers?

We agree to keep in touch and investigate further.

The next morning at the office, alarms go off, and no one takes chances that it's a false fire alarm or anything else: We go by the book, securing all of our material, making certain everything is safe. The drills are built into us from the beginning; I don't even stop for my travel tea flask.

I see the rest of the team doing their jobs and I leave by a side entrance. This serves several purposes: It keeps us from being all collected in one spot and spreads the team out so we can see if there's anything suspicious on the outside.

After an hour, the all-clear is sounded, and Chase and Heath go in first to establish that our offices are secure. I spend my time profitably, scrolling through my phone, doing my best to look like any other tuned-out social media addict. It's taking a while, so I stretch my legs, pace a bit in the parking lot. I take the opportunity to share new data I found with Gina.

The sun is warm and feels good. I don't even mind the humidity; I like the way it frizzes hair and makes shirts cling, an extra layer of humanity. Days like this, it's important to focus on humanity.

A shout, then another. Still, we haven't been given the word to return. More time passes, and an ambulance arrives. Two stretchers go in, and they return with Whitehead and Lee, one unconscious, one whispering to Chase. Both have been fucked up.

Someone rang the doorbell, and it was for us.

The ambulance departs, and then a sweep is done to make sure there are no explosives or anything else. Only then are we allowed to come back in.

I've learned a great deal in the parking lot and the news isn't good. Not for Lee and Whitehead, not for Rogers, not for the Department.

Chapter Seventeen: Amy Lindstrom

At 10:04 on a brilliant spring morning, a week after my surreal adventure, I try to organize my life into a semblance of the ordinary and stop looking over my shoulder. Work helped, though I couldn't hand in the piece I wanted about Kola—a heart attack rates the obits, a piece in international, not investigative reporting. I could work it up into another bit on the lax laws of arms dealing and gun control. A few more industrialists would get mad at me, and I'd start investigating where their campaign donations went. I'd stir up more ire on the Hill, but that was okay. I like to keep my life simple. Friends just complicate things.

I slung the chain with my *Item* ID badge behind my back, to keep it out of the way while I cut away the layers of Saran Wrap swaddling my desk in my cube: My colleagues aren't subtle and they're not as funny as they think they are, but I love them. I was still obsessed with Kola. Since his sudden death, the experts—and I was close to being one—worried that a free-for-all grab for power would erupt. Kola's son—and heir apparent—had died last year. Kola's lieutenants had been too carefully divided and managed to conspire while he himself was alive. But what kept them apart now?

It was strangely quiet. Someone should've made a bid to take over from the inside of his empire. Or outside it. Something unexpected was going on. That scared me badly. The people who deal at Kola's elite level are nigh on as powerful as governmental entities—gross national product, standing army, and all. No one likes uncertainty with them. The whole question of the government's right to wage violence is tricky enough as it is.

Worse, my encounter with "Marie-Cherie" still ate at me. The story I could verify was useless. I nosed around, but there wasn't much to be had. There was nothing to the name Marie Tremblay, either. When I called Jean-Yves, he had several good references, each with a different home address for her, and a Social Security number—fake, as it turned out—and nothing else.

Checking with the Cherrydale cops, there was nothing. Less than nothing. There was no record of *either* of us. The guy who booked me seven days ago looked me right in the eye and said there had been no such incident, and he didn't recognize me, and why was I causing trouble? It wasn't in the computer, so it never happened. I double-checked with the reporter who handled the police blotter for the suburbs. Nothing. If it hadn't been for the ruined dress, I might have begun to question my sanity.

I realized Not-Marie was right. There was no one after me, no noise about the goons in the cars and the bike. Kola's autopsy concluded a not-unexpected heart attack. That left me with nothing...no, less than nothing. I had used up valuable time, spent too much money on an upgraded alarm system, and lost too much sleep over something I couldn't do anything about, all of which infuriated me. As one of the most connected people in a town that judges status by access and contact lists, I shouldn't have run into so many dead ends.

I peeled off the last layer of plastic and checked to make sure there was no other vandalism to my desk while my computer came on. I wadded up the plastic wrap and threw it into the wastebasket. It missed and fell at the feet of my editor, Jacob.

He raised an eyebrow.

I tried to explain, but he held a hand up to his ear. The noise in the newsroom was, as usual, overwhelming. Phones with a variety of ringtones singing or bleeping, keyboards clattering, people shouting. It was no place for either the faint of heart or a quiet conversation. There were no walls—and no doors—to help with the racket.

"I said, it's a joke." I'd complained about people taking things off my desk and not returning them. So someone wrapped my desk and everything on it in plastic. There was a little note: "Sealed and sanitized for your protection."

Other little notes abounded, Post-its declaring "Amy's stapler," "Amy's keyboard," "Amy's Purell—DO NOT TOUCH!" Perhaps my colleagues were suggesting I was territorial or unwilling to share. I was glad to see they hadn't touched my pictures of my family; there'd be a pile of dead reporters littering the *Item's* storied corridors if they had. I set the one of Lucy with my sister Maryelizabeth back where it belonged, and realized I owed them a call.

"If you came in more often, Amy, you wouldn't have this problem." Jacob, my editor, had the uncanny ability to appear as if out of nowhere.

"I come in almost every day. I'm not going to let anyone out there steal a march on me."

Jacob turned toward the center of the room. "They won't steal anything because they're too busy fucking around with practical jokes!"

His voice carried over the din of the newsroom, which quieted momentarily. There were a few nervous giggles, then the cacophony resumed at full volume.

"So." He turned back to me. "How's the profile on Senator Bowen coming?"

"It's coming. I have a few more things to check." There were always a few more things to check. I'd spent time looking up the people around Kola when he'd died and Senator Bowen was the biggest name nearby. I'd dug deep on the senator for the interview that had never gone to print. But my gut told me he had connections to Kola but nothing to do with his death.

"But it will be ready for Monday?"

I nodded.

"Make sure I have it well before. I know your love affair with adjectives."

"Cannibal. Don't chop my closing paragraph."

"Don't go over length. And make sure you go over the schedule for the vlogs and podcasts."

I made a face. "I'm not one of those cable-news Barbie dolls."

Jacob's disapproving frown deepened. "Get the schedule done tomorrow. And wear something decent for the camera." He glanced with distaste at the creased dress jacket I kept handy for trips to the Hill. It was under a pile of files.

I nodded. "Yes, Boss."

He opened his mouth to tell me not to call him "Boss" when help arrived in the form of Michelle, his assistant. "What?"

"Meeting, Jacob. Time to go."

"Okay." He turned to me. "Get it done."

He strode off toward his office. Michelle lingered.

"God, that looks so great with your hair," I said.

She picked up the end of the scarf I'd given her last Christmas. "It's my favorite. It goes with everything." She dropped it again. "You should try some of your color sense on yourself, sometime. Not every reporter needs to look like a schlub."

"Course we do. How else would you take us seriously?"

"Michelle!" Jacob's voice cut across the din of the newsroom.

"Oops. Gotta run. Later." She smiled, waved her fingers, and hustled off.

I followed up on my queries from the Bowen interview, but I kept coming back to the night Kola died, and Probably-Not-Marie, the not-a-cater-waiter psycho who'd landed me in jail that night. I would be looking over my shoulder for a good long time until I knew more about her.

Finally, reluctantly, I dropped a line to George No-Last-Name, a supreme paranoid who was the digital clearing house for every conspiracy going. George had contacted me at the *Item* on numerous occasions, each time promising to blow the lid off some horrific government secret. I deleted his first few emails as soon as I saw them, chalking him up to just one more crank conspiracy theorist. But he kept sending them, and I'd finally read them for the laugh value. Among other things, he's sent me "information" about how the latest version of the flu vaccine contained nanobot surveillance devices, China's attempts to foster global communism via messages hidden in online menus, and the alien infiltration of Reddit boards. Crazy as some of his ideas were, every so often he'd get me looking at a connection I hadn't considered before. Once or twice, I'd reached out to him and he gave me usable information.

We'd never met in person. We communicated through a changing, nearly untraceable set of web sites. Creepily, he'd somehow dropped a security key-fob into my shopping bag last year. It had a random number generator, along with instructions on how to use it.

I decided to ask him about Marie Tremblay and Cherie Deveau. I also inquired about the latest chatter, without mentioning my involvement. Perhaps something would match with Kola.

Right after my night of adventure with "Marie," I wrote down every scrap of information I could remember and put it into my safe deposit box. I mailed a note and a key to my lawyer, telling him if I should disappear or be suddenly, messily dead, to tell my editor about the letter and flash drive in the box. I also left a note and key for Jacob in a fake file in case he had some reason to be worried. I wasn't going to leave a cold trail if I could help it.

Then I made a bunch of donations to my favorite local causes. I don't go to church, not as often as my mother would like anyway, but I do believe in acknowledging I have more than most people. My problems aren't about food on the table or a roof over my head. It's my way of saying to the universe: "Here I am, and I'm feeling scared/pleased/penitent/grateful/bored/selfish, but most of my issues are deal-able, and thank you for that."

I picked a number and divided it up. Since this time I escaped with my life from a very hairy situation, the amount of the donation was large. The donations, as usual, were anonymous. It saves the charities paper on solicitation letters, and I don't necessarily want my reporter's objectivity called into question by leaving a trail to me from my various lefty, feminist-y, liberal causes. My mother says I should get a thank-you note at least. My brothers point out I'm losing gigabucks on tax deductions, so I don't talk to them about it anymore.

I called my sister instead. "Hey, Maryelizabeth."

"Hey, Ames. What's up?"

"Nothing. I just wanted to make sure we were all set for the you-know-what end of next month."

"Lucy's in school—make that dance lessons—now. I have to pick her up shortly. You may speak freely about birthday presents and overly extravagant aunts."

"You're still going to let me give her the computer? I've already got it picked out: awesome screen, latest model, everything."

"For the six-hundredth time, yes."

"And I know you'll monitor her emails and texts and everything—that's only being safe. But I'm so excited about giving Lucy her very first new computer."

"It's the day every nine-year-old girl dreams of. Her uncles are only getting her ballet shoes and ballet bags and ballet tickets..."

"Well, this is an aunt present. So it has to be different and special." I bit my lip. "I've downloaded videos of the American Ballet Theater, though. Just to cover the bases."

"Ames, enough! This kid will be spoiled rotten!"

"And?"

"And." I practically could hear M'e smiling over the phone. "She's looking forward to seeing you at the party. By the way, call Mom. She wants to drive down with you."

"And interrogate me about my love life."

"Make something up. I've done my part to distract her. I've just about decided to go back to work next year."

A lump formed in my throat. Maryelizabeth had left her law firm on indefinite leave when Tommy was killed. "I think that's great. If you're ready."

"I think so."

"And are you going to start dating soon?"

"Amy, one thing at a time."

"I'm sorry. It's just..."

"It's just you're a reporter. Like Mom says, if you just don't ask that one extra question, you'll be much happier."

"Happier, perhaps, but not as reporter-y."

She had to run and fetch my niece, so we said goodbye.

My phone rang, almost as soon as I hung up. No one there. George might be getting back to me, so I pulled out the fob and found the code to access the website. There was a message. Sometimes the oracle got right back to me, sometimes he didn't bother answering.

George apparently was feeling chipper today. "MT probably a cover ID. Nothing there. Chatter suggests short-range travel planning on or near May 7. No details."

Great. Neither "Marie Tremblay" nor "Cherie Deveau" existed, and someone secret was going somewhere else secret in a week. I thanked George, but this wasn't much of anything. I spent the rest of the afternoon trying to find a correlation between May 7, the Kola case, the congressional calendar, and the Pentagon's scheduled news conferences. No luck.

I left the office at five. I'd work at home half the night anyway. A thousand niggling little things were on my mind—my deadline, the details for a potential story, whether there were leftovers for dinner—as I headed back to my condo with my dry cleaning. It felt good to be away from the teeming, steaming Metro stop, and walk down the quiet streets that led to my place just a ten-minute walk from the Ballston station.

I was almost to the stairs when a familiar voice stopped me.

"Amy!" called a woman, perky and upbeat as any breakfast TV blonde. "Amy, wait up!"

I turned, and it was in fact a petite blonde, in business casual: a polo shirt and neat tan trousers. Did I know her from work, college, the Hill, family? Did I know her from behind a counter, from the bank...? "I'm sorry, do I—?"

Then she was on me, and too late, I recognized her. I didn't even have time to yell. She said, "Hey, there!" and grabbed me under the arm, hustling me right into North Taylor Street, heading for the green space there. A car honked at us, and she yelled "Oh, grow up, honey!" She was laughing, like the two of us just heard good news.

I didn't have time to think, to execute any of the plans I'd cobbled up in case of just this sort of emergency. "Look, whatever you want, I haven't told anyone about you—"

"Here's a bench," she called, leading me, stumbling along. It was my favorite bench, backed onto the corner under the wisteria arbor with a great view of everything around, including the tangle of grasses, shrubs, and flowers below the opposite condo building. She sat me down hard, and before I could draw breath, she had the damn gun out and said in her other voice, "Remember me?

"Oh, hell—I swear, I never said—"

"Okay, you recognize me. And I'm glad you didn't say anything; that's good for me and for you. We can take all the usual warnings as read. I need some help."

I shivered. "I'll give you the number of my housekeeping service."

"No, you're the only one who can help me."

"No, I'm serious. Why don't you just call in the Marines? You're government, right? That's the only way you could have waltzed out of the police station like you did. There was so much nothing in the news about the disturbance you caused it was like looking into a black hole. There was so much nothing, it had to be something *big,* and I don't want to be sucked in." At least not without a story and a way back out, I thought.

"That should tell you exactly what kind of trouble I'm in," she said. "And there are more lives on the line, too."

She was in trouble? Still? Oh hell. I didn't like the way this was going. Even if I didn't believe her—and why should I?—this didn't bode well. I needed to get away from here, as fast as possible, curiosity be damned.

I shifted away as far as I dared, as far as I could, from that iron grasp on my arm.

She jabbed me with the gun, invisible to any viewer but me. "Stop fidgeting." She took a deep breath, looked like she was going to change her mind, then said: "I think you have information I can use to prevent Kola's empire from falling into the wrong hands."

Was *she* after the empire Kola had left unattended with his death? The thought of her with the arsenal he'd amassed was enough to make me shiver on an eighty-five degree day.

"Pay attention. My boss tried to have me killed. I don't know why, but Kola told me he'd recently come suspicious of Heath. Which is all kinds of problematic."

"Why should I believe you? You'll have to come up with something better than a gun, this time, to really convince me. How do I know that your accomplice isn't burgling my place right now?" I was babbling, trying to distract her while piecing the story together.

Maybe-Marie exhaled through her nose impatiently. "Why would I need to distract you if all I wanted to do was break in? You don't have anything I'm interested in stealing, anyway."

Before I could reply, my phone rang.

I jumped and Marie took my phone before I could reach it. I felt the gun in my side again. She checked the caller ID and asked, "Whose extension is this at the *Item*?"

"Michelle, my boss's assistant."

A slight nod there; she already knew that.

I swore under my breath. "She'll want to know why I haven't called in for a late phone meeting," I said, trying to decide whether I should sound panicky or calm. I knew what I was going to do. Maybe Marie was telling the truth, maybe she was spinning a yarn. I was going to listen, but there was no way I was going to take that chance without precautions.

"Okay, take it, tell her you can't make it, tell her to reschedule."

"I can't, I—"

She handed the phone back to me. "Do it. Keep your voice calm. I'm listening."

I swallowed. "Hey, Michelle."

"Amy, where are you?"

"I'm running really late. I was running errands and my car crapped out. I'm waiting for the tow. I was just going to call you."

"What do you want to do about the meeting? Jacob's going to be mad..."

"Yeah, I know, but he'll live. I'm not about to do this on a cell by the side of Route 66."

Blonde Marie nodded slowly. This was okay.

"You know," Michelle said slowly, "Jacob's told you not to miss any more meetings."

Good. She understood something was wrong. Jacob was always joking about trying to keep me out of meetings, said I provoked everyone. "Yeah, well, he's gonna have to accept that it's not gonna happen." I took a deep breath. "Michelle, go to my office. Get the Townsend file out of the cabinet and give it to Wendell. Then he'll have all the information I have, and he and Jacob can fake the meeting without me, okay?"

I could hear Michelle writing things down. "Okay, I'll make sure he gets it. Thanks, Amy, good luck...with the car."

"Thanks, I'm fine. I can see the tow truck now. Gotta go."

I disconnected, hoping Michelle and Jacob would move fast. There was no "Wendell." And the Townsend file was a 9-1-1 code, a signal I was in trouble. Michelle and Jacob would know to look in the file to see what I was working on. They could use that to alert the authorities and save my bacon. Or find my body, and those responsible for killing me.

My job now was to drag my feet as long as I could and leave as much of a trail as possible.

I didn't even get a chance. Marie jerked me up by the arm and said, "Move! That little stunt has limited our start time."

"Huh? What stunt—" But my heart sank.

"Bag."

I handed her my backpack. She took the card out of my phone, snapped it in half, and dropped it to the ground.

"Hey!"

"I'm betting the Townsend file is bogus. Kind of people you interview— and piss off—I'm assuming there were other precautions you put into place as well."

I'd put a hardcopy description of my work on Kola and the events of the night of the party, including my incarceration with Marie Tremblay, into a file. I'd also left one of the keys to my safe deposit box there.

She hustled me toward a navy blue Ford sedan in need of a wash. "Kola is dead, and while there should be a fight over who gets his arsenals and contacts, there isn't one. That's strange, and we're going to find out why."

Chapter Eighteen: Nicole Bradley

Heath observes the state of the office suite as he enters for the post-alarm investigation. The attack had been a quick job, no messing about. Two men down, and the rest of the team are fuming. Only after he and Chase have had a chance to survey the office does he let us clean up.

Whitehead got most of the sensitive material under wraps. The file on the reporter is from the library and can be reproduced. The last file is of minimal importance, designed to be a mnemonic, useless in the hands of someone who doesn't know the entire story, he reassures us.

He hears the men grumbling again, threats promised if—when—they find Rogers.

He holds up a hand. "Knock it off."

"I'm supposed to ignore what that bitch has done? To all of us? Whitehead and Lee are both in the hospital—!" Schmidt was almost purple with rage.

"They're not dead, though," I point out. "She could have killed them, easily. Why didn't she?"

"If she's gone bad, it's on us," Heath says, ignoring my question. "We were her nearest and dearest, and we should have seen it before she turned. We're *trained* to see this kind of weakness. We all failed. We failed *her*."

They don't like it, but he's given them something to think about.

When the place is restored to order and after I carefully sweep for electronic surveillance, we resume our work.

"Nothing is changed," Heath continued. We go ahead with our work, which is locating Kola's notebook computer. In my Department dealings with him, I saw it—a flashy thing, covered in diamonds—and it contains all of the information about his business: inventories, contacts, depots, bank accounts. I'm willing to bet Rogers is after it, too. All that's required, given this situation, is renewed and heightened vigilance, so we can neutralize Rogers. We go to her usual haunts, we think like her. Statistics say she'll show up nearby, eventually. We've already started stakeouts on the most likely places. Now we work and wait. It's basic stuff, people. Any of you going to tell me you can't do *that*?"

No one moves.

"We keep an eye on Amy Lindstrom, who may be her next contact. Nothing more—we don't go near that reporter, yet. We're on plan. Any questions?"

There were none.

"Dismissed."

They all leave, but Heath signals for Chase to come into his office and shut the door.

I get to work on my assignment and check the security cameras in the building, and then in the surrounding structures, trying to get a bead on which way Rogers went.

But Rogers knows this is procedure, and so this won't be the way to find her.

"Found her!" It's Schmidt. We've gone out for beers a couple of times. Figured out we have nothing in common but work. Too bad.

"Who, Rogers?" I say.

"Yeah, with Lindstrom. Looks like she swooped in and grabbed her, ducked into a park. Then to a car."

"Got the tags?"

Schmidt looks at me as if I'm stupid. "Yep, and we got a direction. The retrieval team is already on the way."

We do the thing with the cameras on the street signs, ATMs, doorbell cameras, and cellphones, getting a good guess at Roger's probable location.

"Well, all right then! We needed some good news," I say. "Good job."

I close down, pack up, then leave on a pretext. I follow the others, even if that isn't my brief. They're gonna need all the help they can get.

Chapter Nineteen: Amy Lindstrom

Maybe-Marie, having hustled me into the car, was silent as she drove through the District, navigating, circling and doubling back at intervals until she was convinced we weren't being followed. I had no idea what Michelle would make of the Townsend file and my instructions there. Would she be able to get to my safe deposit box this time on—oh, shit—Friday night? Marie—I knew it was probably a pseudonym, but I had nothing else to go by—had done some very careful planning. I began to wonder how often she might have pulled this kind of stunt.

"You try to jump out, I won't follow you," she said. "I'll go straight to Lucy's school, and we'll pick up your sister on our way to someplace you'll never find."

She had the gun on me. I didn't think I could bail...I felt too numb...so I devoted myself to memorizing everything I could about her. She'd given me a lot to think about, too. Much of her story didn't make sense, but she certainly believed it.

Several hours later, we were so far beyond any place I was familiar with that I gave up trying to figure out where we were. The last sign I'd seen was for Fredericksburg, but we'd left 95 a long way back. There were lots of trees and while I couldn't actually see a river, I sensed one was nearby—not a bad guess, in Virginia. Maybe West Virginia. All I knew was we were heading roughly south and west.

"The point of this kidnapping...?" I said. I was tired of worrying about being found by the wrong people and not being found by the right ones.

"Oh, no, this isn't kidnapping so much as...a protective extraction with a noncompliant subject."

Like that made a difference.

"Seriously," she said. "I needed to get you out of the city ASAP. You're in danger because of what you know. I think you have some connection to Kola that'll help me. I need to compare it with what he told me just before he succumbed to the poison."

"He didn't die from a heart attack?" I said, remembering the autopsy.

"The poison brought it on. Some folks think I did it. I didn't."

I tried to keep my voice casual, watching the trees whiz by. First things first. "Who's after us? Who's your boss?"

"As for who is after us, my former employer is an anonymous part of the United States government. Things got...weird and complicated last week, and I'm still trying to figure that out. There's whoever the *Item* sends looking for you, and that'll probably involve even more feds, some of whom don't know about that other, more discreet branch. None of them would have any compunction about shooting me first and asking questions later." She paused. "It's going to be kind of a circus for a while. We're in this together, so you'd best get used to the idea."

She said it so breezily that it might have been agreeing to a blind double date rather than international intrigue with an increasingly high probability of me ending up dead. "So, why don't you start, then?" I crossed my arms. "You said discreet. Tell me about your boss."

She said nothing. If her face hadn't been so perfectly blank, I would have thought she was uncomfortable. Then she startled, peering at me. "Why aren't you fidgeting?"

"What?"

"I thought you smoked. Did you quit? You should be going up the walls by now."

"No, I don't...I never smoked. I just..."

"Just have cigarettes to get people to talk to you." She nodded, satisfied. "They smoke, you smoke, they relate and open up. Nice technique. I've used it myself."

There was no way this was going to be easy: Not only was she not used to giving information out, she was pretty good at reading other people's intentions. Here I was, trying to elicit from someone trained in elicitation. Worse, someone schooled in maintaining secrecy at all costs.

I chose my words carefully. Trying to warm her up, getting her used to answering questions, was time-honored interviewing technique. "When did you become an...agent?"

"Agents are who we recruit," she said automatically. "I'm an officer. An operative."

Good, she was correcting me. If she hadn't, I would assume that she wasn't really interested. "Okay, sorry. It's a fine distinction, I guess."

"It just means that that I'm not openly acknowledged as an employee of the government. I don't 'represent' them."

"So...are you CIA?"

"Kinda."

I glanced at her sideways and she grinned. Cheeky.

"The Department is umbrellaed under the CIA, NIA, NSA, DOD, and State. State doesn't know about it, though. It's a budget thing. We've got lots of covers under State."

"Uh huh. Look, I've been in this town forever. I've spent my professional life crawling around, looking for stories on the Hill, the Pentagon, Langley. I've never heard of the Department."

"Well, then, it's working." She stopped grinning. "For us, a bad day is when you see our work splashed all over *The Washington Item*."

"Seriously, I can't believe I've never heard of it."

"Seriously," she mimicked. "No one's *supposed* to have heard of it."

Was she making this all up? "Okay, so when did you start working for the—what was it again?"

"We usually just say 'the Department.' It's nicely anonymous."

The name was such a cliché, I barely restrained an eyeroll. "How'd you get involved with them?"

"Army."

"You were in the Army?" I said. The car was slowing. That gave me an idea. Maybe it was too late, but her hand was off the gun, and I was more collected than when she first grabbed me, and we were far enough away that it would be difficult to get to Lucy and M'e before I warned them...

"I couldn't join the Navy because my parents were married." She waved her hand, dismissing it. "Sorry. Old joke."

"When were you in the Army?" I prompted after a moment. I couldn't afford to let her see my mind wasn't entirely on the conversation.

"Right after I dropped out of college."

"Where'd you go? To college, I mean."

"Wellesley."

"Bullshit, you went to Wellesley."

"It's true—"

Much as I wanted to know more, it was now or never—

I clicked off my safety belt as I pulled on the door handle. Making myself jump was harder than I imagined. I hit the dirt road in a near belly flop, the wind knocked out of me.

I scrambled from a crawl into a stagger, back to the paved road. If there was nothing behind us, there was bound to be something ahead of us.

Maybe fifteen steps before I stopped gasping and found a stride. Another five, and the damned slide-on sneaker twisted under my foot. I stumbled. I should have taken them off, I should have—

Without warning, Marie stepped out of the woods in front of me. The gun was in her hand, looking even bigger than it did in the park.

I screamed.

She furrowed her brow, raised the pistol, and fired.

I flinched and raised my arms. "What the—?"

"There's no one to *hear* you. No one to be surprised by gunfire out here. Even if there were, they'd assume it was hunters. And—*for* the record—you're a bona fide pain in the ass. Get up."

She frog-marched me back down the dirt road.

About a quarter mile down I saw a shack. The wind brought the definite smell of a river, though I could tell no more about my location than that. I was unnerved by how quiet the woods were, and how unfamiliar the noises.

The shack was spartan, the exterior weathered clapboards covered with pine needles and caterpillar nests. It wasn't rundown inside; the unfinished pine walls reminded me of a fishing camp, a refuge from modern life. There was electricity, but few windows, small and awkwardly placed. The furniture wasn't new but I couldn't smell mildew and there were none of the stains one might expect from long use. The kitchen was modest but functional and an open door led to a bathroom.

"Sit. You move, I'll put one in your kneecap. Better yet, I'll leave you for the others to find. We're going to talk."

She was truly angry now. I believed her. I sat.

She stared at me for a long while then got up, went through her bag, and handed me a thick file.

It was my life. I leafed through the file quickly. Copies of my birth certificate and vaccination records, the reports from the speech therapist who cured me of my stutter at age twelve. Transcripts from every school I attended—hell, there were copies of my high school report cards. My journalism school project, a fat pile of clippings from the *Item*.

The stuff I recognized wasn't the problem. It was the stuff I'd never seen before that worried the hell out of me.

There were also reports on all my family, which I hadn't expected. There was speculation, nearly correct, about how I'd met Tommy at UVA and my switch in majors from creative writing to journalism. The very next item was a report on my grandfather's role in the county legislature and his death by gunshot less than a year after I met Tommy. There were speculations about my visit to him shortly before his death.

I closed it before I could read more. I was drenched in cold sweat; vertigo made the room swim. It took me several deep breaths to regain my composure and stop the spinning.

"Okay. You are what you say you are. Tell me about Kola. Tell me about your boss, and why he wants to kill you," I said, as neutrally as I could. Asking questions helped, professional distance helped. My hand itched for a pen and notebook. No chance of that. The best quotes came once you put your phone or notebook away, anyhow.

"My boss took me off the Kola case, then tried to kill me. He told the guy he sent to do the job that I was rotten. I came back to find out what was going on. Kola contacted me privately, not through Department means. I was at the party at Kola's request. He'd had Mrs. Bolton mention me to Jean-Yves du Plessis—you know him?"

I nodded again.

"Marie Tremblay works for Jean-Yves—as a cover, off and on." She looked around the room, and sighed. "I slide a mean tray of canapés. I can pour wine with the best of them."

So much for Jason Bourne, I thought. But it made sense. Who ever noticed a waiter or bartender? They were omnipresent in elite circles—wallpaper. Anyone could speak to them and never be noticed. "So what should I call you?"

"Stick with Marie, for now. The less you know, the better."

I digested that, a ridiculous thing to say to a reporter. "Okay. So how did Kola know how to find you—the Department?"

"We'd done business with him before."

"What do you mean—?" Oh, of course. A clandestine organization needed to stay off the Federal books. They had to get their gear from someone. "Ah."

"Yes. But now...Kola wanted out of the game. Out of the arms trade."

I stared. I couldn't imagine Kola ever relinquishing that kind of power, not once he'd broken international laws, been a partner to genocide, and fueled both sides of every gang battle, political skirmish, and full-out war in recent memory. Was the birth of a grandson, so soon on the heels of his son's death, enough to change his mind? I know that my niece Lucy's birth had changed me, but Kola and I were two very different people.

Maybe he was just...tired.

Marie continued. "He wanted the Department's help to do it safely, without upsetting the balance of power too much. I was put on the job. Bringing him and his stockpile of weapons in, safely, to our side, was the idea. I'd worked with him before. Then suddenly I was pulled off the job, told he wanted to work with someone else. It didn't make sense. Kola trusted me. Something was wrong."

I digested that. If he didn't want to upset the "balance of power" among arms dealers, Kola couldn't have had entirely altruistic reasons. And could one retire from the arms business? Why not? He was a technically a 'legitimate businessman,' wasn't he, always had the right paperwork, never ran afoul of the authorities? Or rather, never got caught, never missed a bribe, never stepped on the wrong toes, I thought bitterly. Only... "Why? Why would he leave? And why would he want to go to you?"

"You know his background?"

I nodded.

"So you know he's always kept a very low profile, and has been picky about who he sold to. It caused him trouble a number of times. It's easier when you're willing to sell to both sides of a conflict," she continued. "Oddly, people don't get their feelings hurt if you sell to everyone, including their enemies."

She got a box from under the sink, then moved her chair back from mine, ten feet or so. She set the gun she'd held on me on the armrest of her chair, then she took another, smaller one from an ankle rig. After unloading it—she checked the chamber twice—she broke the weapon down and cleaned it with the materials from the box. The weird orangey smell of the lube mixed with the musty, piney smell of the room, and the brush rasped against the hard metal of the barrel.

She continued. "I believed—everyone believed—that his son would follow in his footsteps. Then he died in a skiing accident last year, and I heard Kola started to talk about retiring. However, he also decided he wasn't going to leave his business to anyone. He had everything: contacts, inventory, information on his competitors."

The way she said Kola had stock and files made it sound like any other businessman. It was cheaper for a Hollywood movie company to buy ten thousand real rifles and pistols than it was to make fakes. Someone at Kola's level would also have access to airplanes, attack helicopters, drones, missiles, robotics, land mines, tanks, and hundreds of thousands of small arms and ammunition. They had the power to move all this around the world, almost at will. The scale at which someone could acquire these materials and exploit them, expand the business, was mind-boggling. If Kola had wanted to retire, there would be no limit to what someone might do to gain his empire.

"Why? Why leave it behind, why hand it over to you?"

"He was going to sell his stock to our people, but then he lost faith in Heath. I think he was going to tell me why at the Bolton party but couldn't because he was being watched."

She showed me a crumpled cocktail napkin with a scribble of ink. "He told me the location of his assets was in the files on his personal computer. He told me if anything happened to him, to find that computer and keep it from Heath. The files on the computer were encrypted, the key hidden—presumably, someplace he'd know I'd look. He didn't dare just write the address down. I need to find the computer, the encryption key, and his files before his murderers do."

"You don't think of arms dealers having boundaries," I said. "Worries."

She shook her head. "You're not thinking about his motivations. Remember, he always thought of himself as someone apart. In his mind, he's bettered himself."

"His grandson," I said. "Or maybe his son's death got him thinking about his own mortality?"

She nodded, intent on reassembling the small gun, then reholstered it in the ankle rig. "That meeting at the Bolton dinner wasn't our usual way of communicating."

"Kola didn't trust the Department any longer?"

She nodded again. "At the time, I didn't know why he was suddenly going off script. He wanted to pass me something. Since Heath set me up to be killed, it's clear to me Kola may have been killed by one of ours."

"By someone in the Department? Why? I can see why he'd want to hand it over, but why suddenly lose faith in them? Tell me about your boss—Heath is his name?"

It took Marie a long time to answer me. She automatically began cleaning up her rags and lubricant, then she stretched and rolled her neck, something I noticed she did when she was stalling. Finally, began to speak robotically, all the emotion erased.

"Mr. Richard Heath. Once upon a time, I thought he was the one person in a world of bureaucrats and liars who would always have my back. If he said something, you could take it as gospel. If he didn't tell you something, it was for your own good. And unlike a lot of military guys—a lot of guys, period—he didn't give a rat's ass that I was a woman. I wasn't just there to fill a quota. To be a lure. A piece of ass."

She was silent for a moment. "He made me believe I could change things for the better. Covertly. Expediently. He was rock solid, unwavering—"

I didn't want to interrupt her, but I was forcibly reminded of someone else who'd recently breaking regular habits. "Kola was seen outside of his usual haunts, recently."

"Yeah, I know." She seemed relieved to change the subject, but confused by me stating the obvious.

"He threatened me, last time I saw him, right before the party." I described our meeting at the restaurant. "He said, 'stay away from my wife.' But now I'm wondering...was that a warning? About her?"

"He was always very precise in his language," Marie said. "It certainly seems telling. Maybe she didn't like the idea of him retiring." Her eyes lit up. "Maybe she's the one who killed him!"

Holy moly. It was possible. "It was pretty risky to kill Kola at the party, wasn't it?" I said. "I mean, the murder was so public. It had to be a spur of the moment thing. An act of desperation, before he could talk to either of us?"

"No, no! She knew she was going to kill him. She did it at the party, in the presence of at least two people known to have negative connections with him, in case anyone didn't believe his death was natural!"

"She killed him...so you think *she's* the one taking over his business?

"Yes. Maybe she's even working with Heath. They need each other until one of them finds the computer. Then who knows what will happen."

I nodded. "She would have had access to everything else. She might even have convinced Kola's people that she was acting for everyone's best interest— Kola's hand-picked heir, a smooth transition of power." I frowned. "But...it doesn't make sense to me. It wasn't for money. She has her own. As long as he was alive, she had every kind of security. If he retired, she'd be that much safer. The birth of a grandchild after the loss of a son, you'd think she'd be overjoyed her husband was getting out of the game."

"You're thinking about this like Amy," Marie said. "You need to think like Philomena Kola."

"And that means what, exactly?"

"She knew what Kola was, even behind his legitimate façade, and she stayed married to him. She got something from that. Power? A sense of control? Maybe she didn't want to give it up, didn't want him to give it up. If the timing of her son's death and the arrival of her grandson decided her, just as it decided Kola, her reaction was different from his. The world is an unsafe place, and if you have power, you don't give it up easily. She couldn't dissuade her husband, so—"

"So she took it for herself." I stared at her. "There is absolutely nothing so horrible I can think of that you can't come up with something worse, is there?"

"Probably not."

I was still shaking my head, not wanting to believe any of it.

"I didn't see any other Department personnel at the dinner. I wonder if Mrs. Kola—" She cocked her head. "What's that?"

"I don't—"

But she'd already picked up the gun and grabbed me by the arm, yanking me out of the chair.

"Hey! What's your problem?" Crazy-ass *bitch*—

She hit the kitchen lights and we were in darkness. "Get in the bathroom, lock the door, get down in the tub, don't come out until I come for you," she hissed.

She shoved me toward the bathroom.

I stumbled forward. "What's—?"

"Someone's here. No lights. Get in the tub."

I locked the door behind me, for all the good that would do. There was a little window in there, no more than a slit. It wasn't big enough to climb through, no sill to haul myself up onto, even if it had been low enough. Now I understood why the windows were so oddly configured here: No one could see in, no one could watch as you moved around in the house. I stood in the tub—lip service to my instructions—and looked out. All I could see was the Ford in the woods, twilight descending.

I realized that I couldn't hear anything. Not even crickets.

A flash of blinding light, and a loud crack.

Then the gunfire started.

Chapter Twenty: Jayne Rogers

When is a wall not a wall?

When it's actually a door.

I secure the bedroom escape hatch behind me. No trace of it is visible as I move away from the cabin. Their attention will be on the front door and the windows, small as they are. Amy's as safe as she's gonna get in the bathroom. It's time for me to get to work.

I see one SUV, down the road. No more than four of them, then. I fit the suppressor to the pistol, double back around the side. I can see two. They're second stringers, boys being brought along, not the half-dozen or so guys Heath keeps council with. That's odd; why not send his best if he really wants me gone?

They're treating this like a hostage rescue, meaning they want us for information, not just out of the way. I hear the silence outside, followed by a single crack of a twig. It's not a deer; deer don't scare the birds silent. I know they're getting ready to hit the house, force us out with gas or a distraction. I'm well away from the front door. I hope Amy's smart enough to stay down.

My mistake is thinking faster than they do.

I see one behind my car, crouching, his back to me. Two bullets to the back of the head and he slumps, but something's wrong.

I turn and crouch just in time.

The car erupts in flame. He'd been working on the charge I thought he'd already placed on the door.

I sprint up the path, pause, and finish the one running down the road. Not a brilliant shot, not a great shot, but speed and placement make it count.

Two steps off the path. I wait to see what the others will do. They'll know the charge went off too soon; possibly have heard the first two shots.

The fire burns merrily, an excellent distraction.

One, over by the path to the landing. He's not moving fast, and his position is just a little too open.

Bait.

I turn and see the fourth man as he draws down on me.

I unload one clip into him. He fires as he collapses. Something hits me. We're both empty. I pull the piece from my ankle rig, and make sure he stays down.

I reel over to the guy I just shot. He's still warm, very wet.

I collapse. I decide not to get up, counting on the last guy to come to me.

He's cautious enough, almost to a fault. Circling in on me, to make sure I'm not playing possum.

I'm bleeding from a ricocheting rock. I see the white quartz glinting where it sticks out of my arm, blood rushing over it.

The fourth guy avoids following the path that will bring him in range of my secondary piece. When he's confident I'm no longer holding it, he pauses, just a second, to find the best path between me and him.

I raise the gun I've taken from his buddy, southpaw, and shoot.

He falls, screaming. I limp over, determined to get something from him.

It wasn't a great shot. I aimed for the shoulder of his shooting arm, and probably punctured a lung.

Fuck.

He's going fast.

I scramble over. He's one of Heath's younger lieutenants.

"Rogers...don't do this."

"Don't make me," I say, kneeling down beside him. He's beyond my help and we both know it. I don't need to do anything. I chuck his weapon away out of reach.

"I mean...turn yourself in. Remember what we all used to want."

"Turn myself in." I think fast. "For killing Kola?"

He nods, grimaces. "And Franklin, and the others."

"I didn't do it, Harrison. What's Heath planning?"

He mumbled something. Blood bubbling at his lips, from the chest wound.

"—vate sector" was all I heard.

It's not enough, but at least now I have confirmation Heath's trying to pin everything and anything on me.

All the more reason to get going.

I finish feeding the fiery monster that's the burning car.

Another car pulls up. Shit. Four more men exit, and I realize belatedly, I'm silhouetted by the fire, lined up by their headlights. Another car pulls up behind them, and it's clear Heath has sent every.fucking.one.

I can't catch a break. I'm not going to make it out of here this time.

I remember Amy is still back there, and I hope she has the sense to start running right now.

I don't have time to reload before the shooting starts. Something hits me and—

Chapter Twenty-One: Amy Lindstrom

I was scared and felt so stupid, standing there in the bathroom. There were shots, and then a wall of flame reflected on the tiles and in the mirror. I crumpled back into the tub, not because it was the safest thing for me to do, but because my legs buckled.

I heard nothing but the distant crackle of the fire, and what sounded like breaking branches. I peeked out and saw a burning automobile; it was getting dark where the fire didn't light the shadows under the trees. Who was out there?

I got back down in the tub and hugged my knees. One was bleeding. I'd smacked into the faucet, though I hadn't felt it happen. Next time I get "extracted," I'm definitely wearing something more sensible than cargo pants and slide-ons. It seemed like I'd been there forever but my Raymond Weil I'd been given for my graduation from j-school was still keeping time and it was just thirty minutes since Marie had left me. Why had she gone so suddenly?

Another burst of gunfire. Jesus, it's a war zone out there.

What do I do? If I stay, I may die. If I move from here...

I waited another five minutes after the last burst and then decided I needed to put some distance between me and the cabin. Maybe they all killed each other, but I wouldn't learn anything staying here, and I would *not* be a sitting duck any longer.

A sound so commonplace I thought I imagined it, until it happened again: a door buzzer.

Then pounding. "C'mon, Amy Lindstrom, I don't have time for this nonsense. Would you please get the door? Time's wasting!"

I caught myself going to answer it. Social habit is deeply ingrained, but I paused, when I realized the absurdity of what I was about to do.

Muffled grunts on the other side. Shit, now where do I go?

A click, then the door burst open.

"Give me a hand with this," came a brisk order.

A short, dark-skinned Black woman with a close-cropped Afro dressed in an excellent pantsuit stood in front of me, with Marie trussed up on a handcart, tied with ratchet straps. One hand was free, dangling over the edge; apparently Marie's fingerprint had opened the door. The other woman grunted and wheeled Marie into the main part of the cabin, with her kit piled on top of her.

I closed the door, not knowing what else to do.

"Who are you? Is she dead?" Marie was filthy and bloody, with pine needles in her hair and on her clothes. Her face was slack and trickles of blood ran from her temple.

"No. I drugged her."

"What about the others—all that gunfire?"

"They're no longer a problem for us." The woman rummaged in her bag.

"If you're on our side—or her side—why is she tied up?"

"You've met her, right?" She raised an eyebrow. "In my experience, if she's not expecting you, you either show up when she's asleep or drug her. Like taking a cat to the vet; it's easier on everyone."

"And I should believe you because?"

"You're not dead. *She's* not dead." The stranger nodded to the handcart. "You're not being interrogated by Heath's men, or by Philomena Kola's."

So far, everything she said jibed with Marie's story. For now. My planning for the future was constrained from minute to minute.

"Why are you with her?"

"Marie—whatever her name is—thinks I can help her with the Kola case. She thinks she's being set up by Heath. I didn't exactly come here under my own steam. We're trying to keep Kola's information out of the wrong hands."

That was general enough to let her know I knew what she was talking about, without being so specific as to give anything away.

The woman stared at me as if making a decision. Then she nodded, and rummaged in a small tactical bag. She pulled a syringe out.

"Wait, what's that?" I began to worry she was going to kill us after all.

She jammed the syringe into Marie's neck. "Something to wake Rogers back up. We don't have time for her to nap."

"Wait, that's her name?" I added "Rogers" to the pile of names I was accumulating.

"One of them." There was still no movement from the unconscious woman trussed to the handcart. "Come on, bonehead. Rise and shine."

Nothing, and then Marie's eyes flew open. She jerked violently, realized that she was bound and grunted, plucking against the bands with her free hand. Another grunt, and her eyes cleared, widening when she saw me. I watched her memory of our situation flood back to her, and then surprise as she noticed the other woman. "The fuck, Raven?"

"The fuck, Cave Girl? Here's a clue: You're not dead yet."

"Heath sent you," Marie muttered, still groggy.

They clearly knew each other. I tried to make myself as invisible as possible as I observed them.

"No," the one called "Raven" said. "He didn't assign me to the retrieval team. He most certainly wouldn't expect me to kill the second wave of guys who were so intent on drawing down on you when I arrived that they didn't even register my approach. He didn't request I shoot a trank into your skinny backside. It's so like you gun monkeys: You assume that if one prefers a keyboard as a choice of weapon, that one isn't as competent with the physical stuff."

She shook her head with a gesture of "what can you do?" and turned to me. "I mean, we both survived the same training and made it to the Department, and yet her kind equate sitting behind a computer to being an administrative assistant."

I noticed she hadn't untied Marie yet. "Raven" was still making up her mind.

She turned back to Marie. "Anyway, we have bad news and worse. You know Heath is blaming you for a lot of deaths in the Department, as well as Kola."

"I killed Franklin because he tried to kill me."

I watched her; Marie had a blank look that suggested to me she wasn't telling the whole story there.

"Heath claims you killed Segura, Malmon, Nunnally, and MacLeod as well."

Surprise and horror suddenly crossed Marie's face, jolted by the news. "No! I mean I knew them, but never worked with any of them, much less killed them!"

Another moment where "Raven" seemed to be deciding. "I believe you. I looked into it, and I think it was our own people. Heath's making it look like you're behind everything."

Marie just shook her head. "What? Why?"

"Two things: A while back, he came in all flustered, changed meetings several times. I got curious. Yesterday—you remember Regina Jones? You used to room with her. Yesterday, Gina and I began snooping around in his calendar. We hit pay dirt."

"And?"

"Meetings on the Hill. I hacked the accounts of some of the interns, blackmailed a few aides, and learned that he was there to discuss dispersing the Department. Shutting us down. Because of the budget."

"Yeah, so? They'll blow Taps and we'll go our separate ways. We always knew the program was experimental, that we might have to quickly disband—"

"But he still was negotiating with Kola to buy off his stockpile of weapons, right? Isn't that why you'd been assigned to him?" Raven asked.

"Heath is going private," I guessed. Both women looked surprised to see me still standing there, much less adding to the conversation. "He would close down the Department, take Kola's weapons, and go into business for himself."

"Heath would never—" Marie looked rattled. It was a profoundly unsettling sight. "One of the guys out there said something about the private sector," she admitted slowly.

"Raven" closed her eyes briefly, as if calculating. "Not just the weapons. He's taking people with him, and killing off the rest. The Department was always meant to be efficient and cheap. It's easier to kill off the agents and blame you than to pay out the retirement funds and the like. Horribly efficient."

"But why wouldn't he take me? Take us? I mean, I'm—" Marie suddenly seemed very young, very hurt, incredulous.

"Yes, you are. *We* are the best. But we both ask too many questions, think too much on our own. And I'm sure my doctorates make me suspect with Heath—he doesn't trust academics."

I suspected her humor masked some deeper fear or anger. Marie's whole body went rigid. "Wait—I'm the mopping up crew? I'm his plan?" She shook her head, still thinking, still stunned. "Better yet, if they survive me, kill me, it's like an audition."

"How else to get rid of other highly trained killers? He wants to make sure they're dead. Eliminates potential competition. Another 'good' reason."

Using his own people to kill each other off. Suddenly I was sitting down on a chair. I couldn't get my breath. It felt as though I'd been punched in the chest. I thought I was dying. The world spun and my stomach seemed to roll in an opposite direction.

"How did you find all this out?" I asked. "I mean, that's not the kind of thing that you put on a calendar or to-do list, right?"

Raven—whoever she was—nodded and set a stainless travel mug on the table. "There was an alarm yesterday, and we evacuated the building. I'm assuming that was you?"

Marie nodded.

"The place emptied out, and I decided to check on with what Heath and Chase were talking about while we were out of the building. I left my version of this mug with a camera built into it on my desk, facing Heath's office. I checked in via my phone from the parking lot while we were waiting. And I heard the whole thing."

She played the recording: Chase and Heath discussed the progress of "culling the herd" and whether anyone else had figured out what they were doing. So far, everything they'd planned was on schedule, save that they still hadn't found Kola's computer.

I watched Marie blanch. She didn't even notice when Raven released the ratchet on the band. She just sat on the handcart, her face a mask.

"Cave Girl? You still with us?" Raven's voice was gentle. "I've had…longer to process the news."

Marie held up a hand, her voice under control. "I'm here, just thinking. We need to find Kola's files. We need to stop Heath. And we need to implement Taps before he kills any more of us."

"What's that?" I asked.

"It's a protocol that tells all of our officers to scatter, that we've been catastrophically compromised. I just thought Heath would be the *last* person who'd want to avoid initiating it." The color was returning to Marie's face. "So do they—Heath and company—know that *you* know?"

Raven shook her head. "I don't think so, not yet. I can use that to find out where to get the Taps protocol instructions, before it gets too hot for me, or he concludes that I'm one of the expendable ones."

"Will he believe you?"

"I think so. He underestimates me, and that's worked for me so far. He may twig to it eventually, when he rules everything else out, but I'll be gone long before then."

I was about to argue with that, when I saw that Marie and Raven exchanged a glance. They both knew how dangerous what she proposed was.

"Look," I blurted. "I think we—uh, Marie and I—figured out that it was probably Mrs. Kola who killed her husband." I ran down the story, Marie interjecting details.

"That makes sense," Raven said. "I didn't see anyone I recognized from the Department at the party. And presumably she was the one who told Heath you were there."

"Okay, go figure out how to use Taps to save our people," Marie said. "I'll work on finding the Kola notebook and files."

"Sounds good. I packed you a couple of kits. I can't stay much longer; I need to cover my tracks and get to work. There's some cash, some food, some medical supplies. Couple of burner phones. I'll try to keep in touch." She held up two small packs; I noticed that Marie's was heavier than mine. "Some extra hardware for you, Cave Girl."

"Thank you, uh, Raven," I said.

"Call me Nicole. Only the Cave Girl over there calls me Raven."

"Dare I ask?"

"She was friends with my roommate, Regina Jones, during Department training," Marie said. "The two of them sitting at the keyboard all night, tap, tap, tapping, like Poe's raven."

Nicole shook her head. "I never thought she read books that didn't have pictures of caped superheroes in them. I was surprised at the literary allusion. She doesn't like anything more complicated than fists or bullets."

Marie shrugged. "I musta seen it on *Rocky and Bullwinkle*."

For the first time, Nicole laughed with real humor. "Okay, Bam Bam, don't forget to use a knife and fork in front of nice people."

"I won't. Don't you forget, Raven: The sun is our friend. Crawl out of your basement from time to time and join the meatspace. It's really nice out here."

Raven—Nicole—nodded and left.

"I'm going to clean up and grab my things. Two minutes, and we'll be gone."

I used the loo, then checked out my knee, dabbing at the blood with toilet paper. Made sure I didn't have any splinters in my head. I came out into the kitchen and saw, in addition to my bag and the two packs Nicole had given us, two bundles: one a plastic grocery bag filled with trash and one small rip-stop nylon black bag. Marie's face was clean and she'd changed into jeans and a thin hoodie. There was something red-stained jammed into the plastic bag. My skin crawled.

"Let's go. We'll take the SUV of the second group of guys. The ones Raven took out."

"Wait, where's your car?"

"Same place as the bodies." She nodded at the blazing fire. "And your dry cleaning. Sorry about that."

As we walked past the lively burning wreck, I smelled something that hadn't been there before. Cooked meat. I gagged, recovered, about to throw up. Only by dint of gritted teeth and sheer determination did I keep it down.

"We've got to get going," she said, grabbing my arm. "No time."

"Fuck." I took shallow breaths and tried not to think about the smell of roasting flesh. "They're dead. I got time—"

"Yes, they're dead, and I killed them." She stopped, as a realization hit her. Her eyes wide, but I couldn't tell if it was the effect of the drugs she'd been given, or shock, or emotion, or all three. "I just spent the evening picking off men I've worked with, who believe I'm a traitor. They were part of a group who are—were the closest thing to family I've had...since forever. That smell...anyway. So, get your ass moving."

We walked as fast as I could make myself stumble down the dirt road, to a parked SUV. In the dark, I could only make out that it was a recent and unremarkable vintage.

The keys were still in the ignition. We got in. Marie looked like her old self: calm, intense.

My teeth started to chatter.

"Hey, you cold? The sun's been down a while." She sounded better and turned on the heater. Mercifully, it came on in a hurry.

"Thanks." The heat didn't allay my fears, but at least my teeth stopped chattering.

I could see her teeth reflecting the dashboard light as she smiled. "Hey, my folks were right, huh? Don't go looking for trouble, it'll find you soon enough."

"Sure." Which was kind of strange, us being two people who inveterately went looking for trouble, each in her own way. Then, thinking it might be a way in, I said, "What's Raven's—Nicole, I mean. What's her story?"

"If she didn't tell you, I'm not going to." Marie kept her eyes on the road, made a turn. "Let's just say, her folks expected her to go into academics, like them. She tried that, then tried business. Neither world was big enough—or interesting enough— for her."

"Okay, what about *your* folks?"

"They're dead." Her eyes flicked down to the speedometer. We were doing a shade over the speed limit; she slowed. No sense getting a ticket and drawing attention to ourselves. "Long time now."

"I'm sorry." A thought hit me. "About the time you went into the Army?"

"Right before."

I shivered again. The conversation was officially over. Marie turned up the heat and we continued to drive in silence. The shadows of the trees, and later, streetlights, flowed over the darkened cab. Overwhelmed by how much had just transpired and a series of massive adrenaline dumps, I fell asleep.

Chapter Twenty-Two: Nicole Bradley

At home, after the incident at the cabin, I wash up, waiting for take-out. I check in on the recording devices I've planted on Heath's suits earlier this week. Dry cleaners are far easier to break into than his house, and I've lucked out. He's wearing one of the suits I managed to tag with an extraordinarily small camera.

"The cabin team hasn't made any of their check-in calls." Chase says, barely able to keep himself from pacing. It's as agitated as I've ever seen him so worked up, the guy who prides himself on keeping cool. "And their biotelemetry shows everyone's down. You should have let me go up there, sir."

"I can't afford to lose you right now. We need to keep clearing out the deadwood and bringing the right people on board."

Chase looks like he's going to protest and I wonder about his eagerness to go after Rogers. From a glance that I catch, Heath is too.

"We also need to focus on finding that computer. Philomena claims that she can't find it, but I'm not sure how much I trust her."

"He had a lot of offices, a lot of computers. We'll find it."

Chase is so quick to defend her, I wonder if Philomena Kola has been bending his ear on the subject of the computer. After all, she'd like to have the files her husband maintained on his empire. And maybe she imagines that Chase doesn't want to be taking orders from Heath his whole life.

As if reading my mind, Heath says, "I will, however, ask Mrs. Kola to use her resources to try and locate Rogers."

Chase relaxes, ever so little. Interesting. "I'll pass them the signal we've been tracking. What about Lindstrom, the reporter? She was confirmed at the cabin."

"She barely has any life outside work, and what she has, she spends with her family. At the same time, she limits that, because she seems to take responsibility for her brother-in-law's death, as well as that of her grandfather Bolling—he was in the Virginia House of Delegates when she was younger."

"Why does Rogers want her?"

Heath flips through files, pausing when he finds the correct one. "Rogers must believe Kola communicated something to Lindstrom. Please make sure Kola's men know we want them both alive, if possible. If there's no other alternative, demonstrably dead."

They check their list of folk to bring to the new company. It's very short, and many of the people I like best are on the other, longer list, either dead or about to be.

It's time for me to go, I think. I begin the preparations that I've had in place to close up my condo and vanish. I take a moment to let Gina know she ought to be doing the same thing.

The next morning, at the office, I make the decision to trust someone who's not on the list. It's still tricky; if they don't know about Heath's plan, there's no particular reason for them to trust me. But without that trust, I can't get what I need to implement Taps. So I make the leap.

I stop by Anna-Maria Rodriguez's desk. "Wanna grab a soda?"

"Sure."

Rodriguez, a stout Latinx woman, shuts down and secures her work, and follows me out of the office. We walk past the coffee place without another glance until we get to a small park.

"No cane?" I ask.

"I'm trying to do without this week. The PT is helping."

A little more innocuous chitchat takes us to a bench, and we both look around for anyone who might hear us.

"You've never drunk soda before," she says, settling down.

"Still don't. I have bad news."

I wait for her to nod, indicating she's ready to hear it.

I play her the recording I made from the office, hating to do it. Rodriguez has been at the Department from the beginning, in intelligence for decades before that. She's the one closest to Heath who also knows about how Taps works. I hate the idea that the thing she helped create has not only been morphing into the thing she most wanted to avoid, but is being corrupted from within. I tell her about Roger's role

"Ese cabrón traicionero," she says quietly.

I can see the rage in her eyes, but her face is passive.

She looks at me, trying to decide if she can trust me, but since she was the one who hired me, I think she knows she can. We've worked well together, and companionably. And now I'm trusting her.

Rodriguez nods, focusing on the problem. "My name isn't mentioned on their list of folks to bring to the new program," she says calmly.

"Nope, neither is mine. I once heard Chase describe our hands-off approach as 'witchcraft,' like we stare at goats or something."

"Chase is crafty, but limited in his perceptions of the world." She sighs. "A lot of people will die if someone doesn't do something. Good people, who volunteered to serve, volunteered to die if necessary, but not like this. Not to...save money. Not to give Heath a new job, with no competition."

I nod. "I'm hoping you'll help me prevent that from happening." I run down the information I got from Cave Girl, and what our current plan is.

"That poor kid," Rodriguez says. "I mean, considering what she's been through, I'm surprised she's as together as she is. She began imprinting on Heath like a lost chick from such an early age. How is she?"

"Better than I expected. She's doing a good job keeping it together while we search for Kola's computer."

"Well, I'm not in a position to help with the fieldwork," Anna-Maria says finally. "But I can help you with the security around Taps, and will."

She describes the Taps program setup: two two-factor authentication USBs and Heath's retinal scan.

She pauses a moment, reaches into her blouse, pulls out a chain. It's one of the Taps authentication keys. "Chase has the other one. I don't know how you'll get Heath's scan—"

"Don't worry about that. I'll find a workaround." I take the chain and put it around my own neck. Already, I have a third of the equation, but the other two parts of the puzzle will be much, much harder to acquire.

She stares into the distance and then pulls a foldable cane out of her bag. "I had a fall, trying to push my leg too far, too soon. I'm gonna call in sick tomorrow, explain that I need another operation on my knee."

"I think that's a fine idea. Gonna go back to New York?"

She shakes her head. "Not yet. Once I'm reasonably certain I'm safe—we're all safe—I will. The grandbabies are there, and I miss them like heck. But I'll go to Ponce first. Been too long since I had decent coffee and quesitos. And if anyone tries anything, I'll be on familiar turf." She stands. "Thanks, Dr. Bradley. It's been an honor and a privilege."

I stand and shake her hand. "And for me. Thank you for your service and your invaluable assistance, Ms. Rodriguez."

We walk back to the office as if nothing in the world was wrong, just that now, she's limping. When it's quitting time, I leave for home. And I'm not planning on returning.

Chapter Twenty-Three: Amy Lindstrom

"Okay, I've got another car," Marie announced, waking me. We were in the outskirts of DC in the stolen SUV. It was the last place anyone would expect us to go. Apart from a police cruiser, who didn't give us a second glance, we appeared to be alone.

She checked her gun and magazines, grabbed her bags, and got out. I followed. She dumped the plastic trash bag with the bloody rags from the cabin into a construction site dumpster. She was moving fast, and once again, I struggled to keep up. Stupid shoes.

Every time I felt like slowing down, I had only to look around to put a little more wiggle in it. Metal-reinforced doors and broken or barred windows, the shells of cars, and furtive transactions in the shadows spurred me on.

We'd walked maybe ten blocks to the car she picked out. Another wreck. Maybe this Celica was tweaked, maybe I should just be glad I wouldn't have to walk any more tonight. I went to the passenger side, carrying Marie's black bag as well as my own. She was fiddling with the lock on the driver's side when she spun around, clutching her side. Blood seeped through the fabric of her hoodie.

"Shit!"

Marie threw herself—or was knocked—onto the hood of the car. Another shot. I dragged her to my side. She nodded, got up, and we ran to the nearest building. She kicked down the cheap door. We found the stairs, then cut out the back door of the basement and into the rear alley.

"Maybe it wasn't for us?" I gasped. I was still hoping Marie hadn't been shot, even though the fact we were running again made a good case for that.

"No such luck. Either Kola's underlings just got fantastically lucky—again—or Heath pointed them at you. Keep moving."

We'd turned down a one-way street. It was deserted. Most of the buildings were dark and boarded up. The buildings with lights on behind doors fitted with security bars looked even less inviting.

Then, suddenly, there were five guys who seemed to know we would be there, too.

"Ladies, we don't want to hurt you," said one. "We have some questions."

It was the guy with the port-wine mark on his neck. Mrs. Kola's bodyguard. "Yeah? So why the guns?" Lindstrom, I thought, keep your damned mouth shut.

"Your colleague is too dangerous to ignore," he said.

I felt Marie's arm slip off my shoulder. I wondered what I was going to do with an unconscious spy against guys who really wanted her incapacitated—or dead. Wanted *us* dead. I heard metal on metal coming from behind just before I saw the guns in front of me. If there were more men behind us—I didn't dare look—we were screwed. Worse than screwed.

I felt a weight on my shoulder again. The bleeding woman was trying to comfort me. I turned to her.

She was staring straight ahead. "Don't move," she said barely moving her lips. "Not a muscle."

I was still looking at her face when she fired, using my shoulder as a brace. I couldn't hear myself scream. Unlike the men, Marie wasn't using a silencer. It sounded like an old metal desk being slammed repeatedly from a great height. The concussion was shocking, recognizable in the ways of mythic figures: Even if you've never seen them, you know them instantly. She was six or seven shots in before I unfroze and flinched. Maybe it was all the hot brass cartridge casings jumping out; maybe Marie cursed. But she wouldn't have wasted the time swearing.

Two guys were still standing, and a skinny one looking unsteady and bad when she fired the last bullets. Her arm left my shoulder. She straightened and shoved me right into the arms of a burly guy with a hand-cannon the size of a bazooka.

I landed against Bazooka in a tangle of limbs. He shoved at me, not wanting to take his eyes off Marie, who homed in on the other guy like she was on rails. A brief whiff of sweat and an unfamiliar soap, a feel of rough fabric beneath my fingers, and he flung me aside.

I smacked into the wounded skinny guy. We both went down. I felt the air rush from his lungs. My hands were suddenly warm and sticky with his blood. He struggled feebly under me. I leapt up, gagging. He still had his weapon, but he didn't bother with me. He pulled himself up onto his hip, his sights trained on Marie, waiting for the moment when he could hit her and not his partner, who were engaged in beating the shit out of each other.

I kicked the wounded guy in the back of the head, just below the base of his skull, as hard as I could. He went down with a grunt. I realized I'd just made things worse. By actively taking Marie's side, I'd signaled I was worth attention. Bazooka decided I could wait and took up his unconscious partner's task, waiting for the clear shot at Marie. I wondered if he would wait for his friend to get clear, whether he would think it would be worth shooting through him to get to her. Then I'd be next.

I could run. Maybe I should, but I was far from anywhere safe. I thought about cover—there, the wrecked station wagon. On my way, I wrenched the gun out of the still-limp hand of the guy on the ground. His hand and the gun were both surprisingly heavy.

Bazooka was drawing a bead on Marie.

I had to decide.

I gave up thirty years of protest and pacifism and shot a human being.

I missed—by a lot—but I got Bazooka's attention. He turned and shot at me. I swear I could feel the heat of the bullet as it passed my face. Tunnel vision—it was just the two of us in the whole world. I fired again, and aimed at his chest, the biggest part of him.

"We don't have what you're looking for!" I shouted, my voice high-pitched with fear. Why did I think reason would work?

I missed his trunk but grazed his arm. He staggered and kept coming, unimpressed by my firepower and accuracy. I fired again, and missed. Then I heard a heavy thump, like a load of wet laundry hitting the floor from a height. Marie turned from her opponent and marched on the guy coming at me.

Blood streamed down the side of her face and nose. Her expression was blank. She moved purposefully toward him. If he'd seen her coming, he would have been a whole lot less worried about me. She was switched on—scary power and speed, concentrated violence and controlled grace. I knew she would wade into him before he was able to get another shot at me.

I was only partly correct. I felt a searing pain in my leg as I heard the whine of another shot. A rose blossomed on the cargo pants below my knee and I went cold. Time slowed down. Tunnel vision narrowed to a pinpoint.

Marie came from behind Bazooka, shoving his gun down and away from me. She grabbed the muzzle. She closed the space between them, then turned the gun around toward him. My head started to buzz. It seemed as though I was actually hovering over them. Marie kept moving into her opponent and tried to knee him in the groin.

Why didn't she shoot?

He blocked her knee with his own. She moved to slam the pistol into the side of his head; he reached out and blocked that too. The gun went flying, hit the asphalt, and skidded down a storm drain. The two were left alone with each other.

A flick of her wrist. A wicked looking blade appeared.

They were well matched. He was forty pounds heavier, but his arm was bleeding profusely. Her knife just seemed to piss him off, but she kept pecking away, focusing on his wounded arm and the soft spots—throat, eyes, gut. I heard a grunt. The knife flew out of her hand, a line of blood arcing after it.

It was hard, brutal fighting with very little style. The intensity was fearsome. Neither seemed to utter another sound over the blood pounding in my ears. Once or twice one of them tried something tricky. Both times, the other responded in kind.

Only the growing pool of blood under me and my increasing lightheadedness made me act. Maybe it was the calm of shock, but I just knew if I waited for the right moment, he would pull back from her and I would shoot him, ending things.

The moment came. He slipped on the gritty pavement. I shot him, aiming again for the torso. I hit him this time. He spun around and almost fell on top of Marie.

She stepped back, let him fall into her arms, and snapped his neck as she set him down.

I leaned over and retched. The blank look on her face as she broke his neck, the careless poise with which she killed him shocked me out of my false calm, when the sight of my own blood hadn't. She turned toward me, her face still a bloody mask.

I dragged myself back, aware of incredible burning pain in my left leg and the gun I still held. I trained it on her. She stopped, about ten feet away from me, her face melting into humanity again, filled with concern. For me or herself? Reality had taken a coffee break. All I knew was that she'd thrown me straight into the middle of the danger as easily as she cast aside her promises.

I was the one with a gun now.

"Get away from me! I'll shoot you! I will!" My hand trembled under the weight of the pistol.

Marie didn't stop. "You can shoot me if you like. But wouldn't you rather I got us out of here so I could look at your leg?"

I could feel myself shouting, though I could only hear a little through the ringing. "But...but...you threw me at—!"

"I'm sorry you got hurt."

"Yeah, when you *threw* me—"

"They weren't expecting it. You were no danger to them. They wanted what they think you know."

"No danger...well, now." I giggled. Reality had finished the coffee and was considering a refill and cheese Danish. "I dangered him right in the giblets."

"Yes, you did. Good shot." She knelt down, grimacing with pain, and made a pile of the man's belongings, going through his pockets with practiced ease. She did the same with the next three guys. "Here's the drill. We need to get out of here, get you taken care of, before someone wonders what all the fuss was about and whether they should get in on it. I'll get you out of here. If you still feel like I'm a bad guy, well, you can deal with it then."

The guy I'd kicked in the head stirred. We both looked at him. Marie strode over and asked him something I couldn't make out.

He was too weak to answer. Blood bubbled from his lips.

She took his head in her hands. Suddenly, sickeningly, I knew what was coming next.

"Don't you do it! Don't you just kill him!" My voice was high, quavering. The gun waved around crazily, as I tried to train it back on her. I couldn't stop shaking.

She looked over at me, surprised. "What?"

I coughed, feeling the sour burn of vomit at the back of my throat. "You can't just go around...doing that!"

She licked her lips, took a breath. "Amy, it's them or me. You can shoot me if you like, and then I won't have to worry about anything anymore. But if I don't kill him, other folks will come after us and probably kill me. I mean, you could call Bradley—you've got the phone she gave you, right there—but I don't think she has time to babysit you and rescue the other officers."

Her cold logic and colder voice creeped me out, but I'd already made the choice when I shot the guy. She didn't wait for my reply, just made with the butcher hands again.

And then the buildings and night sky wheeled around and I felt a god-awful pain as the back of my head hit the street.

Chapter Twenty-Four: Nicole Bradley

Kola kept his record clean—since he became a "legitimate" dealer in death and not just a talented amateur—so I find nothing that has even the whiff of impropriety in his paperwork, his organization, not even a parking ticket. So squeaky clean that it should give any investigator pause.

While I'm waiting for a few things to wrap up at home, I use the time to make a careful search on the web for hornets' nest that's the illegal arms trade. I find so much nothing it actually gives me chills. No "going out of business" sales going down, no obscure bids to take over his empire, no gossip about his death, no nothing. It's as though the presence of some large predator has silenced an entire forest.

The sudden demise of any other billionaire, in any other business would have caused internecine alliance-building or power grabs. Speculation, fantasizing, plotting, outright coups, and empire-building—the ether would have been buzzing with it.

It's business as usual, which is telling. Save for that eerie lack of chatter about Kola.

It looks as though I've confirmed that Rogers and the reporter were right. Philomena Kola has taken over where her husband once reigned, moving in so smoothly and efficiently that she's terrified the denizens of a deeply dangerous environment.

I make a note to see who else might have been killed as an example, whose absence is testimony to this transition of power.

The ME's online report regarding Kola is equally unhelpful. Translated into human English, it says he's had a heart attack. I check it for digital fingerprints, to see who else might have looked at it or altered the report, and I am not surprised to find that it's been tampered with, very carefully, very professionally. I trace the tampering back to a lab tech and after a little nosing about, I find that she's not only altered the amount of cardiac glycosides in his system, but she's recently accessed a private bank account in Grand Cayman.

Two things occur to me now: Most lab techs do *not* have millions stashed in tax havens. And I won't be surprised if this lab tech is found dead within a week or so.

I trace the money through several dummy corporations and am not surprised to see it belongs to one owned by Philomena Kola's family.

Means. Motive. Murder.

This at least allows me to focus on her. And I'll be on the watch for any communications between her and Department personnel.

In the meantime, I begin to craft the programs I'll need in order to trigger the Taps dismissal. Rodriguez has given me her authentication key, and I'll need to get the other from Chase. I'll also start creating a list of those officers who're still alive but on the wrong side of Heath's plan. It's a lot to do—very fiddly, very quiet, very secure—and I need to keep it as quick as I can without triggering any other alerts. And more than that, I need to figure out how I can get Heath's retinal scan.

He needs to be alive, and those scanners are so twitchy about matching that I need to find a way to get around them. It's a lot of work, so I focus on the first thing, and plan to meet with Gina for help with the second.

I catch myself whistling and realize that I really do love this work. This would be so much more fun if there weren't so many lives at stake.

Chapter Twenty-Five: Amy Lindstrom

"Amy? How you doing over there?"

I pried my eyes open. I felt stiff and wretched and weak. When I moved, a wave of nausea rolled over me. My head ached, my ears rang. As I sank back into the pillow—an unfamiliar pillow that smelled faintly of bleach—I saw the pistol on the nightstand right next to me. There was one promise kept, I thought.

Marie sat on a chair near the window, watching me. She looked through the curtain briefly, let it fall back into place, and went to the side of the room. I heard her moving and suddenly smelled food. I was ravenous, though I wasn't taking bets on whether my stomach felt as kindly toward food as I did.

I croaked a couple of times before a recognizable word came out. "Where?"

"A motel south of Baltimore. You don't really want to know too much more about the specifics." She stirred something on a hot plate; my mouth watered. "It's well off the radar of anyone who might be looking for us. I cooked! It's canned stew, but plenty of it. You should have some water first, though, if you can sit up."

I gave it a shot, which was a damn poor choice of words, considering. My head reeled, my leg throbbed with pain, but my stomach stayed put, and I was grateful. There was a bottle of water on the table next to the gun, and while my hands still trembled, I found I was parched and drank deeply.

"Take it easy. I have to pay extra if you puke. Don't you ever learn anything?"

"Gee, thanks." I was surprised to see I'd drunk half the water without a second thought.

Marie turned off the hotplate and picked up the can of stew with a facecloth. She handed it to me with a plastic spoon.

"Deluxe accommodations here," I said. The stew was barely hot, but I didn't even care.

"How's the leg?" Marie went back over to her chair once she made sure I was able to feed myself.

I cautiously flexed my calf muscle and spilled a good dollop of stew when the pain hit me. "It sucks."

"The bone isn't broken, the bullet only grazed you. I cleaned you up good, and there were antibiotics in Raven's kits, but we'll need more soon. You lost some blood. You didn't fracture your skull, but you'll have to take it easy."

I made a mental note to put off looking at my leg for as long as possible. I hated the look of cuts, and stitches...don't even think about them, Lindstrom.

"We may not have too long. I set up a few false trails. I don't know how effective they'll be." She raised her hands, in a "what are you gonna do" gesture. "Tough, when the guys who taught you everything you know are after you."

I felt the back of my head. Sore as hell, but she was right: nothing broken. "Those guys—they worked for Mrs. Kola. I recognized the first one, the one with the mark on his neck. They're also working with Heath?"

A thought struck me: What had she done with their bodies?

"How's your side?" I asked, remembering the first shot.

"Coupla stitches. It's sore; I'll live. I could use some sleep sometime soon." She had sutured herself? I shuddered, putting the thought aside. "Sure. What has it been, nearly thirty-six hours since you slept last?"

"Longer. You've been asleep or unconscious since about midnight."

"No kidding?" No wonder I was starving. I couldn't remember the last time I'd eaten a meal.

She shrugged, flinching. "You were a mess."

"Thanks. But I could stay up a bit now, if you want. Keep an eye out, if you want to sleep for a bit."

"Maybe I will," she said thoughtfully. "Between you and the alarm..." Here she nodded at a pyramid of beer bottles stacked against the door to the room. "We should be safe enough. Courtesy of the last occupant. I dislike people who peel labels."

A laughable thought, protection in the form of rattling beer bottles. A few seconds' warning. But...that was all she really needed.

"And I've got the gun." I picked it up.

Marie nodded gravely. "Yes, of course. You've got the gun."

"And don't you forget it." I put the gun down, rolled over, and immediately fell back to sleep.

Chapter Twenty-Six: Nicole Bradley

"When you texted the first time, I was hoping it was just to catch up," Gina says, wheeling back from the doorway as I enter.

I give her a raised eyebrow and she laughs. "No, I appreciate the warning. I was able to get Ellen to safety"

I nod. "Good. I like your wife."

Gina laughed. "Yeah, you know, so do I! She's visiting her mother and from there, will vanish to an undisclosed location. We'd hoped this would be our forever house, but..."

"If you really mean 'forever,' you know folks like us need a couple of options in our back pockets."

Gina nodded. "Fortunately, the private sector has been good to her. And to me."

"But now, you have a plan to close up shop and join her?"

"Yes. And what about our mutual friend?"

"Rogers? She's bloodthirsty as ever," I say lightly. When I see Gina's frown, I hold up my hand. "Not 'bloodthirsty,' but certainly as...keen as any predator for the hunt."

"I worry what the break with Heath will do to her. I mean, even if she was my roommate, I didn't know anything about her background until you dug around. That was a nice piece of work, finding her military tests and assessments. If anyone was ever made for this job, she was. Now Heath's taking that from her?" Gina blew out a breath.

"I don't think she's unstable, but if she shows any untoward reaction, I'll have a word with her."

Gina nods. "We don't want her to go feral. I mean, I owe her a lot, and so do you."

"I never would have made it through the hand-to-hand if she hadn't worked so hard with me. Taught me all of her dirty tricks, bless her heart."

Gina laughs. "So...what are we looking for?"

"Oh, you'll like this. I need to find a way to get a retinal scan."

"Must be interesting, if you're asking for my help."

"You know I've always enjoyed working with you. But yeah, it's...complicated."

"Ah. Then let's away to the library, where we shall become anonymous creatures of the internet."

As we head to the library, I see that Gina's taking my warning seriously and beginning to throw a few things together. At the same time, I know how much she'll miss the house. It's tastefully furnished with antiques and mementos from her travels with Ellen, meant for comfort and not trying to impress anyone. It's the kind of thing I aspire to someday.

Once in the library, we make our way to Tor, which helps hide our IP address by rerouting all of our requests through proxies. After we're sufficiently obscured, Gina asks, "Where to? We need to buy someone's credentials?"

"I don't think those will be available; the retinal scan we need is for Richard Heath."

"You've checked, though?"

I nod.

"I had to ask; no use overlooking the obvious. Still...I might know some enemies of enemies who might be able to help me."

"Give it a shot. Your contacts are more...comprehensive than mine."

It takes forever, as such transactions do. Queries loaded with euphemisms and coded language, hidden identities, the delay of bouncing the information all over the world lagging the responses.

After several patient hours, we're forced to admit defeat.

"Maybe we're going about this the wrong way," I say. "What if we hack the scanning machine?"

"It's not like their machine is going to be off-the-shelf; we're probably going to be looking at some very, very proprietary hardware and software. And generally speaking, even those have pretty robust matching technology."

"No, I'm saying that we don't try to reproduce his scan. We hack the algorithm that makes the comparison between the living retina and Heath's recorded template."

Gina sits back and purses her lips, her eyes wide and unblinking as she considers the parameters of what I was proposing. "It would be a bitch and a half, but I think if anyone could pull it off..."

"We could," I finish. I'm already excited by the challenge. So many levels of security to penetrate, so light a touch needed. In the end, my credentials aren't valid any longer and while that was always a long shot, it would be pretty poor security indeed, if the thing validating the scan could be compromised.

"What if we go low tech?" Gina asks. "Go at this from the other end, and get his scan on a reader that we plant?"

I think about it. "I mean, the scanner hardware itself will be off the shelf, even if the software isn't. The part number..." I tap a few keys and bring up a duplicate of the scanner the Department uses. "We'd have to put it into a door he uses every day. Or replace the door itself, depending."

"Those would be hard to get at now, considering what's going on. What about the doors he only visits occasionally?"

"No way to know which one would be most likely, and even if we picked several..." I shake my head. "That's a lot of construction, a lot of chances to get caught, and, hell, it's sloppy. We'd be letting in everyone who wanted to go in, with the dummy scanner. We need another idea."

"But not tonight. I'm exhausted and will be better tomorrow."

"Of course, I'm sorry. Look, let me cook something for you."

"There's nothing in the house but iron rations: I was planning to leave tomorrow. I'm sorry to miss one of your meals."

I hear her words, but the light in her eyes tells me she'd love me to cook, and it's been ages since I made a meal for anyone but myself. "Look, you get ready to leave tomorrow, as planned. I saw a market on my way here, and I'll stop by and pick up some food. I should have thought of it on my way here."

"Ma'am, I'll gladly accept your offer." Her face breaks into a smile.

Chapter Twenty-Seven: Amy Lindstrom

The next time I awoke in the cut-rate motel room, I rolled out of bed, landed straight on the wrong foot, and made a noise like an outraged wolverine. I had to pee so bad I'd forgotten about my leg. If Marie hadn't been awake before, she was now, at my side instantly.

"Hang on, hang on. Let me give you a hand until we know you're not going to keel over."

She helped me into the bathroom, which was only marginally less gross than your average bus station toilet. At least it wasn't backed up. She barely shut the door before I got my panties down—my cargo pants weren't to be found.

As I hugged my knees in the sheer bliss of a grateful bladder, I opened my eyes face-to-face, if you will, with my wounded leg. I shuddered and looked away as quickly as possible, but the neat strips of surgical tape that closed a jagged tear in the flesh—my flesh—seared an image onto my mind's eye.

"Aw, goddammit!" I clenched my fists and stared straight ahead, trying not to think about what I'd seen.

"Pretty neat, huh?" Marie called through the door.

"Yeah, whatever." I gritted my teeth, pulled myself together, flushed, and hobbled out of the room. My leg hurt like blazes, but I could put weight on it. I saw a bulging plastic grocery bag on top of the trash next to the hotplate. I could see an empty box of gauze and a brown chemical bottle, maybe alcohol or hydrogen peroxide. Marie would have had to stitch her own wound up, without benefit of unconsciousness. My stomach did another forward roll. What kind of person could do that?

I limped back over to the bed and sat down heavily. "What day is it?"

"Same day, three hours later." She paused. "Thanks for spelling me there. I never felt safer."

"Shut up. Where are my pants? What's our next step?"

"I cut them off to fix you up. They were ruined anyway. And the next step is to figure out what to do with you, then figure out how I can keep one covert government entity and a dangerous military corporation from killing us along with several dozen unaware officers who've faithfully served."

I glared at her, and she gave me a ratty smile.

"What do you mean, figure out what to do with me?"

"I can't work and look after you at the same time. Especially not now."

"Look after me?" I pulled myself up straight. "Look, I have contacts we can use. Senators, the Pentagon—"

"We can't rely on them. Not with Heath's word against ours. We need someplace for you to hole up while I get to work. I've got to leave you for a while."

"How do I know you're coming back?"

"You sure you want me to?" Again with the ratty grin, but then it vanished. "No, we need each other a while longer."

I thought about the gunfight, and my part in it. How my mind was starting to work, so utterly contrary to my beliefs. *No.* I still had far too many questions about her past and my future. At the very least, I was going to get the damn story. "Yeah—you owe me a story. What about Jacob Wilson? My editor at the *Item*? Surely there's someone there who can verify what we—"

"Uh huh. Let's talk about that. I tried calling your desk at the *Item* today, and they told me you were out on medical leave."

"Medical leave? What the hell—?"

Marie nodded. "It looks like my former bosses have been speaking to your bosses."

My thoughts rushed forth. Even if coerced, Jacob wouldn't believe whatever they'd told him about me. He'd keep his mouth shut while he did what they said but wouldn't switch his brain off. That might be useful later if I could think of a way to contact him without getting him hurt.

But what can you do against a government? Or, rather, a secret government agency?

A thought hit me, like a punch to the stomach: Lucy. "My family—I have to let my family know I'm okay. I have to warn them!"

She shook her head. "Amy, you can't. You don't want to give Heath any reason to look at them."

I felt the blood rush out of my face. "What...why won't he find them? What if he tries to use them to get to me? I can't—!" I started to get up, but another wave of sickness knocked me back down.

"Amy, listen to me. He's not going to go after your family, not if I know him like I do. For one reason, it would be too public and he's trying very hard to keep this quiet. Tommy was the one he would be interested in, but Tommy's gone so he'll leave them alone. For now."

I wanted desperately to believe her. "What's the other reason?"

"Heath believes we won't be that hard to find." She looked away briefly. "It looks like we're on the same side for a while longer."

I glanced down at the pistol on the nightstand, wondering what I should do. I could smell the citrus-tang of metal lubricant in the room. She'd been cleaning her guns again. When I looked up again, Marie had another ghost of a smile.

"Sure, you've still got it. I have plenty, with the weapons I took off our friends back there."

"It's loaded?"

"There's no point to an unloaded gun. I'll even show you how to use it."

"If you let me keep it, it's because you either don't think I'll use it on *you*," I said slowly, "or because you think it wouldn't do me any good to even try, or so...I won't freak out. You need me to think I've got some control over the situation."

She frowned. "Chances are, I'd probably get the gun back as soon as I needed it. But as you say, if you got resources, you use them, and I need you to be on the same page as me. May I?"

I handed her the gun. "Who's gonna stop you?"

The rodent grin left her face as she hooked her hair over her ear, and turned into Drill Instructor Marie, showing me how it worked.

My hands were shaking as I tried to thumb the bullets into the magazine, and I fumbled it. They were heavier than they looked, and slick, too, in my sweaty hands. The gun itself had a hard elegance that was grimly attractive. It was customized, fancier than most of the guns my family owned, but the horror of guns, for me, is how simple they are to use and how similar they all are.

"Think of aiming the round ends of the cartridges toward the round end of the magazine, flat end toward the flat side of the magazine."

"I know, I know, okay?" She was just trying to break it down to its most elemental parts, bite-sized for someone who'd been traumatized, but it infuriated me.

I took a deep breath, finished loading the magazine, and slapped it home.

"Good job," Marie said. "When you get a little more comfortable loading the mag, I'll show you how to do it without leaving prints on the bullets."

"They can recover prints from a bullet that's been...fired?"

Then it suddenly struck me that she'd done it again. She kept referring to a future in which we were still associated, on the same side, her teaching me things. I had to remember she was a volatile part of this situation, a trained manipulator. But...she could have left me, or killed me, rather than patching me up.

"Okay." I shook myself. "This is the magazine release?" I said, pointing to a button.

"Yes." She paused. "You already seem pretty comfortable."

"Never comfortable. They make me sick. I don't like guns."

"It's them or us, Amy. You've got to get over it." She looked at me thoughtfully. "Your family hunted. Rifles, shotguns?"

"The house was full of them." I shuddered. If she had that file, no doubt she knew all about how Grandpa died, and possibly even my part in it. But she didn't say anything about any of that.

"Well, you can't own just *one*," she said, a light in her eyes that made my stomach clench. "You don't have to like them. I'm glad you know a little about them."

"Dad didn't make me hunt, but he was adamant we all learn proper gun safety."

She didn't seem to notice what I was saying. "Amy, do you remember what happened back on the street? You don't like certain aspects of my job. I can't afford to let your sensibilities get in the way, not of something that may take both our lives and the lives of many others."

Words seemed ridiculously inadequate for what I felt. Keep it simple, Lindstrom. "Being what you are...it's just...you seem to think you can go around killing people. Like it's nothing."

She raised her eyebrows at "being what you are," and almost frowned. "It's not nothing, it's to keep us alive. It's a very small price to pay. A few scumbags who earned a bullet for themselves in return for our lives? Do the math."

"I just don't know if I can be a party to that."

"Too late, Princess." She frowned, then said, "Look, at home, we used to say you show up when we're baking, you get coffee cake. If you show up on chicken day, you help slaughter chickens. You showed up on chicken day."

"What the hell are you talking about? The two aren't at all comparable!"

"You're not being realistic about how we're going to survive," she said. "You would have died, back there, if not for what I do."

"You shouldn't be doing this on your own. There are...agencies, laws..."

"And now the laws are being broken by those agencies, I should just sit back and let them? Let innocents suffer and die? I didn't sign up for that. Wake up, Amy." She clapped her hands in my face, angry. "Wouldn't you prefer me to someone else in this situation? At least I believe in government."

"Of everyone but yourself." It was a stupid thing to say, and I knew it. But I was still hurt by the old memories of guns she was dredging up.

She jabbed her finger at me. "I'm nothing *but* government. I'm nothing but self-control. Lucky for you. And for the record, you're incredibly naive, unable to accept what *you* are." She took a deep breath. "You struggle to maintain your voice, you butt heads with your family, but you still do what you think is right. Is best. But do you get my point? We have to stay alive to save a lot of other folks. That means we do what we have to do."

"I get it." I was exhausted and doubted I was going to dissuade her. Besides, she sounded like my family. "Can't you just...do you have to shoot to kill?"

One eyebrow shot up. "Amy, those men I shot, killed, at the cabin were colleagues. I'm only trying to survive. And they're out to get me. Do you think they'll be likely to leave the field, quietly and never to return, once I've *gently* shot them?"

She wasn't entirely wrong. "Just...just try to avoid it if you can."

Marie nodded. "Avoiding trouble is the whole idea, chica."

It was as good as I was gonna get out of her for the moment.

She took another deep breath, resumed her planning. "You're going to have to stick around here while I track down supplies. You're wounded and need to rest. I need to ascertain whether we have anyone on our side; unlikely, apart from Raven. You can't contact anyone you know, not unless you want them in this, too. That would be spectacularly unwise. We can't trust anyone; they can

Dana Cameron 137

all be compromised. You can't use your regular computer accounts, credit cards, or ATM card, either. After another can of stew, we'll work on disguise."

She heated up the stew and brought out a loaf of bread. Food never tasted so good. After that, we opened a couple of packages of hair color, and soon neither one of us was blonde.

I stared in the mirror, not sure what to do with myself. I wanted to cry. While I prided myself on not generally caring what I looked like above a bare professional level of presentation, I also knew that people saw "white, blonde, fit, tall, with symmetrical features" as "attractive." That had worked for me, all my life, and now that it was gone, I realized that it had allowed me to feel comfortable in my skin. A disguise was necessary to my survival, but I felt wretched about it, and was surprised at how much.

I caught myself staring too long; Marie hadn't batted an eye at her transformation. Sniffing hard, I said, "So, you had a farm?"

"Huh?" She was busy drying her hair with the last towel. She rolled her head, cracking her neck.

It wasn't a very convincing stall. "You mentioned chickens before. My folks have land, animals."

"Yeah, we had a farm. And now, it's sack time. We've got a busy day tomorrow, and I want to look and feel my best."

Without another word, she flipped off the light, flung herself into bed, and looked asleep, dead silent, in under a minute.

Chapter Twenty-Eight: Nicole Bradley

I'm in luck, and the market is still open. Not the time of day I'd ordinarily shop—I go first thing, when all the stuff is freshest—but I'm well provided and begin to hum, anticipating a quick meal that'll be a delight to eat. With so much in my world that I can't control, cooking tasty food is a balm. And if Gina can keep me company one last time...so much the better.

As I'm checking out, the clerk gives me an odd look when I ask for an extra bag for a single can of beans.

The light in the parking lot flickers. I notice that there's an orange parking violation ticket on my windshield.

My brain races through all the things it might be, as the parking lot light directly over my space went out.

I've kept limber and quick through exercise, but I'm out of peak fighting shape. I drop the heavier of my two bags, duck, and twist away and back from where I was.

That doesn't matter, because someone shot me. Maybe it does matter, because I feel the sledgehammer smash in my upper left arm, rather than my head.

I go down. Don't want to, can't help it.

Footsteps approaching. I whisper to my phone to call Gina. My nightmare continues with the ringing, ringing, and no one answering. I leave a voice to text message.

Too late, I was too late, fuck it hurts—

Enough. You're not dead yet. Get busy.

I can't move, without giving myself away. I inch my good hand into my handbag, fraction by fraction. Enough fractions, you get a whole piece. Can't wait until he—it's a he, I recognize a junior guy of Heath's now—decides to finish the job with the second and third shots, and that's gonna hurt worse.

I sit up fast, pulling my SIG from my handbag, firing. It's a crap shot, because the piece catches on the strap of my bag. I manage to slide the strap down my arm, just enough to correct my aim. As prepared as I am, it's not enough. I've been out of the field too long...I can only hope he's thinking I'm going to be an easy target.

He stumbles, and I can't tell how bad he's hit, only that he's still coming for me, just not in a straight line. He gets off another shot, two, and one of them goes wide, the other hits the open trunk of my car. Shit.

Time is officially against me; I don't have a suppressor, but there's a chance no one will have heard it. There's a better chance they did.

I try to scramble up; it's messy, and I hiss when my arm is jarred. I hate that I made any noise, but it's better than a scream.

Free of my bag, I fire fast, three more times, and the bastard is still shambling toward me, a zombie who doesn't yet realize his head has been cut off.

There should be another one, these fuckers usually travel in pairs, but I can't find them. No time to worry about what might be, and focus on what's ahead of me.

I aim the next shots for center mass, but blood runs into my eyes and I chunk it. He swings for me, connecting upside my head. I hook my ankle behind his and slam the pistol into his face.

He goes over, still twitching, still mumbling. "...g personal..."

"The fuck it isn't personal! What's going on?"

Another gurgle, a nasty wheezing sound from his chest, and he's dead.

I like having an innocuous looking weapon on me when I can arrange it, not that it helped this time. I'm tempted to take my bag with the can and bash his head into a paste, but another reality set in:

There isn't another operative here, because that one is at Gina's. They didn't think they needed two to take me down, and since her injury—

Cursing, I slam the trunk shut, and after I toss the body and find nothing useful about their mission, I drive as close to the speed limit as I can. No sense getting tagged for speeding when I'm covered in blood, a cooling corpse in the parking lot of the market.

My heart is racing and sweat soaks my clothing. I've pulled a muscle in my back and I feel the blood running down my wrist, recognizing that I'm steadily getting lightheaded. I'm briefly grateful I'm driving an automatic this week, but then another grim reality reveals itself.

My exquisite Loro Piana blazer is a lost cause, blood-soaked, torn, and filthy.

That motherfucker...

I nudge the speed a little higher. Maybe I can get the guy as he was leaving Gina's. Avenge her, stop him from calling in. Something, anything besides bleeding and cursing.

Chapter Twenty-Nine: Amy Lindstrom

When I woke up the next morning, Marie was already up. She pulled out a phone from the bag Raven had given her.

Panic took me. "Wait!"

She froze, finger poised over the screen. "What?"

"Isn't this...aren't you taking a big chance? Calling someone? Can you trust Nicole?"

She nodded. "It's a burner phone. I either trust her or I don't. She and I went through training together, and I believe her. And you don't get anywhere without getting exposed. Otherwise you're sitting there in the dark, your dick in your hand, waiting for them to find you first. It's a calculated risk. We need help, and AP's our best bet."

"AP?" What did the Associated Press have to do with this?

"We haven't met in person in a long time, and her scale of operations has always been small. Local, you might say." She seemed happier, having made the decision.

She finished punching in the numbers, and spoke, presumably, when someone answered. "May I speak with Ms. Driver, please? Oh, Josh? It's Ms. Jones. I'm just fine, thanks, how are you? How's school? Oh yeah? Well, don't worry about it, you can always take it over. I know your moms isn't happy about it, but she's just concerned about you, you know. Oh? Okay. I know. Is she at work? Okay. Thank you, Josh. Bye, now."

"What now?" I asked. "Ms. Jones" sounded just like some suburban neighbor talking to another suburban neighbor's over-achiever-of-the-month kid. Parlez-vous minivan? Maybe it was code.

She dialed another number. "Ms. Driver, please." A pause, then, "Don't say anything, but if you remember a very special Christmas present several years ago, you'll know who this is. Call me back from someplace private."

She hung up. I looked at her. "Christmas present?"

"You don't want to know."

The phone rang. "Ape? It's me. I'm in a jam." Another pause. "As bad as it gets. Got a pencil?"

Marie ran down a list of letters and numbers, many of which made no sense, but I did recognize "C4," "shaped charge," "d-wire," and "suppressors," though I didn't know the difference between a "D2" and "MULE Folder with a straight edge," and didn't recognize the name of the chemicals—medicines?— she mentioned. And why would anyone need five hundred rounds of anything? What the hell were Danners, and why did she want her old ones? And why she was asking for Triathlons, coins, and her old harness—she wasn't going to go horseback riding, was she?

"I need clothes, too, smart, for DC. I'm still the same size. The other one is female—" She glanced at me. "Probably a size twelve."

"I'm a size ten."

"Yeah, size twelve. Yeah, I know you already have a full-time job and kids," she said, "but my usual supplier and I fired each other." And another pause. "Yeah, I know, 'holy shit'—you think I'm lying? And I need it all ASAHP."

I found myself crossing my fingers this "AP" would be able to help.

Marie didn't look thrilled, but said, "Outstanding. Yeah, yeah, I know it's expensive: a rush job, special orders, and all. And I owe you a chit. Yes, I got money. Bitch."

But she was laughing when she said it. Then she turned serious again. "I figured. Where?" If AP gave her an address, Marie didn't write it down.

"You rock, Ape. Talk soon."

She broke off the call with a look of satisfaction. "We're good. I'll be back later, if all goes well. Good news is, no one knows where we are at the moment."

If they found us...well, I didn't want to think about it. I'd piss in that brook when I came to it, as my brothers say.

Huh. That was a lot like something Marie would say.

"If I need to call you, I'll let the phone Nicole gave you ring three times, then hang up, and call again. Just don't answer when it rings the first time, got it?"

"Right. Telling a reporter not to answer the phone."

She cocked her head, annoyed. "Stay here. Keep your head down. I'll be back as soon as I can."

Before I could say anything, she was out the door.

I tried walking around a bit more. While it was still sore, my leg didn't seem too bad. The water and the food had done a lot while I was awake, and I will never say enough good things about sleeping. But now I had a few decisions to make.

Marie said I shouldn't contact anyone, and while I certainly didn't want to drag my editor Jacob or my family into this mess, I needed to confirm what I'd learned so far. I wasn't taking Marie or Nicole at their word, not entirely. Both were professional liars, trained to be compelling. I had to confirm whether this was a tale constructed for me personally, to draw me along. Provided I could find a pay phone and a library, I had a way to do it. I just didn't trust the phone Nicole had given me, didn't want her tracking me, not even after Marie had pulled the device out of its packaging to enter the other phone's numbers. I may be foolhardy, but I'm not stupid. And I had skills to use.

I went into the bathroom, and when I looked in the mirror, I screamed. I'd forgotten I'd lost six inches of hair and was now an unconvincing brunette. The cheap black dye, way too dark for me, made me look even less like me than a good color would have. I was so much less recognizable as me. Subterfuge was the name of the game, chica. After I showered, doing my best to keep my leg dry, I put on way too much makeup with colors that I never used. Then the ancient phone book that was in the drawer by the bed: it was missing pages, sticky, stained, and ten years out of date. The place we were staying didn't even rate a Bible.

I figured out where we were and where I needed to go. I was almost out the door when I realized a towel wasn't going to be enough once I stepped outside the motel room. Marie had certainly not intended for me to leave. She hadn't even left the rags of my cargo pants behind.

Dry cleaning—gone, lost in the car back at the cabin. Bag—there was some cash in my wallet, but nothing to cover my ass at the moment. Credit cards were out of the question.

Did Marie have anything with her that I could use? I tried to remember what I'd seen when she was rummaging through her courier bag that morning. No extra clothes, not even anything out of the usual, apart from her guns: a fancy corkscrew, same as waiters use in good restaurants, wallet, brush, comb, hair ties, tampons, Leatherman, a fistful of plastic bag ties, a couple of condoms, and a small black object the size of a deck of cards.

Earlier that morning, I'd picked up the Leatherman. They were handy gadgets, with the usual things on a pocket knife in addition to a good pair of folding pliers. "Nice."

"Don't touch that!" Marie had said quickly.

"Don't worry about it," I'd said. "I have one just like it."

"Not like that one. Just put it down, would you?"

I'd set it down carefully. "What about this?" I'd picked up a length of what looked like an industrial sized rubber band, about three feet long.

"For resistance exercises. I'd have used it earlier, but right now, I'm giving my core a break."

When I'd pointed out it wasn't a very convincing arsenal, she'd said, "A waiter or bartender doesn't walk around with a bag full of James Bond, do they? Besides, all the good stuff was lost in the car fire."

So, nothing. In addition to my wallet, I had only my Swiss Army knife and the sewing kit left over from Doctor Marie's surgery. She'd taken all the good stuff, including the cash Raven—Nicole—had given us. But I had my secure key fob electronic encoder from George. Which gave me an idea.

It was a start. After rejecting the curtains—Scarlet O'Hara was an asshole and I didn't want the room to be exposed to prying eyes—I turned to the bed. I tried not to think about what I'd read about the biotic content of motel bedspreads and cut off one of the side panels, wrapping it around me kilt style. I sewed up the side as best I could with me in it, then pulled my T-shirt down over the waistline. It looked like I was wearing upholstery, but if you didn't look too close, it also resembled a couture knockoff from about thirty years ago. My dirty slide-on sneakers had been washed and the blood had dried to a faded brown.

It would do. I checked the phone book and took off.

I got over my reticence pretty quickly. I looked nothing like me, and there was freedom in that. I tried to keep from quickening my pace too much past the low brick homes huddled together. My aching leg helped. I found the secondhand shop I wanted without much trouble. I grabbed sneakers, a shirt, and men's jeans that fit both me and my wallet. The guy behind the counter kindly offered to significantly discount the asking price but I demurred, indicating I preferred to couple with my own species. After the rest of the transaction was completed in silence, I departed.

It took me ages, but I found a payphone and considered who I'd call and what I'd ask, very carefully.

I dialed, held my breath, and waited.

"Emmaline Bolton's office. This is Sarah."

I used my college roommate's Boston accent; at UVA, it stuck out like a sore thumb. It was a pastime in our house to imitate her. "Hi, Sarah, it's Kaylee Faust from *Washington Item* Lifestyle. How are you today? I was wondering if I could ask you a question about a dinner that took place about two weeks ago."

"Of course."

When someone from the *Item*'s Style section calls, you help if you can. Especially when you're the assistant to one of the most socially prominent women in the city. "I've been trying to help Amy Lindstrom's boss while she's on medical leave and wondered if you could tell me whether she was at the dinner to cover an announcement. Something Mrs. Bolton wanted to announce?"

"No, not at all. I believe she was a late addition to the list. Just a moment, please."

Here's where I crossed my fingers and held my breath. Please, don't call Emmaline to the phone...

"No, I'm sorry, I thought I might have a note somewhere, but I believe she was invited at the request of another guest."

"Can you tell me who that was?"

I waited while she calculated. "I'm afraid I can't help you."

It was a practiced lie. I guessed it was Kola, but was hoping she might spill something else. "Thanks for your time. You've been a big help."

"Oh, you're welcome. And please, if you see Amy, give her our best wishes."

"Thank you, I will." I hung up.

Kola asking for me now made sense. If he suspected something was up with the Department, as Marie claimed, he'd want help. When you suspect government misdoings, you go to Amy Lindstrom.

I wasn't going to take everything Marie or Nicole said on faith. It made me a little crazy I'd never heard a hint of a whisper about the Department. I began to consider who I could call. Marie said she was taking a chance on her resources. I had resources, too, and now was the time to use them.

My police and investigator contacts were definitely out. I needed someone even more paranoid than I had to be, someone with deep connections, someone who wouldn't necessarily care about finding me. No one at the *Item*, no one on the Hill, no one with any official connections. You didn't know who'd be listening in or who'd been gotten to. I didn't even want to risk Googling these names.

I had to reach out to George No-Last-Name. Asking him for anything was like going down a rabbit hole, but he was the only person I knew at least as paranoid as Marie. I would leave a message asking about the Department and Richard Heath. I'd give him what details I'd gleaned about Marie and her military career.

A long, painful walk and a bus trip later trip, I found the library and thanked my stars it hadn't been closed. So many were, when budgets and incomes were slashed, exactly the wrong time to close a library. As if there was ever a good time. I changed in the bathroom as quickly as I could. Feeling much better, I headed over to the computers. I thought a while, checked my fob, keyed in the number, then made the message as vague as I could while still trying to grab his attention. I asked about the Department and Heath. Like Marie said, both names were anonymous enough.

Next I went down to the periodical section. Doing the research felt good. Calling Sarah felt good. I hadn't felt this sure of myself in ages. Marie had her groove, and I had mine.

I realized I was hungry and needed to eat. There was nothing left back at the motel room. I had about three bucks over my return carfare in my pocket. Still, three bucks was three bucks, and there was no point starving while I decided whether to use my bus fare to get back to the room or to flee as far as I could before I found a cave to hide in.

There was one other call I could make. It was a real risk, but I couldn't think of anything that wasn't. And I didn't like being stuck with Marie as my only backup. Having been shot, I couldn't be too careful about redundancy.

I thought long and hard, then I went into the library lobby and lucked out again: there was a pay phone there. Maybe I was mitigating the danger by calling Burke, maybe just speeding up the negative resolution to all of this.

Pausing a moment longer before I put the change in, I figured the *Bugle-Courier* was far enough down the food chain from the *Item* to keep him off the radar of anyone looking for me. The fact I had a reputation for being standoffish, especially with newbies, sealed the deal. I put the change into the slot and dug through my wallet for his card.

It took him a couple of rings to pick up. "Burke."

"It's me," I said. "Remember, from Cherrydale? Can you talk? No names."

There was an almost inaudible gasp on the other end of the line as he recognized my voice. "Now's not a good time."

"When would be? I'm in a bad situation. I can't go into it on the phone."

"I'll call you back at this number in an hour. I'll be able to talk then. Are you okay?"

I read him the phone's number. "I'm in big, big trouble."

I disconnected. There was a fast food joint nearby and I rented a table for the next forty-five minutes, making my burger and ice water last as long as I could. Marie would have been proud of me, sipping so slowly. Ten minutes before the hour was up, I returned to the library lobby.

I didn't realize I'd been holding my breath until the phone finally rang.

"It's me. A—What the fuck is going on?"

"Just indulge my paranoia, please!"

I heard a deep breath. "Are you safe, for the moment?"

"Yeah." I felt my eyes fill up. "For the moment."

"Okay. You can tell me about the nature and depth of the shit you're in when we meet. Tell me where."

I was ready, I'd been planning all the time I'd been eating. "Okay, the baseball team you're always rooting against—got it?"

"Yes. Wait—we really need to be this...circumspect?"

"Yes."

"Okay, remember the first time we met, the whole gang all together? The guy sitting next to me all night? You know, our friend with the bad teeth?"

"Got it. Yeah?"

"That's the second part of the name. The repository. When can you meet me?" I heard keys tapping as he worked it out.

"It's gonna be a couple hours, given the traffic. Can you manage it?"

"I think so."

"Okay. What do you need?"

"Money. A burner phone. Clothes. A toothbrush would be a godsend. But I need information, mostly. I'll tell you when you get here."

"Okay, got it." There was a pause on the other end of the line. "We'll talk when I get there. You'll tell me what's going on?"

"Yes," I said. I'd decided: If I was killed, someone else needed to know what I knew.

With exactly thirty-seven cents in my pocket over what I needed to get back to the motel, I had to cool my jets and marshal what resources I could before we met.

We had no gang, but the first time we'd met had been at a retirement party for a mutual colleague. The guy who sat next to me was named Carney. There had been an argument about sports, and I learned that Burke was a Yankees fan; I've always adored the Orioles. So the library—repository—was the Parkville-Carney in Baltimore. I went back and tried to brush up on what I knew about Mrs. Kola, her husband, and their colleagues.

I was hobbled; I couldn't afford to type Anton Kola's name into a search engine on the off chance the government, if not the Department, was monitoring the web. I needed to think about where he might have hidden his computer and its encryption key. Anything might be a clue.

In the periodicals room, I found very little about Mrs. Kola. A piece in *Architectural Digest* about one of her local homes, a few photos in *Vanity Fair* and the *Item*, all from fundraisers. A large piece when her son died, and a sizable obit, where she'd requested donations be made to a local children's organization in his name. A small piece about her grandson's birth announcement. Not much at all, considering the woman was positioning herself to be one of the most powerful people in the world.

That got me thinking about her family. I had to wonder what they were like, for her to consider marrying someone like Kola.

I dug around her father's and brothers' history, learned about their various businesses. Then I did a bit more rooting about, checking into their holdings, corporations, and shells.

I sat back and realized that I had a piece of the puzzle that was all one color. Philomena's family had warehouses and storage containers all over the world—which would make an excellent place to stash enough weapons for several small armies—but I couldn't narrow it down to a continent, much less a city.

I found nothing about Heath, who should've been high enough to have had a presence elsewhere in the government. Disappointment set in.

Using my key fob, I used the code to access the site George created. A chat window popped up, I left a message with my queries, and tried not to think about how much I was counting on him. I'd put my trust in a lot of strangers today, it seemed.

A row of "????" appeared in the window.

"R U there?" I typed.

"WTF RU N2?" came back the reply, almost instantly.

"Bad?"

"Worst. Talk 2 me."

At this point, I hesitated. What if George worked for the Department, or, more likely, had been compromised somehow?

"Hang on. Where was our 1st FTF in RL?" Where'd we first met face to face in real life?

There was a long pause. "Never did." Another pause, and then, "Nice 2 C UR learning."

No, we'd never met in person. Yes, I was learning to be paranoid. At least I knew it was George, though whether he was being constrained in some way was another question. I typed in the names I wanted him to research. "How soon?"

"24hrs," he typed back. "Tough one. Dark places. Rumors only re. Department; weird chatter, interagency."

Apparently George had heard something going on between Federal agencies involving a covert operative going rogue. Maybe this much of Marie's story was true. "K, thx. 24 hrs."

There was another pause. "No, thank u. Careful. Bad things."

Chapter Thirty: Nicole Bradley

I drive around the back of Gina's home and park, drawing the firearm I took off the guy now in my trunk. As I walk through the shadows toward the lit part of the house, I heard the bumping of something heavy, followed by grunts and angry words.

Light suddenly floods the drive. I flinch, raising my hand to shield my eyes; there's nowhere to hide. A motor comes to life, growling with enthusiasm.

Gina's driving the tractor, a shotgun across her lap. There's blood streaming from her nose, and the set of her jaw tell me that she's not in the mood for any nonsense.

Any *more* nonsense.

"It's me," I call out. "You okay? I tried to phone and got back quick as I could."

She waves and cuts the engine. "I'm fine. Your call tipped me off as to the 'who,' when the alarm told me 'where.'"

"Um...where are you going?"

"Back forty. Got a place to stash the trash." She nods at the back of the tractor. There's a cart attached, a bloody arm hanging over the side. I see another arm, a different sized hand, on the other side.

"Nice!"

"Well, you reminded me to work smarter, not harder. I've always admired your little fold-up handcart in the trunk."

It's always lovely when a friend, especially a terribly competent one, pays you a compliment. "Need a hand?"

"No, I'm good. I've...developed a system."

This isn't the first time she's had to move and hide a body on her property. "I'll go in, get cleaned up?"

"Help yourself to whatever's in the guest bathroom. I'll be back in about an hour."

I read the scene as I enter: It's as plain as any printed script. She set the alarm after I'd left. The intruders, who were probably now enjoying a promotion to useful compost, had disarmed the house alarm, but only after they'd triggered the perimeter alarm and cameras.

Gina had rolled up to the side door with the shotgun, waited for it to creep open, then blasted the intruder full of unpleasant and heavy materials traveling at a very high velocity. I noticed a ding in the wainscoting across the room, so the first intruder had gotten one shot off at least.

There's another bloody trail by the kitchen door; I knew she'd killed two of them, but was surprised that three had been sent for us. Huh; maybe they thought they'd find both of us here, or maybe they were more concerned about Gina being in her element, on her home turf. Smart of them, but not successful.

"Whatever's in the bathroom" is a beautifully organized medicine cabinet, with everything someone in our career might need for emergencies. It's a ritual I quickly tired of before I focused solely on intelligence, and one of the reasons I'd first considered crafting that retirement letter: examining myself for wounds. There's a graze on my upper arm—I apply pressure and add layers of petroleum jelly and gauze until the bleeding stops. I wrap it up; it's difficult doing this one-handed, but I'm all too familiar with the process. I examine the antibiotics in the cupboard and grab a vial, taking two of the tablets immediately. I don't dare take a painkiller.

Gina looks drawn when she arrives back in the house. Her nose has stopped bleeding and the trail of blood from her nostril was diluted with her sweat. I've only just beaten her in completing my self-appointed task of cleaning up the blood and patching the wall. It's the toothpaste in the crack trick, but it will delay detection until I can figure out where the spackle is, if we have that long.

"If you'll wash up, dinner will be ready by the time you're done," I say. "We have a short amount of time—"

She nods, tiredly. "I checked them for biometrics—there were none. I think they were just doing surveillance, and then when you showed up, they figured it was their lucky day. Two of us at once."

Adrenaline draining away, it's only by focusing on ingredients and temperatures that I can keep myself awake. I'm ravenous and depleted.

When she returns, Gina and I eat seared salmon and black bean salad. By mutual agreement, we forego what would be our traditional argument over which wine to have; nothing but black tea and coffee now. We need to move out ASAP.

I see tape on her nose. "Ellen's gonna be displeased."

"Yeah, I know." There's a hint of a smile on Gina's face. "I can attest and aver that it's a memento from my official retirement party."

"What about the house?"

"It's been sold. The new owners move in next week; the rest of the stuff will get moved in two days, and the cleaning crew will be in the day after that."

"Are they going to find a recent crime scene on the property?"

"I doubt it. And they're friends; if they did happen on something, they'd know enough to either ignore it or ask me." She sighed and put her fork down. "I did, however, warn them that there was a particularly nasty patch of poison ivy over near the edge of the property, near—or just over—the line with the nature preserve."

A brief smile from me. "I'm sorry. It's my fault, all of this."

"Don't be foolish; if you hadn't come to me, I would've been killed, an unfortunate accident while my wife was away." She shook her head. "The whole thing is shitty."

"I know."

"And you know this is the last time we'll see each other. But if I get any brainwaves about your problem, I'll find a way to reach you."

A genuine smile, now. "If anyone can find me, you can. And *you* are welcome to. Thanks."

We clean up, and I meet her in the garage. We hug, and, settled in her van, she waves once and pulls out.

And then she's gone.

I think briefly about whether I can spend the night here, and that just tells me how tired I am. Time to vanish, again.

Chapter Thirty-One: Jayne Rogers

There's no place like a busy city subway to hide. Lots of commuters coming and going. No one paying attention to an anonymous woman, or anything but their train schedules. I go to one of the larger stations around rush hour.

I realize I feel rusty, and I need a warm-up.

I park the car and get out. A glance at the schedule boards and I realize I've caught my first break in a while. Trains coming in from both sides in two minutes. I duck down the tunnel to the inbound side. As that train arrives, another train comes in from the south with another flood of commuters. Cars jostle for place. Men get out and kiss their wives as they surrender the driver-side seats to them.

I duck onto the first side, walk briskly down the tunnel, looking for my targets. A woman with headphones, her canvas bag on the ground, her wallet sitting right on top. I stumble and scoop out the wallet, stashing it as I recover.

I find a brand-new baseball cap left on a barrier by some conscientious soul and I take it as I go back down the tunnel. It will be just enough to alter my appearance while I make my escape. Plus, it's the Yankees, which will probably annoy Amy, which will keep her from worrying.

On the train, I bump into a guy with bulges in the right places and make a hash out of righting myself. I relieve him of his wallet and cell phone on the way past.

I cut it close. The door closes behind me just as I leave, nearly on my heels. I can feel the air compress behind me. A few more moments of picking pockets on my way back through to the entrance and I have supplies. Not too much, though. The lot is emptying; greed will only get me busted. Plus I don't like ripping off civilians if I can help it. But too much is riding on this for me to feel bad about someone having to cancel their credit cards.

I imitate the gait of a stiff and unathletic commuter and find my car.

I join the queue to exit the lot and drive until I find a place with good exits and without too many cops, too many cameras. I count out the cash and pocket the licenses, not knowing whether I'll need them later. The phones are a blessing: I don't know how long the service will stay on, once the owners realized they've gone missing, but for now, I can use them once and not be traced. I load an app to one of them, then sign in. It allows me to listen in on digital police scanners for several localities. Nothing about me directly, but there's some bad news about Amy Lindstrom's workplace. I have to believe it's connected to us. Another car accident with fatalities—not the first in her life. It lets me know we're getting close and they're closing in fast, but this thing, this public thing, was a mistake and someone will swing for it.

I smell outside talent. And I don't like it.

Chapter Thirty-Two: Nicole Bradley

After I'm sure that I haven't been followed, I go to ground myself. I'm delighted to find that my special retreat is secure and has gone unnoticed in the past two years. A storage locker that, if the door is opened, appears to be packed tight with boxes. Another storage locker, on the back wall, rented in another name, also looks packed to the gills, but shares a concealed door with the first. Both have an outer veneer of bags of clothing that smell strongly of urine, a walker, and beat-up adult diaper boxes marked "Xmas stuff." Another layer or two inside, the boxes are packed with more useful things, and in my concealed space, the tools of my trades. I find my way to the back and open the old wardrobe door. I am, as usual, amused by my choice of entrance. A police call box would have been even better, but less discreet. I've created a small hidden workroom taking up the last quarter of both storerooms.

I lock up from the inside and start the cameras. I'm stealing power from the self-storage place; I have several crates of water and rations, and there's a chemical toilet if I need it. Otherwise...there is one box actually filled with unused adult diapers out front.

I stand on the desk and pull the network cable I've connected to the office and hook it up to my machine. I settle into a chair. The chair is the one nice thing in the room, apart from my tech: posture and ergonomics are important.

Since I still haven't come up with a way to simulate Heath's retinal scan remotely, I focus on finishing my unofficial version of Taps. Rodriguez gave me her list of folks not openly working with Heath on his new project. I compare it with mine; there's good overlap, so I have confidence in her list.

After I open the secure channels, using every trick in my bag to keep hidden, I add their information: retirement aliases, bank accounts, new passwords. Then I start configuring the botnet to reach out to them, with the signal to disperse, and then route their retirement packages to their chosen accounts. Because I'm significantly outraged, I add an extra raise here and there, but not too much; I don't want to set off any warnings.

Now all I need is the other authentication key and Heath's retinal scan. Once I have those, I can send out the signal, save my colleagues, and let them melt into the shadows a little richer, a little less endangered.

That done—it took ages because of paranoia, carefulness, and moving so slowly across the various servers—I close down. I open up another alias, the one that buys the nice clothing and shoes.

I'm about to buy a replacement for the beautiful jacket that was ruined—shot and bloodstained—when I pause. Maybe better to wait until this is all over? Save my estate some money if I don't make it out? Don't risk all that gorgeous cashmere getting shot?

While I'm pondering, I realize I can no longer put off what I've been loathe to do. I start evaluating assets outside the Department to see if there's anyone I trust inside the government to help us stop Heath. Someone who might be capable of stopping Heath.

A bit of subtle prying and I find a name: Matthew Dickens, over in the Office of the Inspector General at NSA. I vaguely remember him from my time there. I'll keep an eye on him and start softening the ground for the shit-ton of unpleasant information he's about to find dumped in his lap.

The tough task done, I realize I should check in with Rogers. I leave a message for her to check our IRC and then ponder our next move.

Finally, I decide to reward myself, and order a replacement for my beautiful coat. Until I'm cold and in the ground, I'll surround myself with lovely things.

Chapter Thirty-Three: Amy Lindstrom

It was quiet in the library. Everyone else there seemed to be sleeping off something. A scraping noise from behind startled me, and I jumped, cursing my sore leg.

"Amy?"

Burke was standing there, a gym bag over his shoulder, looking like the cavalry. Washed-out face and freckles, auburn cowlicks that never rested flat even when he'd clearly tried. His shock when he recognized me and my new look was followed by concern. That turned a key in a lock. I sprang up and threw myself at him, no longer noticing my leg was throbbing, tears coming in hysterical waves.

He was part of the world that I remembered. Work, the job, not this craziness...

I grabbed hold of his T-shirt and held onto the fabric until I heard him actually choke.

"Tight, Amy—ack."

I didn't let go of him, not entirely, but pulled away a bit, unnerved by what I was suddenly feeling—suffocating fear and stress, amplified by all the death I'd witnessed.

He looked rattled, which told me how bad I looked.

"We need to get you out of here."

I nodded.

Burke didn't say another word. I gathered up my notebook, stuffed it into my bag, and followed him as he all but raced out to the curb and his car. He held the door for me and I folded into the seat, my head on my knees.

I was starting to lose it. Oh God. Oh God, oh god, ohgodohgodohgod...

"Are you all right?"

"I...I'm fine. My...I hurt my leg a couple of days ago. I think I might have opened up the wound again, that's all. I'm a little dizzy. I'm probably still a little hungry, overtired, too." I offered him a bouquet of excuses, trying desperately not to cry.

It didn't work. I no sooner gave him the directions then I burst into tears.

He let me cry for ten minutes. "I'm not talking about your leg, Amy. It's okay. The accident has rocked us all. I'm just glad that you reached out—"

"Wait, what accident?"

"The car accident." He glanced at me. "You know Jacob and Michelle are dead, right? That's what this is about?"

I whipped my head up. "What? What are you talking about?"

"There was an accident. Jacob lost control of the car. They were killed instantly." His face went gray, as he tried to look at me and navigate the directions at the same time. "That's why you called me, right?"

"That's impossible," I said slowly, gaining confidence. I wiped my face. "Can't be. You've got it wrong."

"I'm sorry. I heard about it this morning. It's true."

"No, it can't be," I said. "Burke, Jacob doesn't *drive*."

"What? But I'm certain I heard he'd been driving. It was on the wire."

"Oh my God." I felt the blood rush from my face and I was overcome with dizziness again. "Oh, God, they got them, too, like Tommy. They staged it—" I had to get away from Burke. "You need to get out, far from me. I can't tell you anything. People around me get hurt."

"*Who* got them, Amy? You need to tell me what's wrong, you promised—"

"I—wait!" We'd just pulled into the block where the motel was. "Shit! Keep driving, don't stop!" I shouted.

"What? What's wrong?" He whipped his head around, trying to see what had me so scared.

162 *Exit Interview*

"Just keep going, around the corner. Jesus." I sat back in the seat, a cold chill taking me. "The door to our—my—room was open."

"What room, where? Maybe it was housekeeping?"

I glared at him. "There was no trolley or sluice bucket or anything by the door. Someone found us."

"Who's 'us,' Amy? What's going on?" His pale face was ashen. "Amy, we have to talk."

"No, I need to...I have to get out of here." I grabbed the gym bag and scrambled out of the car, running away from the motel, away from Burke.

"Amy!" I heard him call after me, but I ducked into a side street and zigzagged a few more times. I waited in a doorway, hyperventilating, tears running down my face, while I watched the sedan circle a couple times before Burke finally left.

I was trying to decide what to do when I heard another voice call my name. I turned and saw Marie pull up alongside me. She was in yet another anonymous sedan, probably liberated from some poor commuter's workplace. She pulled over and shoved the door open. "Get in."

I hesitated.

"Get in, we got trouble. We need to move, now."

I figured if I didn't trust her now, one way or the other, I was dead anyway. I got in.

She pulled away, but not so quickly that the tires squealed. "Where were you? What were you doing out of the room? Where did you get those clothes, that bag?"

"I left to find something to wear. I had a little money. And the bag, I stole from someone in the MTA." I prayed Burke didn't leave his name on his clothes.

I could see her hands tighten on the steering wheel. "That was incredibly stupid. You could've been caught, you could've been picked up—"

"You talked about assets. I'm an asset, and you weren't letting me—"

"You're not an asset if you get us killed!"

"At least I wasn't in the room. If I'd stayed put, whoever was in there would have—"

"Who was in the room?" She looked at me in alarm.

"Just now. You didn't see it?" I wrapped my arms tight around myself. "The door was open, and it wasn't the turndown service."

Marie sucked in a deep breath and turned the car around.

"Where are we going?" I asked. "I thought you must know, you said we—"

"I didn't know someone was in the room. I need a visual."

I began to shake. Everything started to hit me. "It's too dangerous!"

"Only if you get caught. Keep out of sight. And, for the love of Pete, keep quiet."

She drove around until she found an alley where we could park and watch the room. The door was shut now, but two men who looked distinctly out of place in the neighborhood got into a car and pulled away from the curb.

I gasped, sat up straighter. That particular shade of blue, the seahorse print...there weren't two of them in the world.

"Get down!" Marie pulled my arm, forcing me to the floor.

"But the guy, the one in the doll mask—"

"It isn't a mask," Marie said, her lips compressed, her knuckles white on the wheel.

"He...he was wearing Michelle's scarf!" I could barely catch my breath.

"Wait, your Michelle? At the *Item?*" She looked positively alarmed now, and that scared me worse. "How do you know it was her scarf?"

"It's a silk scarf, I had it made for her...last year, Christmas." I was numb. "There isn't another like it. Hand-painted, it was really expensive, but that shade of blue was perfect for her..."

Michelle had loved that scarf, and now she was dead, and Jacob was dead, and I didn't know who'd done it, but I knew it was my fault, trying to save myself and leave a trail with the Townsend file. I'd killed them just as certainly as I'd pulled a trigger.

Marie sat for a moment, saying nothing as I rocked back and forth, then put her arm over her seat and backed us out of the alley. The color had left her face. I didn't dare disturb her as we made a beeline for the interstate.

"I guess we know someone else Heath put on our trail," she said. "God-damned independent operators."

"Did he kill Michelle? And J-Jacob?" I tried to wipe my nose on the sleeve of my second-hand-store shirt. It wouldn't stop running. "Oh, Goddamn it..."

She nodded, her mouth set. "One of them was Chase, Heath's number two. The other one...if they're dead, and he's wearing her scarf, then you can bet he's responsible. He's one twisted fucker." She shook her head. "It's all bad news."

I stared at her—if *she* didn't think he was right... "What do you mean, twisted?"

She took a deep breath as she found the ramp for 95. "He's got a talent for interrogation and making death look accidental. He's big into taking trophies. They're here for us."

Marie kept her eyes on the road, but her knuckles were white on the wheel. "We need to get out of Dodge."

"We need to do something! Michelle, Jacob—it's my fault! People around me die!" I felt the world spin off its axis. "We need to do something *now!*"

"Amy, you're either going to have to keep quiet or help me think."

"You don't understand—" I fought to keep the memories of the crash away. The smell of gasoline, burning upholstery, the screech of the metal as I was rescued...

"I do. You think because you let Tommy drive your car that night, it's your fault he was killed. Kola—or Mrs. Kola, I bet—didn't care which of you it was, just so long as your investigation was derailed. You think it was your fault about Michelle and Jacob. It isn't. It was Heath and Mrs. Kola. We're going to stop them. Those were all good people, and they were in the world to make a difference. We're not going to let the assholes who did this hurt more people, are we?"

Her tone changed. "I'm sorry about Jacob and Michelle. I heard this afternoon."

"So you *were* in Washington?" I held my breath.

"No. I had a few things to check on and I needed some resources. It looks like someone's been spreading stories to the clandestine services that I've gone rogue. Nothing obvious, of course; they can't afford to be public about it. The stories about me are sifting down to the local law enforcement agencies."

Somehow, the total lack of reality helped. When completely cut off from your normal life, you think more creatively. Once the boundaries are extended—or in my case, eradicated—you just don't have to worry about the usual things the same way. It was freeing.

It made me wonder again about Marie, whose personal boundaries were already somewhat perforated/overextended/flexible/negotiable. She'd been off the leash for way longer than me, and with her skills, that was scary. Then again, she was probably the best person to be sitting next to at the moment.

It's like it was at Tommy's funeral. The rage that came with the pain, the work he left undone, the things we both fought for and against.

Work with that. Work with the guilt.

I'd been on crutches and had tried to apologize to my sister after the funeral. She'd looked blisteringly angry for a moment, then took my hand very, very gently.

"If it hadn't been for you, I never would have met the love of my life. I wouldn't have our beautiful daughter, for whom he wanted to fix the world. He told me once if it hadn't been for you, he might have done rash, stupid, dangerous things. You were the one who kept saying, wait, wait until you had more information, until you could tell the correct authorities. Without you, he would've confronted these people directly. You helped him put some of them away. You helped Tommy live longer."

It helped a little. Sometimes.

Go with that. For now.

The more I hung in there, the more I controlled the situation, the better our chances were, and the more I could make them all pay for Tommy.

"Okay," I said, taking a deep breath. "Tell me. Tell me about the guys we saw. Chase and the one...with the drawn-on cheeks." I shuddered, a ghost with fair, wavy hair and sideburns from the seventies and over-pronounced features still terrifying me.

"Chase always seemed okay to me, maybe a little too devoted to Heath."

"And you weren't?"

"I was, because I believed he wanted the same things I did. I hate how he's used that. But with Chase, I always got the impression he was working more for Heath than the mission. He's good. He'll be a problem." She shook her head. "The other guy. His name's Speitzer. I don't like him, never worked near him, but some people used him for jobs they found too dirty. Heath prefers to do things himself, hands-on—an honor thing, doing the things no one else wanted to—and I thought Heath found him as disgusting as I did. The fact Speitzer is with Chase is bad."

Her description of Speitzer was the first time I'd really ever heard her curse.

"His face...what you saw on his cheeks? It's scars. One is a nearly complete bite mark. Human. He never had it fixed, and that should tell you something about him." She cracked her neck. "I really hate that Heath brought him in."

"Well, it's serious," I said, surprising myself with how calm I sounded. Good. "We don't know who else is on Heath's side. They must be panicking. It's very big news that Heath would do something so bold as mess with the *Item* staff. We can't go to the FBI, the CIA, because we don't know if they're tainted. Even if they aren't, they think you're a black hat. Can't go to another paper—yet—because we don't have enough evidence. We can't hide out until it blows over." I looked at her. "Because it's only going to get worse."

Marie nodded.

I took another deep breath, but it still felt like I was only an observer of our conversation. "So we have to go to them. Who do we tackle first?"

"Hang on there, cowgirl." She actually laughed. "It's a little more complicated."

"How? I mean, we either find the computer and its files and the encryption or we die. Right?"

"That's the gist of it. But we'll do it smart and we'll do it right."

Her confidence was like a tonic. Apart from my leads in the library, I felt I hadn't won anything in about a week. When things go to hell, it's important to remember what victory feels like, especially when that victory's bound to be Pyrrhic.

I tried to keep my mind on our conversation, not on the freakshow wearing Michelle's scarf.

She continued. "We'll pick up the order from Ape. We'll investigate Kola's usual haunts, places he might have been able to leave a clue, even while observed. And we'll take it from there."

The next day we drove to the mall at Bailey's Crossroads, parked outside a giant box toy store, and waited until early afternoon.

Marie's phone buzzed and she checked the text.

She read it and put the phone away, a smile on her face. "We're good. Ape's on her way, no tail. Get in the back, would you?"

A few minutes later, a minivan pulled up and a petite white woman with graying brown hair got out. She wore a white, heavy apron over a T-shirt and jeans, her hair tied in a braid under a white kerchief. She looked like an overworked short-order cook. Although her clothes were clean, the humid summer morning brought a faint odor of grilled burgers. She got in the front seat.

Marie looked positively delighted. "Ape."

"Cara."

Interesting. Maybe Cara was Marie's real name. Didn't matter; I filed it away with the other tidbits I'd gleaned about her.

Ape looked in back, saw me, scowled. "Aw, jeez, C."

"Ape, this is Amy. She's okay."

"Ape? As in April?"

I held out my hand, but the woman didn't appreciate the question. "My friends call me AP or Ape. You can call me Stella."

She turned away, dismissing me from consideration.

"Whatever." I didn't need to be friends with her.

Then I saw she was laughing, and she turned back and shook with me. "AP is fine."

Marie didn't actually smirk, but she might as well have. "And is that a very large box I see in your car?"

"Those are several very large boxes. It's Christmas Day for one naughty little girl." She blew her bangs off her forehead. "Shit. I was up half the night getting it sorted."

Marie held her hands up. "I wouldn't have asked if it wasn't imperative."

"I hear you. Just be careful, would you? I want you to live to collect the favor back. When does it go down?"

"Too soon. We think a couple days."

Suddenly, I remembered George's comment back in my cube at the *Item* about "chatter" and "local travel plans." I did some calculating and came up with a number I didn't like.

I felt dizzy, but now wasn't the time for guesses. The job now was to get out into the heat of the afternoon, transferring the incredibly heavy boxes—one for a playhouse, one for a boy's bike, and one for a chemistry set, which made Marie laugh— to the back of our car. It was a humid scorcher. I realized Marie had let me sleep in this morning because the toy store was open only now. There was nothing curious about three women moving boxes of toys into a car here.

We finished, they hugged. "Say hey to the kids for me, Ape. And don't be too hard on Josh, he's really trying."

"Now you're commenting on my parenting skills? Jesus, Cara, you're still an asshole. You're soft on Josh because he's your godson and you don't have to live with the evil little con artist twenty-four/seven."

"Yeah, well, he takes after his mother."

Ape laughed humorlessly. "And I'll be paying for that for the next ten years—make it ten to fifteen. After that, he's on his own. Here." She handed a brown paper bag to me. "Coffee, some water, couple of sandwiches, apples. Nothing fancy, but all good."

"Thank you, Stella. AP."

I noticed despite the earlier talk of money, Marie didn't pull out her wallet and Ape didn't ask for anything. In fact, I noticed Ape slide Marie a roll of bills that would gag a rhino.

"Keep your shit together, C. The scams Josh's pulling, I might need to call in those favors you owe me. So don't get yourself killed."

"Ah, it's good for a kid, get into a little trouble. Find his depth."

AP shook her head. "He's starting to take after his father."

Marie sobered immediately. "That's another story. I'll make sure I come back."

"I'll count on it. Good hunting."

They hugged again briefly, which surprised me. I scrambled around into the front seat. Ape looked around, then rapped on the hood before she stuck her hands in her pockets and returned to her minivan.

She threw a plastic trash bag AP had given her into the back seat. "Clothes. I think I have a plan, and we're gonna have to look the part. Hey, speaking of clothes—how lucky did you get yesterday?"

My mind flashed to the library, clinging to Burke. I felt the blood rush to my face.

"Yesterday, when you were MIA? You snatched a bag. Was it just someone's dirty laundry?"

She reached back for the gym bag, but I grabbed it. "Give me that!"

I'd been so freaked out by the news about Jacob and Michelle that I'd forgotten the bag. I had no idea what Burke might have left in there, and no idea what Marie would do if she'd found out I'd spoken to anyone. "If I was smart enough to steal it, then I should get the honors. Unlike some, I don't do this all the time."

She handed it over. "Ha! You're the press. You go through trashcans, read peoples' texts, and listen in on their cell phone conversations."

I scowled and unzipped the bag, trying to act as if I'd actually stolen it.

"Clothes, looks like for a guy. At least they're clean. Gym shoes. Toilet bag. Ooh, look at this!" I pulled out a baggie with a roll of cash in it. "Someone was planning a big weekend!"

"Or just getting back from one—what's that?" She pulled out a lacy black bra. "Trophy."

I shrugged. Didn't know where Burke had gotten it or that it was close to my size; all I cared about was that it was clean. I grabbed the undergarment from her and stuffed it back in a hurry. The bra had been caught on something down at the bottom of the bag.

A quick glance confirmed it. Burke had given me a revolver.

She glanced across at me. "Looks like you hit the jackpot, Oliver Twist."

I swallowed. "I just tried to pick someone about my size."

"Anything else?"

I made a show of shifting the stuff around, but shook my head. I'd felt the sneakers rattle. I wondered if there the cell phone was in there. I'd check as soon as I got some privacy. I frowned. That might be a while.

"How much cash?" I asked. She was thumbing through the wad.

"Almost four hundred dollars. Nice one, Princess."

I felt bone tired. "Great. Now what?"

"It's too late to do what I'm planning tonight. Tomorrow, we get to work. For now, we find a place to crash, some food, and make plans. We're doing good. You're doing really good—"

"Don't. Really." I held up a hand. "Just...keep acting like we do this all the time, like this is normal, and I'll get through it. No promises, but let's just try. There's one more thing: I have an idea about where Kola might keep his arms hidden."

I told her about my research at the library, how Mrs. K, through several different companies and hidden by dummy corporations, had expanded her family's industrial interests and created an extensive network of storage facilities and warehouses.

"She has them all over the world, sometimes multiple locations in one city. It's the perfect cover for her husband's arms trade: near the airports and ports, anonymous, busy at all hours of the day or night."

Marie nodded. "Okay...that's something. We'd have to narrow it down to see what Heath might be moving on now, but it's a good start. An excellent start, Amy."

172   *Exit Interview*

I didn't bridle so much at her praise this time. I was pretty fucking pleased with myself.

"We have gear, we have information. It's been a good day."

I hated how she said that, believed it, in the context of recent events. If today was a good day, even discounting the terrible news about Jacob and Michelle, I'd hate to see what she thought a bad day looked like. Her sense of what constituted progress was in a different world than my own.

Chapter Thirty-Four: Nicole Bradley

In spite of my chaotic and occasionally peripatetic life, I have my rituals. I find my flow state with music and tea, then start off easy, like a musician warming up with scales, or a runner jogging slowly. I run down my list of security protocols, and then double-check them and add another when I feel they're too familiar. Easy equals comfortable, and comfortable means slipshod. Poised and aware is the state I need to find, just as I would with physical combat.

I delve into the personal phones belonging to the members of the Department, looking for new signals that overlap with the known haunts. Something useful, not too surprising: It looks like Chase *is* working with Philomena Kola, off the books. Their texts indicate that this is without Heath's knowledge. Ooh. I file that away, and wonder whether I can use it to throw Heath off, and whether doing that is a good idea—not yet. I want them comfortable enough to think they're all keeping each others' secrets, everyone on board. I'll only blow that up if I need to rattle someone's cage.

I start to noodle around the Department's email, prodding the security to see if there's anything new. There is, but nothing I can't handle. Before I feel too pleased with myself, I backtrack and look around a little wider.

I put out a few feelers around the archives, and don't see anything I don't remember. Back when I was working for the NSA's Tailored Access Operations, they loaned me out to the Department so that I could help with their encryption and security. Of course, I left my own back doors in case I ever needed to revisit. Hacking isn't about getting in once, it's making sure you have your own key to let yourself in later.

They'd teased me about being a geek and now I'm making them eat it. But all in the name of a good cause, of course. Revenge is a complicated dish, and you can never tell when you might have it handed back to you.

I'd be silly to think they haven't added more security since they decided I was no longer useful to them, and I'm anything but silly. It's there, I can see it. I can work around it.

Okay, next step: I need to find Richard Heath's personal information, with the hope that either it will contain his retinal images or some other intel I can use to get around that feature. It's not going to be in his personnel file, which of course, would be encrypted, but in the security file that exists in case something happens and Heath loses his password or he pulls a Director Fury and loses the eye he used for the retinal scan. There should be an API to update and reencode this information for him in such cases.

Nontrivial, of course, unless you happen to know of an unsecured diagnostic log only ever accessed by administrators which contains the raw data of the PII. It's been missed over by the audits, an open secret among us administrators.

My credentials are no longer valid, so I choose an administrator's account with sufficient rank to access the log. In theory, such a request will slide beneath the notice of the machine-learning-based algorithms that keep track of such things.

And then—oh, hellfire!

A blip of red on the screen where I'm monitoring the alerts and notifications; the AI's flagged me as a high-priority issue. It looks like nothing, but tells me I've been made.

Shitfuckpissflaps. I log out. Damn and blast.

They don't waste any time with honeypots, trying to lure me to stick around so they can localize my IP address; the data I requested is far too important to leave me near it for any length of time. They block my IP.

I sit back, drenched in sweat, my heart pounding like a drumline, a chill stealing over me. Adrenaline flows freely, and I reassure myself: They blocked me before they could identify where my device was located. They don't know it's *me*. And they don't know I was looking for anything to do with Heath. I was anonymous, I was careful, I was quick and smart. I try to slow my breathing and reassure myself.

I'm safe, for the moment. But unless I come up with something new, I need to take Heath, alive, and his eyes intact. And as much as I wish it were otherwise, it's going to be in RL with a very deadly man.

Chapter Thirty-Five: Amy Lindstrom

Marie and I found a little no-tell closer to downtown Washington. It was humble, but clean, a palace compared to the last place we'd stayed, though I still didn't sit on the bedspread.

We ate at a restaurant; Marie picked a sit-down chain specializing in beef-n-beer. I sighed, but it was a meaningful step up from burgers.

"Can I get you ladies anything to drink?" The waitress looked like she'd been on her feet for about four years.

I hesitated. "A glass of red wine?"

She handed me a list. I could have kissed her. "Just the house cab, is fine."

Marie ordered a diet soda. A steak—"just chase it around the kitchen a little before you bring it out"—and potatoes.

"For you?"

"Could I get the steak and mushroom salad, please? The dressing on the side? And the bleu cheese on the side?"

"Rare, as well?"

"No, please make sure it's completely, totally cooked through. Thanks." I looked at Marie after the waitress left. "I think I love her."

"I can see. Y'know, you could have just had the salad separated by ingredients onto sixteen different little plates. Would've been easier."

A series of exclamations from the next table: a young couple encountering friends in the booth behind me. The wife had a fat baby slung over her arm like a raincoat, and it made noises and faces suggesting imminent disgorgement of something fermented from either end. Its eyes were slightly crossed and its tongue was sticking out and the way Mommy was jostling it reminded me of shaken soda cans.

"Would you settle down?" Marie said. "You're acting like that baby's gonna detonate."

"Well, look at it," I whispered back. "I'm in the line of fire."

"Very maternal of you. Afraid of a little yark."

"Please. I've done my time with diapers and vomit. I've just learned to read the signals about when to duck." I saw an opening, with food on the way and a quiet moment. "How about you?"

"How old is Lucy now?"

Again, she ducked my question. Of course she knew I was talking about my niece. It was all in the file she had found in Heath's office. "Nine," I said. "I'm buying her first new computer. For her birthday."

"Kinda young for that, isn't she?"

The sharpness of her question nettled me. I answered too quickly. "You're never too young to explore the world, find your own voice."

"Ah. And her mother, the attorney, would squelch that, presumably?"

I said nothing. I'd already said too much.

"That's what it is, for you, isn't it? You're caught on the horns of a hell of a dilemma, there, Amy. Having overcome a stutter, you seek to distinguish yourself in a family of orators and politicians with your voice by becoming a reporter. Having become a reporter, you stir up trouble. Trouble that may hurt people close to you. Like Tommy." She paused. "Like your grandfather. That's gotta be tough."

I was determined to treat the subject as clinically as she did.

"He shot himself. Hunting rifle. He'd received a terminal cancer diagnosis that day. He'd always said he'd never go like his father had, and he didn't."

"You just didn't know it was the same day you confronted him about the moonshine, though, did you?"

"How on God's green earth do you—? Wait—never mind. Train schedules, files signed out at Richmond, a little guesswork." I shook my head.

Remembering that day in the library. Tommy had introduced himself—he was in International Affairs, but we had a class in qualitative research methods together. He'd asked me if I was related to Mark Bolling.

Tommy was letting me know his friend was filing a story. About Grandpa Bolling. It was brave of him to warn me it was coming.

On one level, I had understood about the moonshine. But it's one thing to wink at bootleg distilling for personal use and another to do it when you're in the state legislature and moonshine is being sold on a huge scale, in dangerously poor quality. At that level, it blinds and slowly kills the consumers at the nip joints. Grandpa had always been proud of being liberal, but tradition had won out over justice here. He was citing that tradition at the same time he was getting away with things that he was jailing other, browner, poorer people for.

He'd tried to explain it to me, when I confronted him. That moonshine was heritage, an understanding going back hundreds of years. But it was also illegal and killing people, and he had sworn to uphold the law. I was upset, disappointed, and I'd handled the situation with all the tact of a toddler. He patted my arm, kissed the top of my head, then left for his doctor's appointment. Six hours later, he was dead.

"You learn things about your family. Maybe you can change them, or make up for them. I dunno."

"Yeah, but your problem there is that you can't make up for them. And yet you try to. And need people to do your job and you do your best to keep them at arm's length so you won't hurt them. That's messed up. Does anyone else in your family know?"

I was surprised to find myself back in the restaurant with Marie. "When he went to the doctor's, my grandmother asked why I was upset. I told her. She wasn't pleased and suggested I would be much happier if I wasn't so...persistent. She said, 'What you don't know, can't upset you.' She died shortly after. She never said that she blamed me, but..."

"She never had to. You blamed yourself. Amy, Tommy was kicking over anthills long before you teamed up. Jacob had received death threats before this. Your grandfather didn't want to face a long and painful death. If you didn't do what you do, the world would be a worse place."

"And what did Michelle do?" I wanted to ask. But I changed the subject. I'd had enough of Marie poking through my past like a careless anthropologist. Back to her. "So. You know all about me. What about you? Tell me about your family."

"You know already. My parents are dead."

"Any brothers, sisters?"

"Only child of only children."

I saw a dangerous look in her eye and switched tactics. "How about AP? How do you guys know each other?"

She paused, rolled her head around, stretching her neck. "AP is short for 'antipersonnel.' Ape."

"So you met in the Army?"

"Ape and I went through basic together. She ended up in the quartermaster corps, before I got...transferred."

"Ah. So, the 'antipersonnel'...?'"

"We learned pretty quick you don't screw with Ape, not more than once. Not without consequences. There was this sergeant giving her a hard time, really riding her because she was the only other woman around. Ape tried mediation, went by the books, but it wasn't working. Any more and it would just label her 'difficult' and finish her career. So she took matters into her own hands with an IED."

"An improvised explosive device?"

"Well, back then we meant 'improvised explosive dinner.'"

"Okay, you got me."

"The packets you use to heat up MREs? You can rig them to heat up lots of things. And you can rig them to explode. It's crude, but vastly amusing. Most people use hot sauce—gets in your eyes and burns like hell. Ape took it a step further."

"Razor blades?"

"Close. Nair. After taps, when everyone was asleep."

"Oh." I tried to imagine waking up, in the midst of a minor explosion, my hair coming out in chunks. "And Ape's...present business?"

"Her folks left her the coffee shop. She does okay for herself, far as I know."

I gave Marie a look.

"Oh, you mean the other thing. Considering your views on that particular brand of entrepreneur, let's save that story for a more secure location, okay?"

"So what did they call in you in the Army?"

"Posh."

"What, like Posh Spice?"

"No, like POSH, Position on Sexual Harassment. The name of the regs regarding same. One night, one of the guys in my platoon got lubed up, decided he needed to see my tits. Wouldn't back off. He asked me, what's your position on sexual harassment, like he was being clever, making a play on words. So I showed him my favorite position."

She smiled. "He eventually regained use of his arm, but after that no one ever bothered me. Or anyone near me. And to those in the know, I was Posh."

Our food arrived then, the baby moved on, and I could think, under guise of sucking down my dinner.

I hated it. Marie had me talking to her like a friend—or trying to, at least—and I wasn't even sure I knew her real name or whatever name mattered to her. Every time I asked her about herself, she told me about something related, but tangential. Or she turned it back on me. I didn't like feeling so vulnerable, so exposed.

And I didn't want to like Ape—she was clearly just a small-scale version of the arms dealers I loathed. But, if you bought what Marie said, she was doing it for a reason. Everyone has reasons, and usually one of them is money. But watching them together, I thought I saw what looked like genuinely unguarded behavior in Marie. It wasn't so different from her behavior with me.

But Marie was someone used to recruiting friends, bringing people to her side, knowingly or not. She was trained to make me like her, or at least sympathize with her, and she was succeeding.

It had made me mad, and it made me distrustful. But...it started to sink in that we had things in common: rural roots, violent family death, too many guns. She'd been through some serious shit before now, and that same sort of chaos was repeating in our current situation.

As soon as I could, I would check in with George to see whether he'd unearthed anything more about her. I couldn't get away to find an internet terminal while we were in the mall. God knows, the place we were staying wasn't wired for Wi-Fi, but I kept my fingers crossed about the phone Burke had put in the bag. Maybe it was a smartphone. If it was, I might have a chance of finding out more about Marie, because when someone hides from me, I want to find them all the more.

Back at the motel, we gorged again, this time on news. The TV offered CNN, CNBC, *The PBS Newshour,* and Faux News; we watched everything else with a crawl we could find. She browsed other outlets on her phone and none of them had anything about us, which was even more worrying: it was all being kept quiet. I shouldn't have been surprised Marie was a serious news junkie like me. At least while watching the news, looking for anything that might have some remote connection to us, I could keep myself calm until I had the chance to check my phone.

I waited until she was in the bathroom, then looked in my bag. When I saw the high-end Google phone, I swore I'd do everything in my power to help Burke's career, do whatever it took to get him to a leg up in the field. It took me a moment to figure out the navigation, and first thing I did was turn off the sound. Just as I heard the faucet shut off, the screen came up. Before she came out, I stuffed the phone and key fob into my pocket, changed places with Marie, locked the door, and ran a tub.

Typing as quickly as I could, I got the latest random number, and went to the address. A chat window appeared, with a link to a file stored safely and secretly elsewhere if I knew George.

A file about Marie.

I turned off the tub, started stripping down while I considered the possibilities. There wasn't much there that could help me, but it made me wonder about her a little more. I didn't know if it reassured me or helped me in any way to know that her parents had been murdered in what had been described as "execution style." She had no other blood relatives alive. Her father had been a locksmith, her mother a nurse, and while I could imagine several scenarios that might explain their murders, given those professions, the authorities claimed the case was unsolved and unexplained. Marie—under yet another "real name"—had vanished from college, only to reappear several months later on the enlisted rolls of the US Army. A few telling moves from base to base—extra and expert training with teams from other services—as if she was being considered for a specialty. After that, she vanished again, much more completely this time. No wonder she thought of her boss and the Department as "family."

Marie had, in fact, gone to Wellesley College. I would have given a lot to know what she was like then, the rural girl at a posh school.

I tucked the phone into the pocket of my jeans, now in a heap on the floor, and slipped into the tub. Time was going faster than I liked, and I had too many questions.

The next morning, we ate breakfast at a diner, then returned to the motel, where she started laying out clothes.

"What's next?" I asked.

"I spent the day before yesterday scanning Department operatives and their chatter." She held up a shirt, comparing it to me. "Looking for friends."

"And?"

"We have none. They believe I've gone rogue."

"Super. Other agencies?"

She shook her head. "None so far. We have to be careful."

That jibed with what I'd learned from George. "Any word from Nicole?"

"Nothing good." She told me about their chat in the IRC and attack on Nicole and Gina, and that the pressure was on. The way her face froze when she spoke of Gina suggested that the pair had been close earlier in their careers. "On the way back here," she continued, "I tried to figure out where the computer or the encrypted files might be. There's no mark by the dead drop Kola and I used, though it's possible he was under too much pressure to remember. Also, that location was one the Department knew about. We can assume they don't have the computer because—"

"They wouldn't still be coming after us."

"Probably not. But Kola was a thorough guy, and careful—you have to be, in his world. He must have left something where I could find it. The only thing I could come up with was a place near our dead drop. There's an expensive baby store. He was a regular. Anything new for his grandson, he picked out himself. That's why the dead drop was there, so he'd have an excuse to be in the area."

I thought about the camouflage toy boxes in the back of the car. "Could he have left something there? A custom order, or something left to be monogrammed? If he thought he was being watched..."

Marie nodded. "Exactly my thought. I couldn't risk going earlier yesterday and get back to you at the motel when I said I would."

I tried not to think about what would've happened if she'd arrived later, or if I'd stayed in the room.

"We also have to consider he might have been at Mrs. Bolton's party to tell you something," she said. "After all, Mrs. Bolton invited you for a reason, and if you're right, Kola was trying to meet you. He was desperate, at this point, maybe worried his wife was working with Heath, now that he wanted to retire. Maybe he suspected he needed help, if he was going to survive."

I nodded. "Let's try the store. It's a long shot, but we've got nothing else at the moment."

She looked me up and down, considering. "You are...Kola's assistant's assistant?"

"Sure."

"So, new clothes and a new hair color." We dressed me in the part with Ape's clothes, and as I surveyed the results in the mirror—now I was a redhead—I combed my hair back and tied the scarf over it, leaving a few gamine bangs showing. If I was uninterested in all sartorial endeavors between jeans and a red-beaded dress, at least I could tie a scarf. Mother wouldn't let me leave home until I'd perfected the art.

I cleaned the earrings and sunglasses and slid them on. Crisp white shirt, tan capris, navy driving mocs.

Marie glanced over. "Nice job." She'd been busy, too, unloading Ape's boxes and sorting the contents according to some private organizational scheme.

I whistled.

Four SIG Sauer pistols and a little round .38, boxes and boxes of bullets, a gun cleaning kit, medical supplies, and what looked like backpack strapping without the backpack. A pair of small, beat-up, military-style boots. A pile of electronics, none of which were familiar to me save for two radios and earpieces marked "Motorola." Two knives and a dangerous little blade, flat and hooked. There were two watches, black plastic and chunky, and a couple of tokens or coins; I had no idea what that was about. There was a lot of stuff I didn't recognize and didn't really want to be in the same room with. I didn't have to know much to know the materials for explosives were on the bed.

I picked up one of the pistols. It was heavy to my hand, ugly, too. Black matte, textured grip with a small medallion that said "P226R" on the side of the grip. I set it aside and picked up one of the knives, a long flat one in a sheath. Also black. I pulled it out and saw a seven-inch blade, serrations at the base near the handle. It was marked "KA-BAR."

"Kay-Bar. Great knife. Please put it down before you get hurt." Marie loaded a magazine, racked a round into the chamber, then removed the magazine and added another bullet.

I put it back into the sheath carefully. Just looking at the blade's sharpness scared me. I picked up one of the coins. A Sacagawea dollar, but it felt oddly heavy.

"Hang on to that," Marie said. "Don't spend it."

"Why? You got a thing against the dollar coin?"

"No. Inside is a tracking device. If we get separated, I can find you."

I stuck it in my pocket.

"Here." She handed me one of the Triathlon watches after making sure it matched the time on hers, down to the second. "Don't wear it now—it doesn't fit your cover—but hang onto it. And this..." She picked up the little round pistol and thought a moment, then shook her head. "I'm not sure we'll need it, but we'll hang on to it for backup. Ape was thinking of you."

"Great. I get the girl gun." I put it aside.

"Hey, it was nice of her; she wasn't sure you'd be comfortable with a SIG. It's a problem, for women with small hands. Not that it's an issue for you, you damn yeti."

"Thanks a lot."

"My opinion? It's not the caliber, but the placement that counts. And never rule out anything, when you haven't got much." She handed me the smallest of the square guns—she'd holstered the others. "I've got a suppressor and ammo. I don't want to load you down. Just keep this in your bag. Want a knife? No, best not to get too complicated. I just always feel a little better with one. Or three, you know?" She might have been talking about spare keys.

"I'll stick with my Swiss Army knife, thanks." To think I used to worry about overloading my handbag. We arranged things so my shoulder bag was reasonably balanced and the stuff in it was accessible and didn't clink.

Marie looked a lot happier, now that she was heavily armed with her old gear and her courier bag was full of comforting things that scared the bejeezus out of me. We set out the plan. She'd be lookout, and we'd communicate using the radios Ape got us. If everything was fine, I'd walk to the Starbucks on the corner, out the other side, and she'd pick me up. If things went wrong, I walked the opposite direction, then I'd return to the room and wait. If she didn't show up by midnight, or if the place was being watched, I would head out on my own.

"Where? I mean, what happens after this?" I asked in the car.

She shook her head. "Can't tell until we get that clue. If there is one."

My pulse pounded as we neared the square.

"Okay, first make sure you're not being followed. There's a good cut-through, off this side street." As we drove by, I saw a brick-walled alley that ran behind the shops and restaurants. "And remember the contingency plan."

"I keep my finger on the send button. If I run into trouble, I punch it and get out. Keep under the radar."

"You got it. Good luck, Amy. See you in a few."

She dropped me off on M Street, and I found myself alone in the crowd. I did a quick look around to orient myself and see who might be following me, then went down the side street and up the alley. I came out back on M Street: No one was following me. Hey, Baby! was a store so expensive that there was a waiting list to get on their registry. I'd had to restrain myself from spending the better part of my 401K on presents there when Lucy was born.

The store was just a few feet away, along with several other shops. I had to keep myself from running. I felt so exposed. There's nothing like doing something wrong to ignite your sense of paranoia. Every face I saw was full of suspicion, and I forgot how an innocent person walks.

Don't break character, I told myself. You're picking up a teddy bear that contains a nanny cam or a hideously expensive layette set. An organic cotton onesie embroidered with silk. Walk. Act like you're enjoying the day, a little warm, maybe, but...

I was outside the shop. I paused, took out a tissue to blot my face. I made sure I didn't recognize anyone.

I took a deep breath, pushed the door open, and entered.

Chapter Thirty-Six: Nicole Bradley

My next step is a long-stay business hotel, a dreary, anonymous chain that smacks of fatigue and making do with its unsuccessful attempts to create a sense of home away from home. I'd prefer a suite at the nearest five-star boutique property and this is assuredly not my style. It does, however, meet my needs for cooking and coding, and, with my VPN, has Wi-Fi that I can use for my own purposes.

I walk off my hurt pride and the fear that comes from such a close call as I just escaped. After a hot shower, I feel better. It's fine. That's over. Now is now, and time's wasting.

I make a list of the places that the Kolas own and the places Philomena Kola frequents. And then I proceed to visit each place. At each stop, I pause briefly and steal her blind.

Oh, I don't take her money or her real estate or her jewels. I use a "zero-day" exploit to help myself to her passwords, her security codes, her digital life. I install spyware on her tech, so that any time she moves money among her accounts, texts her driver, or looks at porn, I know about it. I add insult to injury, and make her IP address one of mine to put to work for me when I prowl the dark web.

You'd think that someone in her business would keep her patches up to date, but she's a businesswoman and not terribly technical.

With the internet of things, I could probably work out a way to kill her in her sauna or electrocute her as she sits on her very expensive Japanese toilet—even with her ridiculous wealth, she can't avoid the most humbling of human biological processes. But right now, like Heath, I need her alive, because she might be the one who leads me to her dead husband's weapons.

The Cave Girl can keep her crude bullets and blades, because under the right circumstances, I'm empress of my digital universe. States, laws, and money are meaningless to me, because I can reshape them—or my self—to be whatever I need. I only need people, as dull and dreadful as they can be, to muddle along until I find the best way to exploit them from afar.

I sigh. I'm not usually so bleak in my outlook. I must still be feeling the sting of performing so badly in the ambush.

Okay, I also need people to make chocolate chip ice cream.

And I need that delicious young man who works at the high-end butcher shop I frequent. And the exquisite woman who always seems to be working when I visit the wine store for a tasting.

I guess I'm feeling better. Forward progress.

I stay strictly away from anything that has to do with the Department, instead focusing my attention on where Rogers is and what she and Blondie are up to.

After my recent incursion at my old job, checking on the local police and emergency services should be a cakewalk, but I have to assume that most of those channels for two hundred square miles will be surveilled, looking just for me. That, I can work around.

I notice a lot of message traffic around Georgetown, and wonder what could be going down. When I check Rogers' location, it looks like she's right in the heart of it. I try to get a look at license plates and the parties present with the local surveillance cameras, but I don't recognize them. A little research shows that they're probably working for Kola.

As much as I don't want to, I realize that it might be time to join the meat-world again, much sooner than I'd hoped.

Chapter Thirty-Seven: Amy Lindstrom

Refrigerated air washed over me as I opened the door to the posh baby store. I slowed my breathing, then found my way past piles of tiny clothes rolled up to resemble sushi rolls in take-out containers, plush blankets shaped like animals, socks that looked like ballerina slippers, and ridiculously large stuffed animals until I reached the young female associate at the cash desk.

"Good afternoon."

"Good afternoon. How can I help you?"

"I'm picking up a special order. For Kola."

"Certainly. Do you recall what it was?"

"I'm afraid Mrs. Kola didn't tell me. And now Mr. Kola has passed..." I tried to look appropriately somber.

"Let me check in back."

She was gone for what seemed an interminable amount of time. Too late, I worried about a receipt, but clients like Kola probably had an account.

She came out smiling, a moment later, carrying a flat box, about the size of a notebook. "Here we are. Would you like to have a look?"

No, I thought. I want to get the hell out of here. But if it was a special order... "Yes, please."

She removed the cover and pulled back the tissue to reveal a silver picture frame. "And the inscription is correct?"

I glanced down; a blur of initials and a date. I was anxious to leave. "Yes, that's fine."

"We were surprised by the change in the initials. He was always shopping for his grandson, Marcus."

I thought quickly. "Oh, it's a family friend."

The woman frowned. "I thought it was for his assistant's new baby."

"It is," I said. "I'm standing in for her while she's on parenting leave."

"Ah." Her face relaxed into a smile. "Would you like me to wrap it?"

"No, thanks. We want to put a photo in, first. Had Mr. Kola put it on the account?" I suddenly wondered how much the swanky silver frame cost; I had about two hundred dollars. But cash would be suspect, here...

"It's been taken care of," she said.

She wrapped the box in tissue, sealed it with a metallic sticker, and put it in a perfectly sized bag.

I took it, thanked her, and tried not to pelt from the store.

"Oh, Miss?"

I froze in my tracks, deciding not to bolt. I was close enough to the door if things got hairy. "Yes?"

She smiled. "I forgot—did you want a gift card?"

My life, which had been passing before my eyes, quickly went into reverse. "No, thank you."

"Have a nice day."

"You, too," I said. Don't ever do that to me again.

I texted for two coffees, then walked down the street, crossing, and cutting through another store, until I reached the Starbucks. I called. "I'm done."

"Thirty seconds."

I was at the door as she pulled up, the passenger side door unlocked for me. She must have driven around so I wouldn't have to cross the street. Nice move, Marie.

I got in, juggling the package and tray of drinks.

"You stopped for coffee?" Marie was incredulous as she pulled away.

"Well, it was a coffee shop. I...I thought it would be a way to lose a tail."

"Yeah, but..." She shook her head. "Next time, don't waste time we could spend boogeying."

"Does that mean you don't want this?" I held up the cup.

"Hell, no. Just let me get us out of here, first," she said as she navigated through the heavy traffic. We were held up at a construction site. There was no cop to reroute us through the detour.

A moment later, she frowned. "Something's wrong."

"What?"

"This street. I don't know. This construction, the detours...it doesn't feel right to me. Let's get out of sight." She looked around, made a choice. "The office space, over there. It's got the FOR LEASE sign on it."

"I see it."

"There'll be another door on the side of the building. Let's try that."

"Whatever you say." I was nervous. I didn't see why she should be anxious. And what if someone was in the building?

She pulled into the alley, killed the ignition. I followed her to the door she seemed to know would be there. She took the coffee with her, and when I asked why, she said, "People with coffee look innocent. They look like they're where they are for a reason."

"Keep an eye open, would you?" She handed me her cup, then pulled out a small flat package and picked the lock. "Bingo. In we go."

I tensed, waiting for an alarm to go off, but none did.

"Upstairs. Avoid the windows," she said.

The second floor was a shell. Wires and cables stuck out, waiting for some smart young start-up to take residence. She held out her hand, and I offered her the coffee.

"Thanks. I meant, let's see the package."

I handed it over, and she opened it. "'WTT, 12-11-2019.' Mean anything to you?

I shook my head. She took a picture of the front with her phone, just in case.

She removed the back. There was nothing but the backing board, and the paper.

I flipped them over. Still nothing.

But Marie was looking at the tissue paper that had wrapped the box.

"We're hosed." She stood. She showed me the foil sticker that had sealed the tissue paper. There was a minuscule dot on the back.

I shook my head. "What? What's wrong?"

"Footsteps."

She chucked the frame out a window, pulled out a gun, went to the staircase. She came back, silently, shaking her head. She gestured to a doorway across the room.

We no sooner reached it than a guy the size of an armoire with a gun was blocking our way.

"Gotcha," he said. He seemed to recognize Marie. "Where's Kola's encryption key?"

"Huh?" I blurted.

"Rogers, Kola must have given it to you at the party," he said to Marie. "Save your friend here some pain and give it to me now. His people weren't too happy about the knife-job you did on their guy."

"Morris?" Marie looked like she was going to cry. "You can't possibly believe that I...?" She started to tremble. The cup she was holding tilted, spilling coffee all over the carpet.

Armoire's eyes flickered to the coffee—just as mine had—when Marie dropped the cup. She stepped forward, shoved his gun hand against the door frame, and kneed up and into his sternum. Three quick slams, his head into the door jamb. He went down without a noise. Silence bought us time, I realized.

She stuck her head into the hallway. More voices there, none of them tech types shopping for office space. We went up two more flights of stairs.

"That way." She shoved me down the hallway. "All the way to the end."

There was another staircase leading to the roof. Emergency Exit indeed.

There were voices at the bottom of the staircase. And voices closer behind us in the hall.

"Up. Get going."

She didn't need to shove me again. But she didn't follow. I turned back. "What are you doing?"

She pulled a tube out of her pocket and fixed it to the barrel of her pistol. "Suppressor. Go."

I scrambled up stairs covered in dirt and cigarette butts. A series of slamming noises followed. I moved even faster. The door at the top was locked.

"Now what?" I hissed.

"Get your gun."

I dug through my bag and found the pistol she'd given me from Ape's stash, and I slotted one in. Shots echoed down the stairwell.

"Get down here."

I put the extra clip in my pocket; she met me halfway.

"Anyone comes up the stairwell, you shoot them. Got it?"

"What are you going to do?"

"Check the roof. Count your shots. When you hit fourteen, call me. You'll have one left. I'll take over."

"Oh shit."

"You can do it." She was up the stairs in an instant.

It was quiet in the staircase. I wanted to run down the steps or scream, just to break the tension. I kept swallowing, my mouth dry.

I gotta do this, I just gotta keep calm...

Suddenly, there was a guy staring up at me.

"Fuck!" I pulled the trigger, not bothering to aim. He dove away.

More shots. I returned them wildly, praying they'd keep away from me. Then...quiet.

I felt a breath on the back of my neck. I jumped, whirled, and aimed.

It was Marie.

"Jesus! I could have killed you!"

She pushed my hand down, aiming the gun away from her. "No. Your clip is empty, and the slide is locked back. *You* didn't count. Let's go."

I followed her up the stairs, through the door, out into the brutal afternoon sun.

"Take this." She handed me her reloaded pistol. The silencer—suppressor?—made it awkward, unbalanced. She reloaded and affixed a suppressor to the pistol she took from me. "There's a full clip in it. You still got a spare magazine?"

I nodded.

"Good. Get over there." She jerked her head to the air-conditioning unit. "Get behind it. Any of them get past me, you get them."

"Uhhhh..."

The door opened, and something rolled out, hissing, emitting a gas. Marie scooped it up, took three steps, and gracefully lobbed it into the alley. By the time she'd finished, the door opened. Four more guys busted through. I shot, realizing I couldn't really count, aim, and plan all at the same time. At best, I could add to the confusion.

But I hit one of the men. He was so wide, I couldn't miss. He hit the roof like a falling redwood. Marie had disappeared behind an HVAC unit and had nailed one herself. The two who were left split up and began to circle. I did my best, but it seemed all I did was spend a lot of bullets. Thank God for the construction noise; the jackhammers and truck engines were excellent cover for the shots.

I paused when I heard the click. Empty. I dropped the clip, fumbled the fresh one, and grabbed it from the hot pebbled roof with shaking fingers. I finally grabbed the clip and managed to slap it in, which stung my hand like hell.

When I looked up, one of the men was coming my way. The T-Rex who'd fallen after I shot him. I hadn't shot him thoroughly enough.

I shot the gun repeatedly and actually hit him twice more. He dropped his weapon and lurched toward me, zombie-like. Contrary to my expectations, he didn't just drop in a faint. He was clearly used to the sight of his own blood. I emptied the clip as I tried to scoot backward. The last shot hit him.

I held up my hands, but he fell dead on top of me, crushing me into the sunbaked gravel. I almost lost my lunch right then and there. The thought that there might be worse to come kept me shoving, struggling to get out from underneath him, find the other clip, find Marie... I'd heard a crunch in my bag, which was under me...

A short weedy guy disengaged himself from the battle and ran to the door. He vanished. I heard one more body collapse behind me. It sounded large. I hoped it was male...

Marie dashed out, looking around. "Where is he? That little one?"

There was a metallic screech behind the shut door. It took a moment to realize it didn't have anything to do with the guy on top of me.

"Over there!"

She looked around, confused, and then saw where I was pointing. She ran to the door.

I could feel a warm wetness spreading over me. I redoubled my efforts to shove the body away, but it was incredibly heavy. No one relaxes that much when they're alive; they're always trying to move off you or support themselves.

She ran over to the door, tried it. Locked and jammed.

"Shoot it!"

"It won't do any good." But she aimed and fired, twice. No luck. "He's not Heath's! I've got to find him!"

"This one's *dead*." The fucker on top of me would not move.

"I know. Stay here!"

"What are you—?" I grunted and finally dragged myself from under the dead weight. I got up, trying not to think about the blood that was all over me. "Where are you going? Are you *crazy*?"

She ran across the roof, right past me, crunching the gravel and asphalt, then *threw* herself off the roof, arms pinwheeling, legs kicking.

Swearing, I followed, but only to the edge of the roof. What had prompted such a suicidal act? She took forever to fall, but of course she had a plan. She landed on the roof of the building opposite us, almost six feet away and a story below, with the agility of a cat. She got up out of the forward roll, and without pause, found the edge of that roof, and a drainpipe. If I'd seen her up on the roof planning for a week, she wouldn't have looked any more comfortable, any more fluid, almost presciently aware of where her next step must be. I felt my stomach lurch as she snaked down the drainpipe, three stories above the ground, like a squirrel running down a tree. She stopped and extended her foot as gracefully as a ballerina to a railing that was at least eighteen inches too far from her. She clung to the pipe with one hand and one foot for support, then just *unrolled* herself toward the railing. She was there. She paced along the railing of the balcony like she'd been born on a tightrope. She then swung down from that, to the next floor, and then to the first, dropping the last ten feet to the ground. She spun around, tearing down the street, past our building.

It had taken her all of half a minute.

I ran along the roofline, following her progress on the street below.

She came to an intersection and looked up to me, impatience and irritation writ all over her face. She gestured, "Which way?"

I could see, barely, the hooded form of our guy in the distance. "Down two blocks, then a left!" I shouted.

She didn't bother with an acknowledgment, just tore after him. At the turn, I lost sight of her.

I was stranded. I considered following her route down, but immediately dismissed the idea. My stomach did another loop-de-loop just from being so close to the edge of the roof. I'd snap one of my legs off, even if I made it to the other side, and then what?

After a halfhearted shove at the door and a glance at the three bodies practically liquefying before me, I knew I wasn't going anywhere without help. The phone Nicole had given me was crushed, her information lost with it. With Marie gone, there was only one person I could text.

Chapter Thirty-Eight: Jayne Rogers

The jump to the roof wasn't perfect as it needed to be. Something feels funny in my ankle.

Ignore it. One more reason to finish the job.

Focus on breathing out. You'll breathe in with no problem. Keep the upper body still, relaxed. Keep the legs moving.

The guy I'm looking for isn't very bright. He's probably in way worse shape than I am. He's on autopilot. He won't be too clever.

He's got to report in. He can't run all the way. If he knows he's being followed, he'll grab a car. If not, he may find someplace quiet to call.

Getting a few stares. Nothing strange. A woman running, not screaming, will get looks. A guy running will turn heads...like that. A line of heads craning...over there.

And there he is.

Two more blocks, slipping into an alley. He won't go any farther in than he has to, with the cell phone.

There's a dumpster that reeks of rotting vegetables and a few trashcans. One door, rusty hardware, no windows. No other way out. It's a working alley, no place anyone likes to hang out.

Feet under the dumpster and heavy breathing. He's out of shape.

Bingo.

I pull out the knife. Just enough for talk.

One step, then another...

Bad luck. I'm almost around the dumpster when he looks up. No noise of mine. His jaw drops. He's suddenly smart and loses the phone. But he can't quite get the weapon out of his pocket in time, not with the suppressor. Bad form.

Now.

Isolate the weapon. He's using both hands, fumbling with the pocket, good news for me. He sees the knife as it comes up and he jerks.

There's a shot. Not loud, but loud enough.

It hasn't hit me. The guy sags, clutching his gut. Looking at me, surprised. How could I do that to him? Always the same dumb look of surprise.

But I didn't shoot him. He couldn't have been stupid enough to have his finger on the trigger? He shot himself trying to pull his pistol out. Shit, shit—

Never mind. He's not fighting me as I try to see how bad it is.

It's bad.

Again, shit.

He's too busy hanging onto his guts to worry about the gun now, and I get it away from him easily, make it safe. "Where's Kola's computer?" I grab his shirt. "Where is it?"

He's babbling nonsense, in Russian, about his dog. He freaks out when he feels his hands fill up with blood, and, just like a man, his eyes roll up and he passes out.

It's getting too complicated, taking too long. Even if he comes around in a minute, he's not going to last. A noise down the alley reminds me time is passing. I toss him, then ensure he'll never get up again. Take the phone. Wipe my prints off him, wipe his blood off me.

Time to go.

My ankle is throbbing. As I exit the alley, I already miss the adrenaline and endorphins now they're wearing off. I'm a little wobbly, come to think of it, but nothing a shower and some chow and a little rack time won't cure.

They followed us with the foil sticker. Amy's still up there. They'll be looking for us.

I must be more than bright, heading back.

Not a perfect day, but not bad.

Dana Cameron 201

A couple of blocks away, I call Amy. No answer. She must have busted her radio in the tussle. Probably still cooling her heels on the roof. The look on her face when I left...

I hump it over to our room. It's a hike, in the late afternoon heat. Never mind. We got what we needed and are still alive. Not perfect, but a very good day, and the only easy day is yesterday.

A mile later, even with both eyes open for surveillance, even expecting it, I'm shocked when it registers. Someone is marking our building. The overfed and prissy look of the Bureau, Friendly But Ignorant. They're not doing anything, but I'd be stupid to think it's not for us. I keep walking, right past the intersection. Amy knows what to do, if she can get off the roof. I'll try again before midnight.

I keep walking. Were they there at her invitation? She was acting pretty hinky about the gym bag. Something's up. She's not as good a liar as she thinks. Might have been Michelle's and Jacob's death. Or our conversation. She's prickly about her family, and with good reason. Perhaps she's just not answering the radio. Perhaps the fight has triggered her trauma about her brother-in-law's death. All bears consideration.

She's up there. I can see her head. Not too close to the edge, of course.

She's okay. Or if she isn't, she's beyond my help at the moment.

For now, I need to get out of sight. I try Nicole, but she's clearly out of touch, and I worry she's dead.

Now, where to go until it's time to check back?

I keep walking while I cross options from a diminishingly short list, trying to make my brain work, trying to move with purpose. About to take a corner to avoid a place I've been before, I notice the lights are out and a sign that says 'Closed for Renovations.'

I take the corner anyway, the better to think. I never mentioned this place to anyone in the Department, afraid of the connections I shouldn't have made here. If there's no one here, it can't be going to the same well twice, can it? No one will ever know I'm here, so maybe "Uncle Frank" won't feel that I've trespassed too far on his hospitality, especially after springing me from the Cherrydale PD. And I really need to stretch out and rest for a while.

Another block and I'm sure it's empty. Athena smiles on me, and I find the window that was so appealing last time. A shadowed alley, away from the street and John Q. Citizen. The lock has never been repaired. It's as good as a welcome mat, one way or the other. A quick glance around and I stuff my bag inside. Another glance, I hoist myself up and slither through, quick as quick can be.

The alley doesn't let in much sun. I don't need light, as I drop to the floor. The construction is down front, in the offices and showers, the contractors long since gone off to their six-packs. The rest of the place, the part I care about, is exactly as I remember it. The smell, sour sweat driven into leather and canvas, is like homecoming. I scoop up my bag and pick my way through the construction debris, find a working toilet, and make the most of a quiet moment. Bliss. I splash water on my face, clean up the small cuts, check the bandage on my side, and bind up the ankle; it's good. The bubbler still works. I let it run before I drink, swallowing another antibiotic. Thank you, Ape.

The boxing ring is still there, but Frank has added tatami near the weights and bags. He has business savvy, and these days, everyone imagines they can fight in the Octagon. I pull up to a corner of mat, check my gear, set my watch, then pull my hood up and close my eyes.

I can't sleep.

Too much in my head, and nothing I can do about it yet. Sleep's a good use of time, but I'm too wired.

I can fix that.

I stretch, strip down to my T-shirt, then start with combinations on the heavy bag. Nothing too fancy, just punches and knees, working out the kinks,

Dana Cameron 203

letting focus return and mindlessness settle in. I move around, as the bag swings, taking it at half speed and quarter power, not pushing where it hurts, but not wussing out, either. Find rhythm, break it up, find it again.

Someone is there. Standing in the shadows.

I keep at the bag, waiting to see what he'll do. I didn't hear anything, he didn't turn on the light. He knows his way around. He stands there, not speaking, not drawing down on me. Calm, self-possessed, curious.

Unusual.

Another two steps, and I'll be facing him. I keep throwing punches and kicks, calculating exit scenarios. I'm good to go, but would like to keep it quiet. It's already been a busy day.

"Holy shit!" I scream, when I finally "notice" him. "Omigod, you scared the shit out of me!"

He doesn't say anything.

"Look, mister, I was just messing around. I can leave, and no one will ever know I was even here, right?"

I move toward my gear, to distract him. He doesn't say anything, doesn't move. "You can even check—I didn't steal nothing."

"I saw," he says. "The alarm wasn't tripped, either."

His voice is measured, calm. Accent's Georgia, near Atlanta.

I get my first good look at him.

Trouble.

White male, short black hair, six feet, one seventy-five, no flab, no bulk either. Posture and poise. His nose has been rearranged a couple of times, but he's dished out more than he's taken. A T-shirt and sweats, sneakers and gym bag. He doesn't appear to be carrying, but there's something in his pocket.

I shrug and scratch my side, still moving over to my bag, like I'm gonna jam, opting for the knife under my T-shirt rather than the ankle rig for speed and quiet. "I'll just get going."

204 *Exit Interview*

"One thing. You came in through the back window, didn't you?"

"And I can leave the 'zact same way, mister."

"Mr. Frank told me about the last girl who came in through that window." This could go either way. Fifty percent. Best odds I've had all day.

He reaches for his pocket, and I tense for a takedown. He won't make the shot before I get him, and then it'll be too late for him.

He pulls out a cell phone and hits a button. I know for sure it's not the cops.

"Mr. Frank? Joe here. Sorry to disturb you, sir, but it's about that back window." He looks at me. "You know, the one I keep wanting you to get fixed."

I wait a long time while he listens. He watches me. Sizing me up. Then.

"Yes, sir. Yes, sir, I understand. Thank you. Good night, Mr. Frank."

He puts the phone away and takes his hand out of his pocket slowly, reassuring me, he thinks. "Mr. Frank sends his regards. He also said I should give you whatever you want, and I quote: 'If she needs a doctor, get her a doctor. If she needs a helicopter, get her that. Get her a pizza if she wants it. And be polite about it.'"

"That was nice of him," I say. "Bar Harbor puts him in a good mood."

That reassures him I am, in fact, the last girl who came through the window.

"He also reminded me it's sometimes useful to leave a small hole in your defenses, to see what'll come through."

Sounds like Frank.

"So," he says, "what can I get you?" His gaze lowers to my strapped up ankle. "You need a doctor?"

I shake my head. "I just want to crash for a couple of hours, then be on my way."

He nods, not going anywhere. "You hungry?"

"No. Thanks. Really. I'm just gonna..." I nod toward the heavy bag.

"Okay. Let me know."

He stays put as I work. He doesn't relax. This is too easy.

"Did you want to have a turn?" I step back from the heavy bag. There are two others he could use.

"No thanks."

I nod, get back to it, loosening up because something's about to happen. I keep an eye on him, but he's just standing there. I mix it up, throw in some showy stuff because I don't know what he knows about me and I don't want to give away the farm. I pull back, scratch my side like I'm resting. The D2 is still where I want it.

"You know..."

Here it comes.

"Your balance is a little off. That's why you're not getting the height on those standing kicks."

I step back, make a show of breathing heavy, tilt my head. "Yeah? Oh. Thanks."

"Come on. Let me show you."

Maybe Bar Harbor wasn't doing it for Frank. Maybe he decided I used up my last favor at the Cherrydale police station—was it only ten days ago? "Naw, that's okay, thanks."

"No, seriously." He nods to the mats. "And your kicks are flashy, but you're in the air too long. On the street, anyone with real skills would just knock you down."

The street. Real skills. "Oh. Okay." Is he really talking to me like this, after what Frank probably told him about me? Something's up.

"It's not difficult."

If Frank is playing me, he's gonna find parts of his boy nail-gunned all over his office. I take a sip of water. I thought we had a better relationship, more respect.

Might as well find out. Mats are easy enough to clean.

I go to the mats, getting just the right mix of reticence, distrust, and curiosity. It's not hard. Joe's already slung his gym bag down and dropped the cell phone. Doesn't look like there's anything else on him, but I'm ready.

"Okay, your stance is good, but now try throwing a kick at me."

Dear God, he's serious. He thinks he's being helpful. I hesitate, still not wanting to break through the fourth wall. It can't be what it looks like...

"Go ahead. I won't let you hurt me."

I do the same high-falutin', show-off flying kick as before, and he does what anyone should and steps in and mimes a shove to my trunk. "See?"

"Oh. I get it."

"And when you're moving from a standing position, you're not quite..."

He moves in quick to correct my stance, but I'm tired and if he's not going to try and kill me, I wish he'd just leave me be. His hand flicks out to my side—to my bandage or to my knife?—and—

I block it, hard, step in and plant it, land a sweet one to his jaw and then, as he stumbles back, slam the flat of my foot straight into his sternum.

He goes all the way down and rolls with it. He's back on his feet, lightning quick, looking surprised.

I don't stop to admire my work, but I back off. Because it's not "I got hit by a girl" surprised, or "you're going to be hard to kill" surprised, but "why'd you do that?" surprised.

Aw, hell. I just kicked a puppy.

"I guess I should have asked first," he says.

His guard is up. I never dropped mine.

"I guess."

"Bet you can't do it again." He grins and touches his jaw. "Not when I'm looking."

I shouldn't have been able to do it when you weren't looking, friend. Not if you work for Frank the way I think you do.

I'm tired. I don't want to get into a pissing contest.

"Come on," he says. There's something about his grin that makes me want to act stupid. "No eyeballs, nothing that hangs, dangles, or pokes out. Everyone limps away largely intact."

I shake my head, then turn away. He almost buys it, and I spin in with a backfist that should take his head off if he's still there.

But he's not. He's back and low, waiting to get in with an uppercut to the body. I block it, try a couple of hooks, land one, muff the other. He takes it, makes me pay for it with a knee to the body I should've anticipated. I make a noise, and try to keep my game face on, but I just can't keep from smiling.

It's fun.

I've forgotten how much fun it is with someone who knows what he's doing. We're pushing each other, not out for blood, not fooling around, either. Joe's in shape, he's got ability. We dance for five minutes.

But I'm tired. I need to break this off before I get clumsy or he gets frustrated with not winning and acts on it. He's headhunting and lines up a nasty kick. Yeah, it looks like he's going for my ribs, but he'll whip it up at the last second and try to conk me one with his size eleven. Now he's showing off. I go low and sweep his supporting foot out from underneath him.

He doesn't fall as well as before; he's getting winded. When I don't follow him down for the ground game, he looks annoyed. Then he looks disappointed.

I hold up my hands, shake my head again. "Joe, we're done, okay?"

For a second, I think he's gonna bounce back up—he's got that guy-look in his eyes that says he's revved up and not done, not by a long shot, no *ma'am*.

I don't want to convince him he should have stayed down. I tense, then shake it off, give him a little more game face, the one that says we're done playing. He gets it.

He's not stupid.

He slaps the mat—whomp—and gets up—slowly—and offers me his hand. I take it, promising myself, only half-serious, that if he fucks with me, I'll just cut him and leave him there. But he's cool, and we're good.

He walks it off and I realize the damp on my T-shirt isn't just sweat. The stitches have pulled.

I'm looking at it, and he's right there. "That bad?" he says. Calm. He's seen this sort of thing before, knows what's what.

"Just a nuisance."

"Need some help?"

"I got it." I go to my bag, pull out the medical kit I've got in there. "Medical kit" is a fancy name for a baggie full of useful things to keep it together in the field. I rummage for the hand cleaner, tape, and antiseptic. Pull off my T-shirt, wipe the sweat from around my athletic bra.

Joe watches while I work. "Wow. A Girl Scout." He looks right at me. "Marry me."

He's not entirely kidding. He likes what he sees.

"Can't," I say. "I have my career to think of." I don't even want to think about what his career involves.

"How about a kiss, then?"

"Sure. Get over here." He leans over, and I'm planning to give him a peck on the cheek, a joke, a brush-off, a boundary.

But his hand is on my good side, burning right into the skin, and I linger, longer than I mean to. I stop, he starts. He kisses my temple, a line down the side of my face.

It's an hour off the street.

It's an alibi.

It's an alliance.

He pauses to move the damp hair stuck to my cheek. I should stop this now. His eyes—

It's been a long day.

It's been a *long* damn time.

He shifts his weight and puts his hand on my thigh. A line of firecrackers goes off up and down my body. Suddenly, I'm not tired anymore. I ache only in good places.

I kiss him back, meaning it, and I grab his shirt, plant my foot behind his, and pull.

He goes over onto the mat, and I follow, straddling his hips—damn ankle, *what* ankle?—and we manage to keep kissing while we sort things out. I pull off his T-shirt. There's an interesting shiny white scar running from his left collar bone down to the top of his stomach. I trace it with my tongue, feel him arch up beneath me, breathless. It's all muscle. It's not vanity sculpting and it's not prison bulk, but the sleek cabling of muscle that's used hard, often. His hair's lighter than I thought, and there's a slight cauliflower swelling in one ear.

When his hand slides under my battered jog bra and finds skin, I almost pass out. I rock forward, giving it right back to him, and the back of his head hits the mat, not daring or willing to move. I lean back, and instantly realize there's movement across the room. A hunched form, bulky. It tenses as I do, and I'm about to spring—

"Hey, it's just the mirror," he says. He grabs my side with his other hand.

It's the wrong side, the one that's bandaged. We both know it at the same moment.

"God*damn*," I say. It hurts like hell and breaks the mood like a martini glass hitting marble.

He jerks his hand away like he's been burned. "Where? What? Oh shit, I'm sorry."

It's a reality check. For both of us.

Joe says, "We can't do this."

He looks like he's ready to cry.

I'm on the verge of killing someone or crying myself. Keeping a cool head is everything now.

It's been so long...

"Okay, if it's this—" I reach over into my bag and pulled out a little foil envelope from the baggie. "—if it's just this, we're good. If it's something else, tell me right now. Right now, or so help me, I'll—"

"No, that's it..." He looks at me. "Marry me, Girl Scout."

"First things first."

We're back in business, with a few workarounds: My bandaged side is out of bounds and his jaw still hurts. We pick up the thread of things right away. Mouths inspire bodies and small movements instruct us both.

Suddenly I forget how sweatpants come off. That doesn't last long.

Neither do we.

I no sooner climb on top of him, then it's over for both of us. I feel like I've exploded, shattered, and then been rebuilt anew.

I feel consciousness returning with some regret.

"Hmmm?"

I feel warmth and chest hair against my back. "Hmmm."

"I swear to you," Joe says, "with even just a little warning, I can do a lot better."

"If you were any better, we'd both be dead." An exchange of clichés, yes, but the niceties matter in such situations. I snuggle back into him, a blissful moment.

My watch alarm goes off. Time to go. I whisper into the crook of my arm, "You cannot be serious."

"Back to work?"

I nod, unwilling to look at him.

"Then we were lucky to get what we did. Thanks."

Sensible. Polite, too.

"No, thank you." I get up, stretch, get my act together. It's short work.

He's dressed, and his hair's messed, and suddenly, I'm tired to death and I hate the Kolas and Heath all to hell. They can sort their own mess out. I've done more than my share. No one could fault me for getting out while I can. There are others who could—

But Amy's still alone. Might still be on the roof. There's an army turning on itself, and my people's lives are in danger.

"Gotta go," I say.

"I wouldn't mind seeing you again," Joe says. "In the daylight, even. If you wanted."

It's raining outside, dark now. Maybe it's been raining for hours; I never noticed. "I'd like that. But I can't make any promises." I think hard before I speak again. "I'd like to make promises, but I can't."

"I get it." And he does get it. He's something else. No unnecessary chatter, no complications.

I swallow. "Just...don't fix the window latch."

He shakes his head. We're either going to stay there forever or I'm going to get back on the job. I pick up my bag, gear up, and walk to the window.

He gives me a boost out, then holds his hand up against the glass as I leave.

It was easier than killing him, I think as I leave the alley, dodging the puddles as best I can.

You can think that if you want. But you never would have taken so long to do it.

Chapter Thirty-Nine: Amy Lindstrom

After broiling on the roof surrounded by bodies for fifteen minutes as I collected myself, I realized I needed to act on my own. Meet back at the room, she'd said, right before we started shooting people and she jumped off the damned building.

My radio was a pile of plastic and electronics sticking into my butt. So much for that. Calling out to someone on the ground didn't seem like a good idea. I glanced over at the two bodies within eyesight and sighed. I tried not to remember what my mother had always said about being judged by the company I keep. These guys weren't good company, and they weren't aging well. Better sooner than later.

I texted Burke, using his phone, and got to work.

I started on the smaller one. He'd died first and the most messily; he wouldn't improve with time. I tried to avoid getting more blood on me. Breathing through my mouth didn't seem to help as much as everyone always said it did. Phone, check; gun, check. Extra ammo, good. Wallet—? There might be receipts or something, so I took the whole thing. He didn't have anything else on him, and while I thought about the jewelry he was wearing, I figured it might be too much trouble to pawn it. Besides, if we needed cash, Marie could get some. She always seemed to be able to get what she needed.

I'd finished a whistled rendition of "Bad Romance" and was halfway through "She Works Hard for the Money," when I frowned. What if Marie didn't come back? Same plan as before: Wait at the room until midnight, then hide somewhere else if I was on my own.

Next came T-Rex. As bad as he'd smelled when he was alive, it was nothing compared to now. I had to get off this roof. He had a few more interesting things in his pockets, including two knives. One opened with just one hand and one made out of something I assumed was some sort of industrial glass or ceramic. Huh. The things you learn when you leave the house. I pocketed them. I pulled the bodies out of sight as best I could. By the end of it, I smelled like noontime at the slaughterhouse. I thought about doing this guy's phone in the way I'd done the others, then stopped. It was worth going through the call list and address book first.

Then I went through the whole pile of wallets.

Banging started on the door a half hour later. I stopped my imaginary target practice, got up, and slipped over to the door, pistol ready. One final crash, and the door opened, revealing Ted Burke, his face streaked with sweat and filth. He wiped the cobwebs off his hands, then tried to wipe his face, which only made things worse.

"What the hell is going on..."

"Let me get out of here first, then we can talk," I said, taking the shirt he offered me. Turning away from him, I pulled off my once lovely, crisp white blouse, now covered in dried blood. I changed into the clean shirt, which covered the worst of the blood on my capris.

He grabbed my arm. I swung around at him, but he let go, stepped back.

"No. Amy you need to stop this. I'm not a ride share. I'm not your concierge. We're not friends—we're not even collegial. You must have friends, people at work, family—"

Tommy's face, Michelle's and Jacob's, crowded my mind. "I'm not putting anyone else into danger—"

I froze, turned red, immediately realizing my reasoning as soon as he did. "I...I didn't."

"Yeah, you did. I'm no one. We're not close. I don't matter." He was quiet for a minute. I moved for the door but he held up his hand. "You make a kind of sense, given recent events, what I know about... But it doesn't mean that calling me is not truly sociopathic; you'd probably even do it again, without a

214 *Exit Interview*

second thought. I'll get you out of here, you'll tell me the story—because if the shit you're in is this deep, then you're going to need someone else to tell, someone *not* tied to you, if people need to know about this. And since you've volunteered me as tribute, that's the trade."

"Burke—" He was right, though. "I'm sorry," I said finally.

"Okay, that's fine. But you survive, we share a byline and you get some fucking help—and I mean, the best shrink you can afford—and you do *all* the work, three times a week, whatever. People can't live without...other people." He shrugged. "Well...if you die....I get the story and we're even."

"Okay." I could barely look at him. "Thank you."

He held the door, and we left. I counted the steps down, holding my breath and praying he wouldn't go farther out to the roof, seeing the bodies. He didn't need to be an accessory to that, as well. I got as far as "six," when I heard him close the door and follow me down the stairs.

"Amy—" he began. "You need to tell me...the blood—"

"Please, Burke, I swear I'll tell you everything, but if I don't get a shower soon, I'm going to scream."

The edge in my voice wasn't a trick. I was hanging on to my sanity by a hair. With toenails and teeth. Burke looked really furious, but he only asked one more question, and it was the right one.

"Where to?"

I told him how to get to the motel, and he nodded curtly. We drove in silence for the duration. A reporter's mantra is "confirm and confirm and confirm." To do that, I needed my own reinforcements. Marie said herself if you have assets, you use them. Maybe I didn't have soccer-mom arms dealers in my contact list, but I did have one thing going for me: Burke's willingness to take a chance on me to get the story.

Keep telling yourself that. Try not to remember you're killing him, by telling him the truth.

There wasn't anyone else, I repeated to myself.

Without me asking, Burke drove around the block a couple of times before parking down a cross street. The room looked okay from what I could see. I checked the various safeguards Marie had put into place. They were intact: The talcum powder was undisturbed on both the outside and indoor knobs and the toothpick she'd taped to the door frame only broke when I entered. I closed the door and reset the "alarms."

I'd done very well. I wasn't going to lose my cool or burst into tears. I was managing.

My knees gave out just as I reached the bed. "She just jumped off the fucking building!"

Burke had glanced around the room. The way he looked at me suggested that now he was pretty sure I was having some kind of mental breakdown. "Who did? Amy, you've got to tell me what's going on! The things I've been hearing. And the last time I saw you. I mean the car wreck that wasn't an accident and the—well, it's only gotten more confusing since then."

"I'm sorry, I'm so sorry," I said. "But...I don't know where to begin."

"Start with *who* jumped off what building," he said. "Nothing like a punchy lede to get the reader hooked. Build the inverted pyramid: who, what, why, when, where. You remember that, I'm sure."

"Bite me, Burke," came automatically. That felt better, for a moment, but then came a sudden rush of guilt. The man had come to my rescue, again, and I was about to dump him into a whole world of shit. He didn't deserve that. Nice going, Lindstrom. I could feel the backs of my eyes burning.

I was not, was *not*, going to start crying again. I got up, went into the bathroom, and splashed some water on my face. As I was wringing out the facecloth, I heard footsteps behind me.

"Enough. No more. No crying, no washing, no...nothing else. Just sit down and start talking."

I don't know why I should have felt...rebuffed, but I did. Burke had a right to be impatient. So I did what he asked and started with Marie's stomach-clenching display of free-running, bringing all the detail I could remember. I needed a backup of what I'd learned, apart from George. "I mean, it was like being at the monkey cage at the zoo. I didn't know humans could do that!"

"Wait—her name's Marie?"

"I honestly don't know what her name is. I thought it was Marie or Cherie for a while, or possibly Cara Jones. It may be Jayne Rogers. I doubt she even knows what her real name is, anymore." The name in the file George had sent me matched the one from Kola's gang, and Nicole had called her Rogers, so the latter option was possible.

"Makes sense; the way she fights, the parkour? She's had some very serious training, somewhere." He shook himself. "Okay, sorry I interrupted. Tell me about her."

I went back to the beginning. The Bolton dinner. Why I had been there, why she was there, and what we knew about Kola's murder by his wife. Then her reappearance. Heath, and his probable plans to take over Kola's armory and start up a private security firm—and how he planned to downsize his loyal staff. Jacob and Michelle. Our attempts to find the encrypted computer with the location of Kola's resources, the lives of the innocent operatives. How time was going by, too quickly...

Telling what I knew to another reporter went against everything in my being, but as I spoke, it got easier. Maybe just hearing my own story out loud, all of what I'd been going through, helped by giving me a familiar perspective. Telling a story, getting the facts straight, imposing order on the world. Except the world was running out of order, getting stretched too thin around me at the moment. We still didn't have the Kola files or the location of his arms supply.

When I got to the picture frame from Hey, Baby! and the tracer on the ribbon, I put my hands up. "And I wasn't sure what else to do. So that's why you're here."

"There was nothing else in the frame?"

I shook my head. I heard a faint tapping at the door. It had started raining.

"Maybe they just left it there as bait. To see who'd come for it."

"I don't know," I said. "I'm too tired to think about it."

"That's a good start. I'm willing to bet you're hungry and thirsty, and I'm starving. You get cleaned up. And in the toilet kit I got you, there's some...you should get some burn cream on your, um...that."

He gestured and I looked down; sure enough, there was an angry red mark, about an inch long, at the top of my left breast.

"Yeah, well, I'm lucky if that's the worst of it." I got up. "Give me a few minutes."

"I'll be back in a half hour. Pizza and beer."

I nodded. I could feel myself welling up again. Just two more minutes, and I'd be in the shower, and I could have as big a fit as I wanted.

I held onto the edge of the bureau. "A half hour."

"Yeah." He looked at me. "Amy, I'll be right back. Honest."

"I know."

"It's just...I will be back. I just want you to know."

I nodded. "Got it."

He paused by the door. "I promise. Thirty minutes."

I locked the door behind him, and began to strip down, surprised at how much work it was and how much I ached from the day's events. I glanced at my watch—watches, I should say. The very demure Raymond Weil Parsifal was now unrecognizable. The other, the Triathlon, was scratched but fine. I was astonished to see it was nearly nine at night. A faint metallic ring on tile. I glanced down and saw the brass casing from a bullet—cartridge, Marie would have corrected—had fallen when I took off my bra. Now we knew where the mark came from. I skinned off my panties and hit the shower.

At first, it just stung everywhere the hot water hit. Eventually the relief at washing the grime and sweat and odd spatters of blood took over. I soaped up and heard another ping. Another casing at the bottom of the shower. It had been stuck to the underside of my breast. Okay, well, that's why Marie wears those crew-necked T-shirts in warm weather instead of a scoop-front. No more cleavage when we're expecting gunplay, I lectured myself sternly. I closed my eyes, but this time the hysteria came in the form of laughter.

No more V-necks, no bikinis, no strappy sandals or short-shorts, not when there's going to be a firefight. Turtlenecks, crewnecks, fine, but no more skin, Lindstrom, it's not smart, not professional.

I finished the shower and started checking for cuts, scrapes, burns. Too late, I realized I hadn't brought clean clothes in with me. I didn't want to go parading around in front of Burke with just the skimpy motel towel; doubtful he was back yet, anyhow.

I shoved the door open.

Marie was there, dripping wet. Holding a pizza box. "How'd you get off the roof?"

"How—what's going on?" I stammered. "When did you—? I had the chain across! Where'd you go?"

I went a little dizzy: What had she done to Burke?

She slid the pizza box onto the bureau. "How'd you get off the roof, Amy? Who saw you up there?"

Chapter Forty: Nicole Bradley

The drive out of town takes a while, but it gives me a chance to clear my head. A little mom-and-pop corner store in a Black neighborhood in North Philadelphia. The owners think I'm the niece of the landlord, who owns most of the block. They think that I have an apartment on the second floor and use part of the basement for storage. They don't know I'm also the landlord, and that nice old man who stops by every month for the rent (and to catch up with neighborhood doings) works for me. There's much to be said for human intelligence, curiosity, and gossip. There are few things like a corner store for keeping an eye on the neighborhood.

Up in the apartment, it looks nice, tidy, lived in. None of my alarms, digital or practical, have been tripped, and I checked the cameras right before I arrived. There's time for a cup of tea while I make lists and gear up.

Things are about to get crude and wet, and I'm not about to show up at this party empty-handed. As much as I used to joke that I will just stand behind Cave Girl in a physical fight, there's something in me that's hungry to finally end this betrayal, the disloyalty. Punish the ones who take the easy way out of a problem that was already solved for them for the sake of small savings to the taxpayer and a much larger personal aggrandizement. Look them in the eye and let them know that I know what they did. I find myself surprised that I want that, but I'm only human.

I'm delighted to find that I have my period. That's usually when I'm at my sharpest, my eye-hand coordination the best.

I've done all I can to get Taps ready. I need to get close to Heath now.

Chapter Forty-One: Amy Lindstrom

"Answer me, Amy. How'd you get off the roof?"

Marie was asking me questions? Making *demands*? That made me incredibly, stupidly angry.

"You ran off! Ran off the roof of a building—and how fucked up is that, by the way?—leaving me with a pile of stinking, rotting bodies. What the hell was I supposed to do?" I strode forward. "I bashed on a door, and a contractor or someone opened it, eventually. When I saw it wasn't one of Heath's men, pointing a gun, I pushed past and ran out of there like my ass was on fire!"

"I'm sorry," she said. She went into the bathroom and I took the moment to stash the shirt Burke gave me and get changed. She emerged with the last threadbare towel. "Things got out of hand with the runner I went after. Then I saw Feds watching this building. I thought it best to give it a few hours. As we agreed."

I nodded. "Well, that's what *I* did, too." I wasn't sure she believed me, but on the other hand, I'd spent all day on the run, firing guns, picking over corpses, and watching feats of aerial gymnastics that upset my stomach just remembering them. I wasn't sure how I should sound, but I've lied my way into and out of lots of situations before. I thought I sounded pretty good. The borderline hysteria didn't hurt. "What's that?"

"It's a pizza, Amy. You eat it," she said, wide-eyed. Her sarcasm vanished. "I figured you'd be hungry if you were here, and I knew I was starving."

My stomach flip-flopped with relief, then consternation: She hadn't killed Burke and taken the promised pizza. But now I had to worry about when he did arrive.

I got dressed, as quickly as I could.

There was a knock on the door. We froze, then Marie motioned me over to answer it. "WTF?" I gestured. "I gotta be bait?"

She rolled her eyes, gestured with the pistol that appeared out of nowhere.

"Whaddya want?" I bellow.

"Delivery," a muffled voice said behind the door.

I tensed up again, worried how this was going to play out. I put the chain back, opened the door, bracing it with my foot so it couldn't open and more.

Burke was there, his face blank. He blinked. "Pizza?"

"We didn't order anything," I said, grumpily as I could. I tried to keep the emphasis off "we."

"Yeah, but this is room twenty, right?" He sounded exactly like a delivery person who was behind schedule, losing ground on his route, and blaming me for it.

"No, it's not, and we didn't order anything."

"Motherfucker...now I'm gonna be late. Okay, whatever."

He glanced at the ticket sticking out of the pizza box, and walked away, muttering to himself.

"Okay, good. I was worried that was going to be one of the Fibbies from down the street." Marie relaxed, took a deep breath. "I don't know about you, but I gotta eat."

I felt close to vomiting, but nodded. "I can't even think straight, after today." I glanced at the box. "I'm getting really sick of fast food."

"Okay, well, I'll send this back and order a beef Wellington and a nice Bordeaux." She frowned at my complaint. "Anonymous is good, so that's what we do for now."

We dug in. "Anonymous, right. So what's your real name?"

She snorted and grabbed another slice. "Don't worry about it."

"I'm serious. What am I supposed to call you? It's not Jayne Rogers?" I said. "Not Cara Jones? Not Marie Tremblay? Cherie Deveau?"

That surprised her. Nicole Bradley had always called her "Rogers," but how did I find out about "Jayne?"

I reached into my bag and pulled out the grisly packet I'd stashed in there. The photographs were stuck to each other. It took a couple tries before I could work up an edge with my fingernails and get them unstuck again. Cheap photo paper from a home printer. Blood-and-sweat-soaked. "Here."

One was me—recent but in a setting that told me I'd been under surveillance for some time. I shivered to think about how close they'd been without me knowing. One was of Marie, much younger, an ID photo from the Department, her State Department cover. A young, idealistic, earnest woman, heartwrenching in every way. With the name Jayne Rogers. Same as the one I'd had from George.

She raised an eyebrow. "That's from the guys on the roof?"

"Yeah. The T-Rex I took them from wasn't into scrapbooking, I bet."

"We'll stick with Jayne Rogers." She filled a coffee cup from the bathroom tap. "Mr. Heath presumably sharing intel with Mrs. Kola's gang."

"So I'm assuming you added to that body count after you left?"

"Three on the roof, one in an alley. One left down below, maybe alive."

"And you took your time coming back because you saw the unmarked car?"

Did Marie—Jayne—it was going to take me a bit to remember that. Did Jayne blink? Something. I saw her stretch, shrug her shoulders, something I knew she did to buy herself time.

"Yeah. Okay, here's the drill."

We'd hit Kola's guys' hideout—we now had an address from the licenses—and look there for the computer.

"Time's getting short," Jayne said. "They're the most likely people, besides Heath, to know where the computer or the encryption key is."

"Whatever." Suddenly, my eyelids felt like they were full of buckshot. The day hit me hard. "I'm gonna sleep."

"Good idea."

I was dog-tired, emotionally wrung out, and mad at the world. Tomorrow was one day closer with too many questions and no results, and the possibility of encountering a well-armed private force who had beef with me.

I didn't bother changing out of my clothes and I didn't bother saying good-night.

Chapter Forty-Two: Amy Lindstrom

I awoke the next morning stiff and sore from dehydration and sleeping with clenched muscles. And for the first time in our acquaintance, Jayne snored. Like a band saw. Maybe it was the pizza. She'd had a busy day, yesterday, what with the killing and jumping and hiding and God knows what else.

I sat up and reached for a bottle of water on the floor next to me. I was parched. No matter how good pizza sounds at the time, it's not health food. Soul food, maybe. I'm sure the salt did me good after my stint on the roof.

If I get out of this alive, I told myself, I'm going to a spa for a week to get refurbished. Retrofitted, if need be.

I went into the bathroom, prepared for the day, then filled the none-too-clean sink with water and stuck my head under. I was profoundly grateful Burke had taken my hint. I had no idea whether I'd see him again, but at least he knew what I knew.

The cold felt good on my face and neck. I was scratched and sunburned, and still sore from the fight. Since I wasn't breathing, the noxiousness of the basin didn't bother me. It was quiet here, calm...

Banging on the door was audible, even underwater, and I reluctantly came up for a breath.

"Yo! You taking up residence in there or what?"

"Bite me," I muttered. I took the largest towel, which was still damp. Screw her.

I opened the door, drying my hair.

"Jeez, Princess. Takes you long enough." Jayne pushed past me and slammed the door. It caught me on the heel, and I cursed as I limped over to the bed.

I pulled on socks and running shoes from AP's stash. A pedicure, definitely, when this was over. And, screw it, I was going to buy Lucy a phone to go with the MacBook Pro—she needed to keep in touch, with all of her after-school activities... Look forward, Lindstrom. Promise yourself everything to get through the end of all this.

The bathroom door opened, and there was Jayne, looking downright perky. Where'd she find that good mood?

"Okay, kiddo. Up for breakfast before we take on the enemy?"

There was an ancient, cracked-linoleum breakfast joint around the corner. The food wasn't bad. I ate ravenously, and ordered a second side of toast. We didn't talk much, which was fine with me. I concentrated on shoveling it away like there was no tomorrow, because who knew?

"Wow, you can pack it in there, Lindstrom," Jayne said. There was admiration in her voice. She'd ordered twice as much as usual and her own plate was scraped clean down to the glaze. She'd asked the waitress to leave the coffee carafe.

I slid out of the booth. "Be right back."

It was a little past the time I was supposed to get in touch with George, but I figured it was close enough. I had to try, anyway.

The signal was pretty weak in there, but I was able to get the random number and a browser.

I frowned. There seemed to be something wrong with the address. A dialogue box came back: "Error, page not found."

I tried again. Same result.

I logged out, and started from scratch. A cold sweat broke out all over me.

The screen was insistent. There was no such address.

"Whatcha got there?"

I jumped a mile. Jayne had come in without a sound and was looking over my shoulder. I was so wrapped up in what I was doing I had no idea how long she'd been there.

"Uh..."

She took Burke's phone from my hand and scrolled through the last several items in the browser drop-down.

"It's not mine; it was in that bag I stole," I started to explain.

"Who's this?"

No trace of emotion in her words or on her face. She clearly knew what I'd been doing. I didn't bother lying. I told her about George, emphasized his mania for security, how I'd found out from him about who she was. That I'd asked him to look into the Department and her. There was no reason, now, to conceal what I knew about her past. I waited for the explosion when I finished.

It didn't come. "Looks like he's been compromised," she said.

"It could be the computer's down."

She gave me a look.

"He might not be dead—" I insisted.

"It's not a bad assumption."

My hands went numb. I was freezing.

"If he was as careful as you say, they probably won't find us," she said, relieved.

"What?"

"That kind of guy thinks he's fighting a war. He lost. You can't let that be for nothing. I mean, I can check in with Raven, next time we connect, but...yeah, don't get your hopes up."

I groped for an answer. There was none.

She nodded. "We gotta get going." She opened the door, then paused, her back to me.

I nodded, still unable to speak. Jayne must have assumed I was cool, because she said, "I'm gonna let Nicole know what we're up to. Five minutes." Then she left.

It occurred to me this was the kind of thing she lived with all the time. She'd probably seen "resources compromised" before. I thought about her relationship with Ape. How they both knew what they were doing, and what the consequences of exposure would be, but they trusted each other. They had to. Jayne had been through all this, kept the secrets, did the job, and went on.

I had to do that, too.

I washed my face, stared into my blank eyes, and tried not to think too much about George. I took a deep breath, then tried a smile, then tried another one. After two minutes, I had it about right, and I returned to the booth.

Twenty minutes later, we were on our way to the address from the licenses of two of Kola's men, assuming that it was a base of operations. Waiting across the street, Jayne hesitated.

"My Spidey-Sense is tingling. I just can't see why," she said.

"You got me. So what's the plan?"

"You go to the front, take your time. Ring the bell. I'll check the back, break in that way, let you in if it's all clear. We have a look around, and we're out ASAHP."

"What are we looking for?"

"A computer, anything with technology that might hold Kola's files. Other than that, we'll know it when we see it."

The place was nice enough, from the outside. When Jayne let me inside, I saw that the mail had piled up over the past day or so. They hadn't rented it furnished, or if it was their building, they hadn't done a whole lot of nesting.

Jayne and I moved on to the living room. Couch, big TV on a crate. Another couch had a fold-out bed, and the sheets hadn't been changed in some time. The plastic they'd come in had been flung on the floor next to the bed.

A humming began, and I couldn't place it. "What's that noise?"

"Refrigerator going on?"

"No."

"Then we find out."

Upstairs, there were two bedrooms, one of which had a large, empty animal crate in the corner. Jayne stared at it.

"The guy I wanted to question said something about a dog," she said. "Went on and on about it, even as he was dying. Be careful opening doors. You start in the other bedroom, I'll take this one." The one we were in was the cleaner of the two.

"Thanks a bunch," I muttered. The entire place smelled like a locker room that had never known bleach. Guys had lived here who weren't expecting guests and didn't care if any were coming. Dirty laundry, everywhere.

"You want to start with the bathroom?" she asked, amused.

"Probably not."

I glanced in the bathroom, which was even nastier than I expected. Why wouldn't these guys lift the seat or sit down? Why didn't a filthy bathroom bother them?

I realized dirty laundry was better than blood-soaked clothing. I'd already shaken down these guys up on the roof, so there was nothing much more to be bothered by here. I looked in the closet, even poked at the floorboards for a hidden door, but there was nothing. A chair stood in the middle of the room, and the laundry on it was just laundry, nothing in the pockets. These were guys living in the present, no thought of the past, the future measured only in hours or days. Maybe that explained the bathroom.

I was just pulling myself up and dusting off my hands from looking under the bed, when Jayne came in, frowning. "Anything?"

I shook my head. "But there's an attic."

I glanced up, and she followed my gaze to a recessed door. The chair under all the clothes was directly under it, and just the right height.

Jayne looked at the ceiling thoughtfully. "Good girl." She pulled the clothes from the chair and climbed up on it, then paused.

"Booby trap?" I asked. "The dog wouldn't be up there, would it?"

She shook her head. "Haven't heard any barking. But if I find what I'm hoping to find here, I'd expect a little more trouble."

"We killed four guys last night—I assume you...got the one you jumped off the building for—"

She shook her head, waving her hand. "Amy, that's...not really just jumping. It's all just steps, one point to the next. You just need to look at the world differently, think about it a little differently."

She'd said something like that before, on the fire escape. "Anyway, I'm just saying. We might have gotten them all on the roof."

She pulled the door down and abruptly jumped off the chair. "Omigod!"

I stepped back, clutched my heart. "What? Oh, Jesus, what the hell—?"

"Nothing. I'm just messing with you, Princess."

I stared at her. "You're such an asshole."

She grinned and scurried up the ladder like a squirrel up a tree.

I swore again under my breath, trying to slow my heart. "It's not funny!" I called up the stairs. Ghostly laughter floated down from the attic. "And stop calling me 'Princess!'"

"You need a sense of humor," she said. "Helps keep you loose."

"I've got a fabulous sense of humor. *You're* a psychopath."

"Yeah, yeah. C'mon up, take a look at this."

Since my palms were sweating just being on a ladder, I focused on getting upstairs without falling off. Free-running would have to wait.

Upstairs was the humming and bumping I'd heard before. A large air conditioner cooled the attic room and now I understood why. A lizard-skin and blinged-out notebook computer looked desperately out of place on the cheap cafeteria-style table next to a cable modem hookup and printer. The only other thing this expensive in the house was the television, and that wasn't in the class of this gaudy billionaire's toy. Next to the computer was a pile of CD-ROMs, an external CD-ROM drive hooked up to the notebook, two flash drives, a mug holding some pens, a homemade gadget that looked like it might fit into a port, and some commercial software. The room was freezing. No one had been up here to open the door and let the cold air out for some time.

"Bingo," she said. "That's Kola's computer! No doubt about it!" She laughed.

I wasn't sure. "Would he have done all that bedazzling, though?"

"Those are real diamonds."

My jaw dropped. "What?"

"I didn't even think they really made those things. Customized Luvaglio notebooks. Run over a million bucks." She crawled around the floor, examining a tangle of cables that led from the equipment to a surge protector.

Then she sat at the keyboard and started going through the commercial stuff. "This stuff might crack a Windows password and maybe some store-bought accounting software, but that's about it. I'm betting Kola had something more effective protecting his files."

"Government grade," I agreed. "At least. He could afford it."

She picked up the homemade gizmo and said, "This is probably meant to spoof commercial security devices. Judging by the locks on those little file icons, it didn't work. I can't do anything with it."

She glanced at the CD-ROMs. "Russian encryption crackers. And the flash drives are empty. No dice there, either. You don't happen to have a quantum computer on you?"

"Huh?"

"Nothing. Makes me wish Raven was here. She could—"

A crash downstairs. We froze.

I glanced at Jayne, who was as focused on the machine as if she was trying to get a term paper submitted under the wire. "Amy, check the rest of the room."

I had a quick look around as she shut down the machine. There was nothing else I could see. The room was virtually empty. Glancing down, I saw the mug full of pens.

Jayne's fingers flew over the keyboard as I dumped the mug out on the floor. Pens, pencils, styluses—and two labeled thumb drives.

"Done." She closed the computer, pulled the cords out carefully, shoved them and the notebook into her courier bag. I grabbed the two flash drives and held them up.

Jayne smiled. "Nice one! Now out!"

A muffled thud and crash downstairs. The sound of breaking glass. Jayne shoved me toward the ladder. "Don't think, get down, wait for me."

I did what she said. It was easier to focus on orders than to think.

In the bedroom, the sounds of struggles downstairs were more pronounced. Another crash came from the side of the house, louder than the first, followed by a shout.

Jayne shoved me back against the wall.

"Front door is out. Kitchen is out. Window."

"What window?"

She pointed to the bathroom. "Move."

The window was nearly painted shut, but she heaved it open with a creak and a shudder, just as I thought we'd have to resort to breaking it.

Looking down, I balked. "Are we just going to drop?"

"It's not far. I'll go first, help you."

She was right, it wasn't as far as I thought because there was a shed roof beneath us. Still, it was a lot harder getting myself through. The window was an awkward distance above the floor. I had to go through headfirst, and let her half-catch me, half-break my fall. She'd shot through the window like water from a squirt gun.

"Now what?" I asked, panting, once we'd hit the ground.

"I gotta see who's there. Take this." She shoved the courier bag into my arms. "Don't lose it. Get around the fence, then stay put. If I'm not back in five minutes, you hear anything that doesn't sound right, you get the hell out of here."

I looked at my watch, and realized that, like the guys who lived here, I'd been living my life in bursts of seconds, minutes... "Got it."

She was already too far away from me to hear. She went to the back door, the one that led into the kitchen through the shed we'd just climbed off. I would feel every inch where the shingles had rubbed and scraped my belly.

I wriggled through a hole in the fence, made it a little larger as I felt the bag grabbing splinters from the ragged pickets I squeezed through.

I looked at my watch again—

Gunshots and screams. Did that count as "didn't sound right"?

I had to assume so.

I was alone. I started running.

Chapter Forty-Three: Amy Lindstrom

It took me a moment to realize the gunfire in the gang's house had stopped.

My legs felt like Slinkies, and I buckled. I finally figured out the ground itself wasn't shaking. I got up, kept my back to the fence.

I knew I had Jayne's "orders," but I couldn't just walk away.

If I was truly alone, I was probably as good as dead, anyway.

I stumbled toward the front of the house and ran across the street—after a fashion. I got three honks and was almost hit by a rubbernecker but kept moving, somehow.

I saw a small figure in a hoodie, jeans, and sneakers materialize from nowhere. Jayne—I was never so glad to see anyone in my life. She was limping slightly. She'd emerged three doors down from where I stood.

I began to walk down the street, the opposite direction from the way we'd come in, assuming Jayne had seen me.

She found me before I had a chance to think of what to do.

"What happened?" I said.

"I don't know. I think a stray of Kola's came back. Or maybe Morris, the one I took out after the coffee stunt; I don't remember seeing him up on the roof. I just kept shooting until I could get out. We need to get moving."

She put her hand around my shoulder, startling me.

"Don't hug the reporter," I said. I was scared out of my wits.

She nodded. "You're feeling better. Time to roll."

We made it all the way back to the car. There was no going back to the motel room. We had no idea if the same people who were at the house would be waiting for us there.

Too many questions.

I was dizzy with questions, and the loud ringing in my ears persisted. "How can you do that?"

"Do what?"

"Jump out of a window and escape a firefight, and then just...act normal. It's like you don't care."

"I care." She fiddled with the car's air conditioner, but it was no longer working. "Nothing's changed, really, in the equation, just brought the situation a little closer to home. *And* we just hit a big payday."

She glanced at me. "We need to see what's on the computer. Amy, we may have the location of Kola's files. Everything about his operations. Heath wants this, and we have it!

"We have Kola's data here!" she continued, abominably upbeat. "We know we're a step ahead. The bad guys came home too late, and I took care of them. Either way, we can replace more unknowns in the equation."

"This is *not* a math problem," I said. I wanted to scream, but I was tired and she was right.

"It's all math. There's no emotion in solving an equation. Try it."

"I can't believe you're such a...such a..."

"Such a what?"

"You're an...an optimist."

"Of course I am. And you should be, too. We're gonna do this, we're gonna beat Heath. Trust me."

I was too frazzled to argue.

We drove to George Washington University. The urban campus offered plenty of places to duck in and out-of-the-way nooks that weren't surveilled. There were power outlets and unprotected wireless access points.

"You'd think kids this smart would be more careful," I said after Jayne logged in with no problem.

Jayne looked at me. I had a lot to learn.

Dana Cameron 235

We found a place outside that suited our discreet purposes and plugged in. I gave her the flash drives and flicked through my phone, looking for news, yearning for the reality I thought I knew. I felt infinitely older than all the students wandering the green space of University Yard. I resented them for not having the weight of the world on their shoulders.

"Stop glaring," Jayne said without looking up.

"I'm not." How can it be sunny out? How can they only be worried about finals and stuff? Graduating? When such terrible things were happening in the world.

Horror was always looming, I told myself. I just happen to know about it this time. You can't stop living because you're afraid of what comes next.

"I'm not glaring," I repeated.

"You are." She looked around and smiled, almost, before she went back to work. "They're just kids. Let them be."

"You couldn't have been much older than they were, when..." I couldn't spill just how much I knew about her. "When you joined the Army."

"My job found me a little sooner, that's all."

"And you don't resent it?" I personally was resenting the hell out of my present situation.

She shrugged, then frowned at a file that wasn't behaving as she wanted. "Why would I want any of them to go through what I did, if they didn't have to? If I can make those choices so they never have to, I'm glad."

There's a Zen Buddhist concept about sudden comprehension or revelation: satori. Like a whack upside the head, I got it. I didn't like it any better, but now I understood: She believed she was taking responsibility when no one else could.

Her motivation wasn't so different from mine.

About three minutes later, she said, "Okay, we got nothing for clear files— files that haven't been encrypted. There's no personal email in the program, no other files. As for the files that are in here, they're encrypted to at least 1024 bits."

"That's bad?"

"With a supercomputer, we wouldn't crack this before the sun burns out. We need the encryption key. But I can try this..." She hit a few more keys. "Bingo."

"What have you got?"

"This is definitely Kola's computer. One of his people must have liberated it after he was murdered. I checked the paging file, what the files go through as they're encrypted? It leaves fragments, only fragments, but enough to tell me this computer was Kola's. I mean...apart from the diamond-encrusted case. And it does, absolutely, contain the information we've been looking for."

"How do you know this? How are you so good at the technical side of things? Nicole said you were...not tech-friendly."

"I bet she said worse than that. And I'm definitely not in her league—far from it. This is basic stuff, the kind of training we all got." She took a deep breath. "This is a very good day, Amy. We're winning."

"You could have fooled me. And what about the security key? We still need that."

"We do. Any thoughts about the picture frame we got from Hey, Baby? Could that have been something?" she asked.

"No. We didn't have that long with it, before you chucked it."

She nodded. "Let's look at those thumb drives you found at the house."

They were nothing. Too much to hope for. One was blank, the other just a backup of what was already had on the notebook.

She paused to check in with Nicole on the IRC chat.

We checked the phones I took from the men on the roof. Nothing. Some of them were locked, but Jayne got around them. All they had was the numbers for each other, nothing more. She tried hacking the phones, bringing up configuration screens I'd never have found without help from the manufacturers. Nothing.

The computer wobbled on her lap. Jayne went rigid.

I looked around, couldn't see anything amiss. "What's wrong?" Was she having a seizure?

"Nothing, I—" It happened again, but this time she laughed. She twitched again, then started to pull the cell phones back out of her pockets. They were all vibrating, chattering around on the ground like wind-up toys.

Each of them had "private number" in the screens.

The computer beeped at the same time. This time I jumped. It was turned up way louder than we'd realized. A message in the otherwise empty email box.

"Is it...is it Nicole?" I asked stupidly. How could she have reached this machine?

Jayne shook her head.

A string of meaningless letters in the "From" box. In the subject line, only "Text me. $$$ for you." There was a local telephone number. There was nothing in the body of the message.

I shivered. It was like a William Gibson novel, this anonymous electronic outreach.

She put the number into one of her burner phones, and shut down the computer. It seemed to take forever.

I couldn't help looking around, as if we were about to be besieged. "What do we do now?"

"We'll call them, but I need a minute."

"Mrs. Kola knows we have the computer. Encrypted or not, we should destroy it!"

"No. Even if we do destroy the computer, she and Heath would never believe us." I could practically see Jayne thinking. "We need the encryption key.

We need it all, so they can't ever figure out the location of all of Kola's assets. Then we have to meet them."

"What? Why in God's name would we meet them if we get the key?"

"Quiet down," she said. "You're drawing attention to us."

She leaned back against the tree and sighed, clutching the closed computer. Any curious onlookers would think it was a lovers' spat. It was like she could give off vibes, tell them what they should be seeing. The stage lost a star when Jayne opted for a life of mayhem.

"This is crazy!" I hissed. "They'll find us!"

"Not by the time we're gone." She busted the phones' chips. "We have to do this on our terms. That's the only way we'll survive. Believe me, Amy, I want this to be over. But it has to happen the right way, or there's no reason for us to have hung on this long. We have to make sure it's over for good. Our terms."

I sagged, the tension in my shoulders no longer even enough to keep me together. "Shit."

"Let me think this through. You go stretch your legs, get us some food from the union, if you want." She rummaged in her bag. "Here's some more cash. Anything for me. Water. And stay—"

"I know: Stay under the radar." I nodded. My stomach was growling, but I was terrified she wouldn't be there when I got back.

"Sure. Don't be long."

I rolled my eyes. "Yeah. I won't dawdle."

While I was waiting for the food in the Marvin Center, I watched a clutch of kids arguing good-naturedly about who texted whom and who else they should invite to what. It made me think of connections, again, and the party. I couldn't put my finger on it, but I kept coming back to the party.

How did I get invited to this party? Not Mrs. Bolton's party, which turned my life upside-down, but how did I get into this situation in the first place? What started me on the road to writing about the illicit arms trade, the

Dana Cameron 239

international business of weaponry, Kola? It was Tommy who'd started me on this project.

If I could just frame the questions properly—

Holy shit.

I stopped dead in my tracks. My brain raced to think over the idea, check it out, feel for holes. It was nearly all holes. It was a long shot, but at least it made sense within the context—

The clerk at the counter called my number again, and people were starting to look around for the person slowing things down. I grabbed my order and hurried out of the union, trying not to act as suspiciously as I was sure I looked.

When I got back to where I'd left Jayne, the sun was going down. "I was getting worried about you," she said.

She looked tired, I thought, and that worried me. "Ma—Jayne?"

"What?"

"You okay?"

"Sure. Just low blood sugar. Been a hell of a day."

She grinned, and I knew she was lying. Something in her eyes wasn't right, even though she looked me straight in the face when she said it.

"I think I got something. It's improbable, it's weird, but—"

"'When the going gets weird, the weird turn pro.'"

It didn't seem fair she should quote Hunter Thompson to *me*. "The silver frame—you took a photo of it, right? The inscription was initials. WTT?"

She checked her phone. "Yeah, WTT. And a date: December 11, 2019."

I shook my head and pointed at the image. "It's November 12. Like a lot of Europeans, Kola used the day, then month."

"And?"

"It was my brother-in-law, Tommy, who got me started researching Kola. Right before the car crash."

"Right."

240   *Exit Interview*

"Well, those are his initials: Ware Thomas Thornton. And that's the date he died. I think Kola was making a reference to Tommy."

"Tommy was using you to 'name and shame' Kola, wasn't he?" Jayne asked.

"We were cooperating on that, and a couple of other projects, yes."

She sat up. "Would he have left anything with your sister? Something Kola might know about?"

I shook my head. "No way. Anything like that, he would have kept out of the house, away from Maryelizabeth and Lucy." I was filled with bitter memories of having failed my family.

"Would Kola have left the encryption key in New York?" she said. "At the UN? Some other place Tommy had? I just don't think Kola ever had the time, was never off the radar for so long."

I swallowed. "I think we should look at Tommy's bench."

"Bench? Where?"

"Arlington. We bought a memorial bench and put the plaque up there a year ago. It was in the article I wrote about Tommy. Kola would have known about it. He was most likely the one responsible for the hit and run. The one...Tommy was driving when he crashed." If I'd been driving, I'd most likely be dead now. I still remember the terrible shudder of the car, the crunch of impact...

Jayne cocked her head. "I don't know. He would have found Tommy's efforts—and the UN in general—annoying, at worst. Mrs. Kola was more likely to think him a danger. She might have acted on her own, even then."

My stomach clenched. I didn't like that thought much better. "We should at least look."

"I agree. It wasn't one of our regular drops, but it's a good spot. A busy place, a reason for lots of people to be there. We don't lose anything by trying."

We packed up and found our way back to the car. I concentrated on the outside scenery, trying to calm my mind. All those people wandering around, with no thought of what was going on. When we arrived, we struggled to find a parking space. It seemed ludicrous to worry about it, but we couldn't afford to get noticed with a ticket or get towed.

I found the bench readily. I'd been out here frequently since we put it up. "What do we do?" I asked as we approached.

She smiled, talking without moving her lips. A good trick. "Well, don't start crawling all over it, acting like you're looking for something. Do you see anything from here?"

I shook my head. "Some trash. There's some bird poop on the back."

"Okay. Walk up casually, check out the bench as if we're trying to see whether we'll sit on anything nasty."

It's quite an art—one I'm sure I didn't master—walking and keeping your eyes open for clues, for enemies, and trying to look normal all at the same time. "It looks clean enough," I said, perhaps a little too loud.

"I see a mark," Jayne said, much lower, much more casually than me. "The one Kola and I used. I was hoping to see that. You've done it, Amy!"

"Holy—" I felt a rush like when I got a lead on a story. "Okay, now what? Where's the key?"

"I don't know for sure."

"So what's the point of having a mark, if you don't know where to go next?"

She gave me a look. "We never used this bench when we were working together. But that's Kola's mark. Other times, if we couldn't use a regular drop, we agreed to meet at a hotel bar."

"Do you have any idea how many hotels there are in the area?"

"Yes. But how many of them could a man like Kola enter and not be noticed, especially if he was being watched? It has to be nearby." She sat, stared, almost as if she were scanning a map of Washington that no one else could see. "Pentagon City Excelsior Hotel. I bet it's there."

A short but agonizing trip later, we were there. Jayne, despite her jeans and hoodie, had me convinced she belonged there: over-privileged, a renegade rock star. She used posture and attitude like a costume. She could have taught a clinic in character projection at Juilliard. She strode into the swanky lounge and signaled the bartender.

"I believe my employer, Mr. Pastorelli, left his wallet here," Jayne said.

He blinked and said, "Please let me check."

He reached under the counter and handed her something small—definitely not a wallet. "I'm so glad we found it."

"Thank you very much."

It was only because I was watching so closely that I saw a flash of green as his hand disappeared. She'd handed him a large tip.

I tried not to think about what we might have until we reached the car, parked at the lot at Fashion Centre.

"What is it?" I said as I locked my door.

"It's a security key, with two-factor authentication."

I could barely keep my voice down. "See if it's the encryption key to Kola's computer!"

It was nothing fancy. A bit of black and gray plastic two and a half inches long. She removed the cover to reveal a USB connector.

She slotted it into the computer. Clicked on a file.

It opened.

Simple as that.

"It works," she said. "Fuck me sideways, it works."

I wasn't so sure. "Shouldn't...shouldn't we see something more? More screens or something? Shouldn't it take longer?"

"You've got to stop watching so many movies," she said as she scrolled down through the file indexes. "It's like putting a key in a car."

I had to admit, I was kind of disappointed.

Jayne whistled. "It's all here. Places, numbers, names. Kola was very businesslike, very thorough. Jesus, fifteen Sidewinders in one depot? Smart grenade launchers, robotics—I wouldn't be surprised if we found a nuke or two tucked in his wife's warehouses somewhere."

I took a moment to digest that.

"I suggest we go across the street, to the gym, over there. They'll have lockers in the ladies' changing room. We get a membership and leave the USB with the real files and the encryption key there for the time being. It's random, not a place either of us is associated with—is it? You don't happen to go there, did you?"

"No. You?"

"I used one downtown." She shook her head and looked a little sad. "I can't go there anymore."

She shook herself. "Okay. We copy the data, stash it and the security key, then we'll set a rendezvous with Kola's computer, and something that looks like the encrypted files. We bug the computer to see where it goes. We act from there." She thought for a moment. The plan was as good as it was gonna get. "Let's go."

We stashed the thumb drives in the locker at Fitness Freak. It looked so lonely, there, two small pieces of plastic tucked in the pocket of the complimentary sweatshirt. The key to a military arsenal fit for a small country.

Chapter Forty-Four: Nicole Bradley

After the goat rodeo convergence on the gang's house and the following chatter, it's clear matters are coming to a head. In addition to backing up Rogers on the ground, I'm also stocking up on details for every possible situation and setting, looking at traffic patterns (around DC?—almost always shitty), house plans for Philomena Kola, and the makes and plates of her various cars.

And then I see the chat that tells me that Rogers and Blondie have found the fucking computer. Of course they have. I grin at my disappointment that I wasn't there. I mean, I know Kola's security is probably good, but I also know that he'd been trying to reach out to both of them and would have left clues as to how to decrypt it. They don't need me for that. I just wanted to see how many different ways the machine might have been spiked and how many foreign entities might have been spying on him through it. That would be *neat*. And maybe I could then get access to them? Cooler than cool. Maybe that will still be possible.

I have almost all I need to launch Taps. I've done everything I can to try to get around Heath's retinal scan, but now...now I have to get to him.

Time to be on scene. I text Rogers and let her know I'm incoming. She lets me know her present location and plan. If I can get there in time, I'll try and cover her when things start to happen. Otherwise, I'll try to catch up, follow whoever has the package.

Showtime.

Chapter Forty-Five: Amy Lindstrom

"So now we...set up the meeting place?"

"Yep, we'll do that, then call them. We act dumb, like we found the computer or something. We give it to them, but they won't know we've already taken the encrypted files off and left them fakes. They'll want to know how we got it, try to reconstruct what happened at the house, maybe even think they're being double-crossed. If they're so keen on it, we'll give it to them for...fifty dollars? One hundred? We tell them where to meet us and we get there well ahead of time to see who shows up. Should be very informative."

"Okay, what do we want to sound like?" she said. "Opportunistic junkie? Homeless person?"

"Who would go into that house, and know how to use an email? Be greedy enough and stupid enough to risk facing the owners?" I shook my head. "A burglar. They're not too bright."

"You got it."

We arrived outside the garage that would be our observation point, and Jayne pulled out the burner with the number and called.

"I got your message," she said in a voice nothing like her own. "I found some stuff in the trash. What do you want?" She held the phone so I could hear.

A man's voice said, "I just want the computer. I'll make it worth your while."

"Are you cops?"

"No. I'll give you one hundred dollars. When can we meet?"

"After dark. Nine o'clock." She gave directions to the busy intersection near Gallery Place. "You go there, you show me you have the money, and I'll bring the computer. And make it five thousand dollars. All that bling must be worth something."

"Are you *crazy*?" I whispered.

"No," she said, covering the phone. "Just trying to sound stupid and greedy."

The voice answered immediately. "I only have five hundred. It's yours."

"Okay." She turned off the phone. "We got a date."

I shivered. "We're not actually going to meet them, are we?"

"Hell no. But we'll be up here watching them, ready to see who shows up."

The flesh at the base of my back crawled: What she said sounded simple but I knew it was dreadfully dangerous.

"We needed to draw them out. We can keep ourselves concealed. There's no reason for us to go down range."

"What about Uncle Frank?" I said desperately, thinking of the guy she'd used to bail her out of jail the night of our first meeting long, long ago. I really didn't like anything about this plan. "Was that Heath, or is he someone real, someone else who could help us out?"

"Frank...isn't from the Department. Not by a long shot." She smiled. "He's a mob boss who owes me some goodwill. He's the last person we want involved in this and he's only marginally less bad than Heath because he's not actively trying to kill my friends as well. But yeah, imagine Tony Soprano with his own private military-grade arsenal—not a 'legitimate businessman' like Kola."

She rolled her eyes. "Anyway, he's on vacation in Maine this time of year. There's a guy—" She looked thoughtful, almost hopeful, for a heartbeat, but then shook her head sadly. "There's no one. Don't worry, Amy. We can do this on our own."

The parking garage gave us the best situation we could hope for. There wasn't much traffic this time of night, after the offices emptied. The few security cameras suddenly, mysteriously went on the fritz a moment after Jayne located them. From our position, we could see the two major roads leading into the area. Depending on the traffic, we'd have no problem following our quarry. There were too many places we could be hiding for them to cover them all, so I'd stay here. Jayne would be on the other side of the floor. She'd given a new burner cell and half of a hundred-dollar bill to one of DC's many unhoused people. When he got her call, he'd bring the wrapped-up computer to the corner. Someone would give him more money, and he'd be on his way. If no one showed, he got the other half of the bill when we got our package back.

We'd bugged the notebook and its case. Its GPS would point us in the right direction.

There were still four hours to go till the rendezvous. She told me to rest up while she kept an eye out for anything novel happening at the intersection.

I couldn't sleep. I sat drinking in the perfume of urine, motor oil, and exhaust fumes that clung to the concrete of the parking garage. The humid day cooled to clamminess when the sun eventually went down. Staring at my fingernails, I saw what had once been a seventy-five dollar manicure was hastily clipped or bitten down to the quick. Thick scabs of what had been pale polish were almost unnoticeable, but were ringed with dirt. The flaking around the edges was starting to show just how hard their use had been. A long, ugly scar was healing over the back of my left hand. I still had a dirty piece of gauze around my finger from the fight on the roof.

"Those aren't the hands of a lady," Jayne said, coming to wake me.

I shivered. I swear to God, she sounded exactly like my mother. "Nope, they're not."

"Don't worry, Princess. We'll get this sorted out and book you a couple of weeks at the Hotel Del. You'll be perfect again in no time."

The Hotel del Coronado is near San Diego. Pristine beaches; quietly beautiful and comfortable rooms. The lobby gave off a feeling of safe, luxurious seclusion. Being on its own peninsula didn't hurt. I had distant memories of a long ago visit, a handcrafted margarita on the patio under the palms, crystalline waves on a silver beach, the day a gentle golden blur, the rest of the world infinitely far away. A lump formed in my throat, the peaceful memory almost too painful to bear.

And somehow she knew about this, too.

Damn it.

And I just hated it when she called me "Princess."

I knew from her file I wasn't the only one with fond memories of southern California.

"Miss training with the SEALs?" I said. "The danger, the testing without the consequences? Maybe they have a refresher course. Play in the bay, followed by brews and tattoos?"

It came out harder than I meant, full of pent-up resentment and fear.

Jayne started, then shrugged, stretching her neck: I'd hit a nerve.

"It was one of the best times of my life," she said simply. "I'd love to have some of those ugly swabbies at my back about now. Thing is, they'd think I'm a traitor. You don't come back from that."

Then I realized she hadn't been trying to be mean by calling me "Princess." My face burned. I'd never been so horrified at finding a weak spot in someone's armor. Her utter lack of emotion told me everything. Coronado was one more place she could never go. What kind of life would she have, if, despite the long odds, we survived? No family, no one to trust, her life always in danger? And she'd been willing to give up the little she did have when her boss went wrong.

I am such a dope sometimes. Everyone in the military gave everyone else nicknames. "Princess" was just her way of saying we were friends.

By now, I guess we were.

"I'm sorry—that was an...unnecessarily mean thing to say." I looked her straight in the eye. "I'm way, way out of my element, and you know so much about me, and I don't know anything about you. And...I'm sorry."

She looked off across the garage and took a deep breath. "I get it." She cleared her throat a few times. "You know my family was killed. A local gangster tried to get my father—who had a side gig as a locksmith—to do some dirty work for him. My fath—Dad refused. And I got a call while I was away at college that he and Ma were found, shot to death. I left, figured out who did it, and then went after the killers. It felt good, knowing I could do...what no one else could do. Would do. But I felt exposed, so I hid myself—I thought—in the Army. And that's where the Department found me. Heath offered me a chance to refine my skills."

"Holy shit," I whispered. "You were what, twenty-one?"

"Just about."

Well, Lindstrom, you got what you asked for. "Screw the Del, then," I said. "We'll go to the Four Seasons on Lanai. My treat." It was prohibitively expensive, out of reach, but right now, staying alive was equally long odds.

She smiled for real. "You're on." She stood up, stretched, and cracked her neck. "But for now, how does scoping out a filthy parking garage in anticipation of an ambush sound?"

"Absolutely delightful," I said.

It was two hours before the agreed-upon deadline when Jayne got the shivers and thought something was about to happen. We finalized our preparations, expecting someone to arrive at any moment.

"All you have to do is sit here, watch the area," Jayne said, after a final glance at her phone and a hasty reply. "No one sees you, you're in no danger. Just keep your head down, your eyes open. That was Nicole. She's incoming. With any luck, she can provide us some backup. And I let her know the location of the Kola's data and encryption key...just in case."

I nodded and took up my position behind one of our two cars. We had one parked near me on the floor below the roof, and one on the street, stolen for what Jayne called contingencies. If anything went wrong, I'd take a car and scram.

"Don't worry," she said. "No one should even know you're here, but if you have to go, you've got the rigged dollar coin. Wherever you end up, I'll find you. I'd never leave one of my people behind."

I looked at her. "I believe that."

"Okay, bring it in." She hugged me, thumped me on the back as if we were going out onto the playing field. I hugged her back.

"Time to get to work. Eyes open," Jayne said. She took her place up the ramp from me.

A few moments later, I saw a guy in a suit approach the corner. Suddenly, my fatigue was replaced by pure adrenaline. I struggled to keep my eye on him, while at the same time, scanning the area for clues.

The homeless guy made his way across the street, the package under his arm. It was clear he wasn't the caller the men had expected. He handed over the computer, was paid, and left. Probably they thought they were going to follow him to us, but Jayne never intended to take the money. Once they had the computer with its fake encrypted files, we could see who we were up against.

Then a barrage of gunfire.

I hesitated. I didn't want to leave Jayne in the lurch. Maybe there was something I could do—

I saw a blur outside the parking garage, as if a giant bat had swooped down from the floor above.

No time to scream. I ran.

Light footsteps echoed behind me. The sound of grit on cement scratching and reverberating.

I ran faster.

Something brushed by my shoulder. This time I did scream. I started to spin around, but was propelled forward, a fist bunching the material in the back of my shirt.

"Keep moving," Jayne said as she practically hauled me to the car. "Stop screaming."

The doors were open, the keys left in the visor for whoever needed them. There was no discussion. Jayne was driving.

I slid into the passenger seat. I hit the lock before I fastened my seat belt.

The other door slammed. Before I had the chance to turn around, we were roaring down the ramp.

The brakes screeched. I felt a sudden pressure on my chest as I lurched forward. The safety belt had locked up.

A car was pulled across the down ramp. We knew we'd been discovered.

"No use us both going back up the ramp, so here's what we'll do. I'm going to pull up to the next staircase," she said, ridiculously calm, like this was some kind of exercise. "You hit the stairs, get to the other car. Meet me."

"Where? What about you?"

"I'm going to cause a distraction." She looked over her shoulder. "Aw, shit."

She said it like she'd forgotten to pack extra socks. Men in matte-black body armor with ridiculously large guns were coming down the ramp toward us.

"Feds, and damn it, I see Chase."

"Now what?" I was pleased I was so calm. Maybe if I treated it like an exercise, too...

"Same. I slow. You bail. Distraction."

"Got it."

One last glance behind me. I unlocked the door. We slowed infinitesimally, then stopped abruptly.

"Now. Go!"

I tore the door open, hit the ground, ran for the stairs, my footsteps lost amid slamming car doors and shouts.

No luck. Someone was coming out of the stairwell, not a civilian, not with that gun. I skidded to a halt.

A crash behind us stopped us both cold. Jayne had rammed our car through the crowd of armed men behind her. A split second to realize this was my chance. I ran across the ramp as Jayne drove backward, up to the roof, a lead-storm following her.

I was sure I felt the tug of the car as she passed within two inches of me.

I kept running. The other side was clear. I could hear more footsteps and shouts.

But there were no stairs over there. Only a narrow walk along the ramp, and a twenty-foot drop to the ground below.

I ran down the ramp to where I'd seen a drainpipe. If she could swing out of the sky like a bat, so could I. Acrophobia be damned.

I sat down on the low wall, grabbed onto the drain, and tried not to think about what I was doing. *Please hold. Please don't shift.* I looked down, only as far as the space directly beneath me. There was a toehold—if you were a gibbon. I took a breath and tried to swing my weight off the wall.

I froze.

Come on, Lindstrom, you're better than this. Do it. Do it now.

But it wasn't fear. Someone had grabbed on to the back of my shirt.

For a moment, I thought it was Jayne: She'd dispatched them all and was back to save me.

It wasn't Jayne.

It was Speitzer, the scarred man. He'd clamped onto my shirt. With a strength that belied his narrow, reedy frame, he grabbed my right arm. Not only could I not jerk myself free—falling to the pavement seemed like a fine alternative—but I could feel myself being pulled back into the garage.

No thought of climbing now. I hugged the pillar for dear life, my cheek scraping against the cooling surface. It was too wide, I could barely reach my fingers across. My face slammed against the pillar. He'd punched my shoulder. I lost my grip. My fingernails dragged across the cement. I grabbed for the drain, caught it, but he pulled me back. I tumbled into the parking garage, landing smack on my tailbone.

Pain shot up my back, but I rolled over and kicked at him with everything I had. The angle was off, but I was able to wrench myself from his grip. I could almost hear his fingers snap closed. The agony in my arm was incredible, like a chunk of flesh had been ripped away.

I tried kicking again. He jumped out of the way. I scooted up, almost like I was Jayne. I was learning.

I could do this, I realized. I *can* do this.

I pulled the gun out of my pocket and pointed it like I'd been doing it all my life. Like I'd been enjoying it all my life. I aimed it at his chest. No way I could miss from this distance.

A rush of euphoria took me. I felt sixty feet tall. I must be getting the hang of this. *Please,* I thought. *Give me a reason to put a bullet in you. For Jacob. For Michelle. For Tommy...*

For the hell of it.

My knees weakened. It's all right. It's all good. Just the rush of adrenaline. I straightened myself, my confidence returning, blooming, erupting.

Speitzer didn't move, those washed-out blue eyes just following me, his bite-mark scar livid from exertion. I frowned. He should be more concerned. I was in control here. My back hurt, but not like my shoulder, which ached with a cold cramp. I rolled my shoulder—

Exquisite pain. So bad I couldn't find my mouth to scream.

I reached back. Maybe I'd landed on some glass. My fingers brushed something, like a pencil was stuck into me. I pulled at it, ignoring everything I'd ever learned in first aid class, only needing to get whatever it was out of me.

It was like a knife tearing through my muscle.

It wasn't a pencil. It wasn't a knife. As it dropped to the ground, bouncing in slow motion, taking its time shattering, I recognized it as some kind of syringe.

All Speitzer did was watch.

He loomed in front of me, his scarred face and pale eyes eerily close to mine. I felt the weight of the gun leave my hand, was surprised I'd held onto it that long.

I was in deep, dark trouble.

A white ground fog rose around me, the taillights from the cars suddenly urgent, red and orange—what was wrong? Swirling colors and Lovecraftian shapes played out against the backdrop. I couldn't make any sense of it.

I saw the roof of the garage over me and realized I was being dragged. Looking down, the ramp folded, a sheer drop beneath me. I couldn't feel my body, couldn't scream, couldn't fight. Suddenly there was a huge white void in the world in front of me, a tear in the fabric of reality, and then it vanished, and it was only by smell I realized I was in the backseat of a car.

I tried to scream, but made only a bleating noise again, my face pressed into the backseat. My eyelids were too heavy to keep open. It was more comforting not to see the chaos around me.

Chapter Forty-Six: Jayne Rogers

Amy doesn't have long. I limp from the parking garage to the car on the street. They'll find out she doesn't know anything but Kola's message to her on the silver picture frame, then they'll kill her.

I have to wipe my hands before I can hot-wire the ignition. Blood is slippery.

Cold settles in my gut. They'll kill her or they'll give her to that clown-freak Speitzer to practice on. That gives me more time but won't do her much good. I can't let Heath kill my family for his own private gain. His family too, or so he'd once have us believe.

The lights continue to pulse on the screens as the GPS on the seat next to me relays changing coordinates. The maps shift with passing miles. There's still time to do this. Just enough. All I have to do is follow the transmissions. Determine the extent of the rot. Get Amy back.

Doesn't matter. Soon, but not yet. Find out where they're going first, move from there.

Banging on the glass. I almost leave my seat; it feels like I've been tased in the ass.

"You look like shit." Raven is pretty beat up herself. Her jacket is torn, and I can see her rig. "Let me in, we gotta plan."

"Yep." I could barely form an entire sentence. "Appreciate the added eyes and cover."

"Chase has Kola's computer."

"And Speitzer has Lindstrom, and since he works directly for Heath, they'll all be together." I tell her about Amy's idea about the arms being at one of Mrs. Kola's warehouse lots.

Her eyes light up, and she does a quick search on her phone. "There are three in this area."

"And we'll know which one Heath has when we follow Amy's tracker."

"One more reason to get to the warehouse." Raven looks as tired as I feel. "I have Rodriguez's Taps authentication key, but we need to get Heath's retinal scan. Gina and I weren't able to hack the biometrics."

"Shit. So we need him alive?"

"Yep."

I sigh. "Okay. As soon as soon as anyone with any talent boots Kola's computer, they'll know they don't have what they want. Even if they get the location of the real data from Amy, they won't get the encryption key and the copy of the data." I tell her about the sweatshirt in the gym locker.

Raven grins. "You palmed them."

"I palmed them. I couldn't risk leaving the copy and the decryption together back at the gym. Do you need anything else to deploy Taps?"

"If you can get me Chase's Taps authentication key, Heath will be the last part."

"Shit." I hate what that means.

"It makes more sense this way. You're in no shape to take on everyone at Mrs. Kola's warehouse. If you get the computer away from her and Chase, or take them out, if you have to, that'll be plenty."

I can't say anything, watching the blip on the screen.

"I'll do what I can to get Amy out of there, if she's still alive, but she's not the first priority."

"No, of course not. But it's just—"

She gives me a stony, knowing look. "It's just you wanted to be the one to go after Heath. I get it, but trust me, I want him as much as you do. Maybe more. If you're still alive after you get the computer and Chase's key, you join me there. If I get Heath's retinal scan, and if he's still alive, and if you're still alive, I'll even give you a chance to take your shot."

"That's a lot of 'if,'" I say, but I nod.

"Our lives have been nothing but 'if,' so this makes a nice change." She raises a fist and I bump it, smiling tiredly. We exchange gear, intel, Amy's tracker coin, the flash drive. When she finishes telling me the plan of Kola's house and disables the alarm, she says, "Okay, go make 'if' into 'when.' See you on the other side, Cave Girl."

"Good hunting, Raven."

She takes a deep breath, nods once, and leaves, vanishing almost instantly.

I check the coordinates from the tracker coin in Amy's pocket then the one on the computer. They're heading in different directions. I watch the blips move farther apart and as I follow the car with the computer. I figure out where it's heading and catch up. I know the location well, so I can take a shortcut and catch up, giving them space. They won't be looking for me, not this soon, but there's no sense blowing it by being sloppy.

Amy, you're on your own. Hang in there.

The Kolas' nearest house outside the District is in Potomac, Maryland. The tracking device I put on Kola's computer led me here, to Mrs. Kola. It's an exclusive suburb, and things like what's about to happen certainly don't happen here.

I park away from the lights and do a last check. Right house, shoelaces, full clip and a couple of backups, all administrative loads. Suppressor? Probably buy me a little time. A glance up and down the street. I pick my entrance. A side window, unlighted, nicely screened from the road, but not obvious to those inside. It won't take me long, and then it's on. I pause, just long enough for a quick prayer.

Dear gods. I better not fuck up. Amen.

On my way past, I stick the KA-BAR into the tires of the SUV in the drive. Doesn't matter if they have more, because it's blocking the garage. Cocky. Amateurish.

Raven took care of the alarm, and they're not expecting anyone while they're there, armed, awake, and ready to pull out for good. It is a very nice neighborhood, after all.

The window lock's a good one, but I'm better, and I'm in without a sound. It's an office or a library, and it's been stripped. As my eyes adjust, the only thing I can see left are unplugged computer peripherals and expensive carpeting. The house is being packed up, closed down. Maybe they're upping stakes, heading out to some event more private home, probably on an island somewhere, on the promise of a big payday.

Someone's coming down the hall past me, toward voices at the front of the house. I visualize the layout from Raven's description—damn these open-plan houses—and figure the long way around to the front. I don't want any more surprises than absolutely necessary.

I'm right. There's Nash in the kitchen, reading the paper when he should be watching the door. Lazy, too confident his side has already won. Just waiting for the next order. I wait until he turns the page, glances around, and settles back into his chair. Two steps, one hand over his mouth, one with a long, hard draw across the artery and larynx. It goes with a minimum of noise. I don't even give him a chance to rattle his coffee cup. I can tell by the way my left arm's pulling I did something bad to it in the last scrap. It's okay. The time for knives is now over.

I set him down, wipe my hands dry, frisk him, and take a deep breath. Bless the fine, thick rugs in the hallway. I move toward the lighted front room, sneaking and peeking. A dining room, on one side, also dark, and then the front room. I can see Chase and Mrs. Kola sitting. She's studying Kola's computer, the diamonds on its case glittering in the lamplight. She's not happy with what she sees. Good. Frustrated means it's still encrypted. That's one bit of good news.

I hear the creak on the stairs opposite me a second after I need to. It's Pisco. He takes an instant too long to register it's me. I shoot, earlier than I want to, but he's smoke-checked with a hole in the forehead. I'm in the front room.

Philomena Kola startles but is calmer than you'd expect when an intruder shoots an armed assassin dead in front of her. She closes the notebook and looks to Chase, who's still standing. Her hands are now folded in her lap, patrician. The SIG feels heavier than it should. I'm tiring, my hurts catching up with me. I'd like to take both of them alive, but that seems overly optimistic.

Before he can draw, I shoot the man who used to be my friend, my team-mate, my partner in saving the world from itself. "Sorry, Chase. You're done."

He screams, collapses, clutching his leg just at the knee; if he doesn't have the key on him, I may need to make him tell me where it is. I pocket his weapon, pat him down, and find his secondary. I tell the woman to keep her hands where I can see them.

Chase gasps, tries to collect himself. "You're in this, deep as we are, Rogers. But you lost. Heath has his new team, and the Department will be gone as of tonight."

"Yeah? Why would he cut me out of that plan? Think about it. Also, Kola's data and the location of the encryption key have been copied and given to a lawyer. He checks that I post a notice online every day," I say. "If I'm still alive after you're in custody, that's gravy."

I turn to the woman, who is still watching us, expressionless, and pull the ties from my pocket. "Use those. His hands in front. Then yours."

"Thank God you're here," Mrs. Kola says. "This man...he's a monster. He killed my husband—"

"Tighter," I say.

I watch Chase wince in pain as she tightens the plastic cuffs, white marks on his wrists.

"—and he's held me captive, trying to get Anton's business papers—"

"Keep talking your bullshit, Philomena," Chase says. I see doubt in his eyes; maybe he'll help me yet. "Maybe she'll shoot you, too."

"Monster!" She hauls off with both hands clasped and smashes him upside the head. A torrent of swearing follows, and she hits him again. This time, he lunges at her. I see they're both going for the side table and something there I can't see.

It has to be a weapon. I don't really want either of them dead, so I have to do things the hard way.

I wade in and kick Chase hard in the knee where I shot him. He keels over in agony. As I grab Kola by the hair, she turns, a pistol in her hand.

Her free hand automatically goes up to her head. I yank harder. "Drop it!"

I shove the gun under her chin. She might be armed, but there's no way she's getting out of *this*. "Drop it—now!"

She lowers her hand, every kind of hate in her eyes. She tenses when she hears Chase moan—I've broken his leg. She glances at me, nodding, slumping.

She reaches out and fires two shots at Chase.

Shit.

If I wasn't in such a close tangle, I'd kick her. I can't get my footing and I'm trying hard not to get shot myself. I bring the butt of the SIG down on her head. It's not perfect, but she grunts and slows down. She drops the pistol. I nudge it away and cuff her.

Then I check the chain around Chase's neck, which has his authentication USB on it. Thank God, she didn't hit that. The second thing needed to deploy Taps is now slung around my neck. I turn to her.

"We don't have much time. Call Heath. Tell them to let Amy Lindstrom go. If she's hurt, it comes out of your hide." I hear sirens, and I sense my time is running out.

"No."

I look at her. "It wasn't a request."

"As it stands, I can blame everything on Heath and Chase over there. Or you. There's no reason for me to help you. You've killed and tortured my men in a sadistic spree. Moreover, we have your friend. Give me the encryption and she goes free. All it takes is one text from me, with the correct wording, of course."

"No."

"It wasn't a request," she mimics me. "And the more you play tough, the longer Miss Lindstrom suffers. Remember, Speitzer likes to keep his skills honed. And when she's dead, there's the rest of her family. I've had quite enough from them."

I keep my face a mask. "Heath will kill us all," I say. "And as soon as he has what he wants from you, you'll be the next on his list."

"So you say. You're desperate and pathetic. Killing me won't help you."

"Hurting you might."

"Not with those sirens so close. Remember, *you're* the one they're looking for."

I don't have the time to waste to make her comply. I can't leave her. And she's right, I can't kill her. We need to get out of here, and then I can work out the next part of the plan. "Okay, let's go."

On our way out, I kneel and feel for a pulse. Chase is going colder by the minute.

"You can't afford to kill me," she repeats as I hustle her into the car. We drive. She doesn't need to tell me where. "One way or the other, you need me alive."

"You're right."

She smiles, and sells it, which is quite a trick. "I've ruined your plans."

She's trying to rile me, find a way out for herself, which is smart and ridiculously dangerous. She thinks that, bad as her situation is, she's still got it all over me. She doesn't know about Raven, and I plan to keep it that way.

"I have new plans."

I pull over to a deserted parking lot. There's no one within shouting distance. There's one light a long way off. I saw how controlled she'd kept herself from the moment I entered her house. She wasn't going to make life easy for me. I pull out my bag and rummage around in it. I pull the Leatherman out of its case and look at it for a long minute. She glances at it, clearly doesn't like the look of the thing, but doesn't give much away.

"You haven't the time for that," she says.

Her voice is still steady. If I had time, I'd be impressed. She made the decision to kill her husband in a roomful of people, has taken over his business, and subverted and killed one of the most powerful men in American intelligence. She's standing up to me.

I shrug, extend the saw blade, and examine it. She doesn't move, doesn't say anything, but she can't keep her eyes off the saw and she swallows.

I pull the tiny hypodermic from the space where the bit-driver would usually be and stick it in her neck, maybe a little harder than I need to. She's pissing me off. And she should have known: If it had come down to fingers or ears or nipples, I would have used the KA-BAR.

She curses and scrabbles for the syringe, but it's already too late, and I pull it out before she can grab it and maybe stick me.

I wait until I know it's working, then drive to within striking distance.

I take her phone, press her thumb against it, then snap a picture. There's a number for "H" on speed dial. I press that and send the picture.

"I've got someone here you don't want to lose. Make sure Amy Lindstrom is alive and waiting for me when I get to the warehouse by National—yeah, I know about that. If not, your lady friend goes straight to the Feds. Wave to the man, sweetie."

I hold the phone up to her, but she's giggling even as she tries to talk to Heath. It doesn't matter. It's her phone and it sure looks and sounds like her, even if she's a babbling mess.

I take the phone back. "One hour. And I don't want to see Chase anywhere. I'm not in the mood for his bullshit." I hit the off button. Since his biometrics are down, that may confuse them.

Maybe Heath will want her back, if only to keep her from testifying. Maybe he'll want her back because she's scared her people into worrying what will happen if they don't act on her every order. Maybe Heath and her people will be glad to see the back of her. Maybe they'll be rattled, which will make some cover for Raven.

But maybe they'll keep Amy alive, just a little longer.

Chapter Forty-Seven: Amy Lindstrom

I'm in freefall forever. I have no idea where I am, and can't tell whether I'm hallucinating. I see faces, hear questions I'd like to answer, but it all strikes me as a little ridiculous. I struggle to speak and make sense. There's nothing worse than not being able to express myself. I flash back to a time when I was a kid, hobbled by my tongue, and it only makes everything worse.

When I try to explain about the boxes, I hear a man say, "Enough. She's talking about toy stores and ballerinas. Speitzer overdid it. We're not going to get anything out of her yet."

There's arguing. I can't tell if it's one voice, or two, or six. I strain to understand, get past whatever's keeping my brain and tongue from working.

I was trying to tell someone else something. Not so long ago. That feels familiar. I cling to it like a shipwreck victim to a fallen spar. Was I in an accident?

"It doesn't matter. We're going after Mrs. K soon as we're done with sweeping up the last stragglers who aren't on board."

I try to speak.

"She's making noises. Try again."

That's just rude, talking about me like I'm not even here. They find out who I am, they'll be nice enough. Until then...screw 'em.

I give up. I see ceiling lights flash past me. I sleep.

Chapter Forty-Eight: Nicole Bradley

Outside the container warehouse, I slink in unobserved, and conceal myself among the rows of crates. I don't dare try to find an empty office. The folks here don't know where I am, and that makes me smile. I'm not sure who knows that I've been "re-org'd," but it doesn't matter. My goal is to find Heath while not being caught myself. Ideally, I can find him with enough time to get Taps deployed and add his scan without too much trouble.

Without too much trouble. The thought makes me laugh to myself.

And yet...he's right there. Getting coffee, tired but feeling like he's already won.

I launch the first part of Taps, using Rodriguez's key. If I'm lucky, Rogers will meet me with the other. If not, I'll have to figure out another way to spoof that.

And that's just one more reason I have to keep Heath alive, as much as I'd love to shoot him. Killing him before we get his biometrics would be catastrophic; killing him too early would raise the alarm. For now, I'll see what I can do to cause trouble, and maybe find Amy Lindstrom. If I'm lucky, if she's lucky, if, if, if...

In the meantime, trying to look like I'm doing an inventory, I spy a router. I can damage to their communications and plans, maybe save a few more lives before I figure a way to get Taps working without the last two pieces of the puzzle.

I start in on the service accounts, the infrastructure, cutting some lights, some cameras, just enough to make them think it's a fault in the wiring or in their software. That gives me a look at who's in and around, and I calculate how I might take them down. After a bit, I feel comfortable with it all, and give myself superuser status access. Now I'm basically a god to the site's computers.

That's fun; I know Schmidt's code, her tricks, her habits. I know how to flummox her, and it ties her in knots while I carefully peek around the system, causing tiny disruptions and failure messages as I go. I don't find anything about the other operatives, those who didn't meet Heath's standards, whom he's opted to murder, but I can keep moving the problem with the communications among his team around so they're in chaos.

Interesting: I see that Chase's biometrics are down, flatlined. But I also see that the location of his tracker is moving, heading toward us. That gives me hope that Cave Girl managed to get his key off of him. I hide the fact of his death as soon as I find it, just to fuck with Heath. If I can, I'm gonna thin out her welcome party, make her a hole to climb through.

"Wait a minute, Bradley! What are you—?"

Fuck me; I was too intent on my work. I'm exhausted, but now charged with adrenaline. "Hey, Cooper. Just checking up on the diagnostics Mr. Heath mentioned to me."

He's smart enough to think he might not be privy to all Heath's instructions, but takes too long to realize that if I were indeed doing such a thing, I'd be in an office, not tucked away among the containers and crates. While he's figuring out that he should either shoot me or confirm with Heath, I hold my finger up—just a sec, please—and then set my notebook carefully aside, acting as if I want to chat with him.

It throws him off and that gives me enough time to close the space between us and get my favorite knife to hand. Still want to keep it quiet.

I smile at him—it's another unusual occurrence, and it buys me a few more seconds. I smize like mad and put my hand up to his mouth as if I'm playing naughty with him.

Too much—it's way too far out of my character for him to believe. His eyes narrow, and I speed up my plan: instead of a finger against his lips, I'm shoving my fist into his mouth as I stab upward. My knife travels along a rib—

Dana Cameron 267

I'm hurried, and sadly out of practice—and he opens his mouth further to scream.

I stick my hand in farther, and he bites down. But he's doing well, too, in spite of this: He's realized that I'm probably not heavy enough to muscle my way through this, and he stops reacting and takes initiative.

He gets his left hand between us, trying to shove me away. I stab that instead of his chest or another rib. It doesn't tickle, but he's still breathing.

At the same time, he slams his fist into my jaw. I see stars and stumble back. At least he's insulted enough to want to hurt me for having caught him unawares. He still doesn't raise the alarm.

He makes the most of my disorientation and kicks me in the knee. It's bad, and I'm losing ground, so I grab onto him, dragging my knife down his leg. He knees me away and falls himself.

I pull myself up and gut stab him; when he folds in on himself, I stab him in the throat. Pull him out of the way.

That's it. Time to get shit started.

I wipe my hands off, and claw my way up to my notebook, hit a few more keys. I notice that "Chase" is nearly here. I hit the fire alarm, then stash my notebook in my pack, and pull my piece.

I plan to take it one room at a time but hit gold on the first one: There's a series of monitors. I see a blurry struggle happening in one of the rooms and I know it's Amy Lindstrom.

I scan the room and find keys—metal and magnetic—in an open lockbox. I study the labels, scoop them up. The next door is metal and locked. It takes a few moments for me to find the right magnetic card. I slow my breathing, concentrating on the job at hand and keeping an ear cocked behind me.

The green light flashes. I hear a click in the wall and push the door open. An office, posh, maybe for customers. If I had time, I'd go through it. On to the next room.

This one is also metal, with a magnetic lock. I feel vibrations behind the door. If there was a chance I'd be heard I'd call, tell her I'm on the way, but I have no breath to waste.

It takes forever to find the right key... I pick up the key, try it, and get the green light—but the door doesn't open. I shove against it, and it moves a little, but not enough. Something's jammed against it, but I can see shadows moving. I holler for Amy—hang on—then haul back—

Chapter Forty-Nine: Jayne Rogers

I have to assume Heath and his men know that Chase is dead, so I have to haul ass. They'll be looking for me anyway. The whole trick is to make sure Heath wants to see it's me with his own eyes. He'll wonder where Chase is, whether I've killed or turned him. Maybe worried Mrs. K has corrupted him and me.

I've got to keep her safe, so I pull over and pop the trunk. The great thing about these earlier models is there are no modern escape latches. She'll be out for a while, and out of harm's way. Besides, I may need her for biometrics. I may have to use the knife after all.

I take the chance and text Raven: I'm alive, on my way in, with Chase's security key.

I hope I'll see the three dots meaning she's typing a reply, but I don't, and I can't wait. Either she'll know or figure it out or she'll be dead, and they'll be waiting for me.

Finding the right way into the cargo park takes longer than I like, but now is not the time to go off half-cocked. Half-cocked, hanging fire, all of those terms from so long ago still mean the same thing to a soldier. As Amy learned in the library, Mrs. Kola's family fortune is in shipping and storage. She knows the business, still kept her hand in from a distance, once she got wind of Kola's plans to retire. Lots of airport traffic at all hours of the day and night. Lots of on-site security to be expected. Expensive in the short term, but the long-term benefits? Almost incalculable.

Heath's there now, I'm sure of it. Amy's there, too, according to the trace.

These places are pretty standard. Offices at either end, shipping bay on the side, storage in the center. Crates stacked neatly throughout, loaded with death and waiting to be deployed.

I park and grab a few things. I check the laces on my Danners, load then slip into my rig, snap the buckle at my waist. Black electrical tape is already on the metallic parts that would show or clank. Everything else battened down and guaranteed silent, jump proof. I've been working on this kit for years, grateful that AP held onto it for me. I feel good, which is worrying considering how beat up I feel. I decide to chalk it up to adrenaline and the excitement of action, and not some kind of shock. I'm nearly invisible, black jeans and hoodie, a smear of dirt to dull my sweat-shiny skin. There's an area near the back of the warehouse that is shadowed and darker than the rest, and I head for that. I count on the notion they're still reacting to my call. Racing around in a panic trying to locate Chase or Heath. Not posting extra guards or dogs. I frown. There *is* a dog barking, off in the distance. It could be the fire alarm, but it sounds like it's in pain. Puzzling.

I look for cameras and see nothing I can do anything about. Scurrying across the lot, I hug the wall and move to the front. I listen for a moment, then set up the first of the little shaped charges AP got me. Still no response from Raven, so it's time to assume I'm on my own.

I circle the building, working carefully—slow is smooth, and smooth is fast. I finish with a little flashbang. Guaranteed to stir up the hive—but the hive appears already to have been kicked. I hear shots fired.

I grin. Raven's been fucking with them.

I count off as I run for the back, the long way around, away from the loading dock and the front door. The explosion is far louder than I expect. I hope I'm right about where they have Amy. But these assholes are idiots, too, if they're prepared for anything less than what I'm bringing. They've earned every bullet.

I find the back door. It's locked, but not for long. The barking I heard before is louder but still contained. Maybe I'll catch a break there. I don't count on it.

Dana Cameron 271

There's one bright boy who stays by the monitors, just long enough to realize where the real trouble is. He reaches for a radio, swivels, and draws. I'm already there. There's no need for the suppressor over the ruckus out front. It's now or never. I don't want any of these shitheels to get away if I can help it.

Done.

I hope there's a fire company on the way to handle whatever is stashed here. I hope I have enough time to find Amy and scramble on out of there. I hope if they're storing any of Kola's goods, it's small stuff: a few railway containers of rifles and handguns. Ammunition. No missiles with shoulder-mounted launchers. No drones, or God forbid, radioactive, biological, or chemical weapons, not this close to the civilian population.

Another man, someone I don't recognize. He's really huge; suddenly he realizes I don't belong here and shouts. My bullet tears out his throat before he makes much noise. It's not a great shot and he's still reaching for his piece, so I finish the job. I'm getting wound up—this is taking too long—but I take a deep breath and regain control of myself. A quick look down the hallway created by the containers reassures me all the action is still down front. I move quickly to the first in the row of locked rooms.

I hear barking near the first door, and it still strikes me as odd. I can't risk not investigating. The door isn't locked. I open it cautiously, but there's no rush of fur and teeth. There's a dog in there, a gorgeous shepherd, in a crate far too small. Whoever put the poor thing here hasn't had it long or meant for it to stay. The shepherd looks out of its head from thirst and immobility. Its bark is hoarse. I'm about to put a bullet in it—I don't have time, but I can't let the poor thing suffer like that—when something occurs to me.

"Hey, dog," I say, remembering the guy in the alley, the dog bowl, and empty crate at the empty house. "Good dog," I say in Russian.

The barking stops. There's an alertness to the eyes that wasn't there before, and the tail tip thumps.

Damn it, how do you get through life like this? Rogers, you candyass.

I look around, and I'm still alone. I go to the crate and find the catch. The dog whines, then its eyes shift and it barks again. Someone's behind me. I pull the latch free, and roll out of the way, shooting. The dog erupts out of the crate, and follows the bullets, throwing itself—herself—at the man. I recognize Fellowes behind me.

His shot goes wide of both of us. Whatever the dog was suffering, she's visiting it on Fellowes in the hallway, who's stopped screaming and isn't going to make it. If the dog is as smart as she seems, she'll find her way out easily enough. I slip by both of them and try the next door.

Locked.

Yet another explosion and screams from the front; Raven's messing with them good. I can feel the heat now. I pull a mask out of my kit and slip it on. It's hot and it stinks, but it's better than breathing fumes and smoke. I need to find Raven—and Heath before he takes off, before this place is overrun...I have to get him alive. My people—my family—are depending on me.

The door is nothing special, with only a hollow core, so I don't bother with finesse. It takes two kicks, but in it goes. I'm using a classic stack-up entrance on several filing cabinets, a desk, and a copier. I frown. Something's weird here. I don't have time to consider why. The files are full of paper I can't take with me. The desk drawer has a few memory sticks. I grab them and stash them in my bag, praying they tie this mess to Heath.

As I exit, I'm slammed face first into the door, pain drilling into my back. I turn to see Pinky Whitehead, a look of hatred and concentration on his stitched-up face. He's angry enough to shoot while he works it out. I return fire. It takes the rest of that clip to slow him down.

I catch myself admiring my handiwork, and shake myself. I'm tired, the initial burst of endorphins gone. I make sure he's done, dump the clips, reload, slot one in. I keep moving. I don't think I'm hurt bad, but I can't stop now. I'm not about to burn to death wondering.

It's getting hot and I'm feeling woozy. I have to finish this now, or it's going to finish me. I'd like to win, one last time, even if it's the last time—

That thought brings my natural cussedness to the surface, enough for one more try. No point in leaving with a blot on my copybook, no matter what it might say on my permanent record.

Once more, then. I shake my head, trying to clear my vision, then—

Chapter Fifty: Amy Lindstrom

"Amy." There's a whisper against my cheek.

I awoke to something cold and hard against my temple. My vision was still bleary, but everything else... I felt a hand close around my throat, remarkably strong. I couldn't breathe. My hands flew up to my throat, my legs kicking. The pressure against my larynx eased up ever so slightly as the pressure against my head increased until it was absolutely painful. I couldn't think about anything else.

The whisper was no more than a breath against my ear. "No kicking. No fighting. Do you understand?"

Blond hair and bite-scarred cheeks. Oh, sweet Jesus. Speitzer.

A stabbing pain in my temple. "Do you understand?"

I nodded, not willing to sacrifice breath to speech. The pressure against my throat eased again, infinitesimally. Tears slid out of the corners of my eyes, down the side of my face and around the barrel of the pistol.

"You're trembling like a little leaf," said Speitzer. "So sweet."

I clamped my teeth together, stifling a moan. Now that I could breathe again, I realized he was kneeling, straddling my hips, his feet locked inside my thighs. The pressure left my throat entirely. I gasped, gulping in the air.

"Oh, Christ, whatever it is—"

A tremendously sharp blow caught the side of my face. He'd hit me with the pistol. I screamed. He leaned forward, jamming the gun under my chin.

"No talking. Ever."

I couldn't have if I'd wanted to. I could barely breathe, with the pressure on my chest and my head tilted back so far I thought my sobs would break my neck. When I tried to tilt my head forward, I felt the pistol at the base of my chin.

A shifting of weight. I tried to move my leg. Instantly the pressure increased and I was choking again. "Be still. I'm working."

I couldn't breathe. My head was swimming. Not only was my air cut off, but I could feel his fingers clamping onto the sides of my neck, the blood flow being cut off. Panicking, I tugged at his hands, but he was so strong... He didn't even notice my increasingly feeble struggles. There would be no moment when the grip relaxed. My death was just the start of his project.

Dizzy, spots flying in front of my eyes. The pressure only increased. The pain was incredible... Maybe the gun was...

I saw a flash of blue. He was wearing Michelle's scarf.

He's killed my people. He's stealing my voice. He's killing me...

I see red, anger boiling over in me.

With a last, desperate hope, I bucked my hips up as hard as I could.

He was just a little too sure of himself, maybe a little too caught up in the moment. He toppled to the right, his grip loosened just that little bit, and I rolled as hard as I could. Breath came again, and I pushed us over onto the floor. Every moment I expected the pistol would go off.

It did.

The blast was so close. It had to hit me.

It did.

I felt the heat of the shot along the side of my jaw line and the roar exploded in my right ear. It was like nothing I'd ever heard or felt before.

But the dulling fade into unconsciousness and death didn't happen. I shoved at him again. I pushed him away from me, as he raised the gun to shoot me in the face. Adrenaline cleared my vision, narrowed it.

The door opened into the room, smashing his head backward. It might have snapped his neck. I didn't care. It hadn't decapitated him.

Without looking to see who was at the door, I scrambled over to Speitzer. I wrenched the gun from his hand and shot him in the face. It wasn't until I shot him three more times and was kicking his bloody corpse that I realized someone was yelling at me.

"He's dead! He's not coming back, Amy!"

It was Nicole, bloody, in black tactical gear, with a rig like the one AP brought Jayne. "We have to get out of here now!" She said something else I couldn't make out.

I had no hearing in my right ear. "What?" The syllable tore at my throat. I raised the pistol, confused, but she disarmed me. Impatiently. Not gently.

"For fucks sake, will you focus!"

I reached for my throat then hastily dropped my hand. It had been badly crushed, and the exterior was tender to the touch. I was spattered with blood, in addition to my bruises, and now that the most immediate danger was past, I was now free to realize that the side of my face hurt like vinegar in papercuts. Not all of the blood on my shirt was from Speitzer. I sank down. "Oh...oh shit, oh shit...ohhh."

"Okay, Amy?" Raven shouted. "Amy, you've got to stick with me now. You've had a bad time, but right now, right *now* we need to get out of here. Okay? Can you do that?"

"Oh...give me a..." I leaned over and threw up. I hadn't had much to eat and my throat muscles rebelled at the effort. I was so dizzy I thought I would fall over, but she steadied me. Being sick helped, somehow. I looked at my shirt-sleeves, but they were too filthy to be of any use. Nicole handed me a hanky—where did she get a clean hanky? I wiped off my mouth.

"Okay. But later..."

"Later, you can freak as much as you want, I promise. I'll *help*. But if we don't leave now..." She nodded at the faceless mess on the floor. "If we don't leave now, that wins. The people who hired him win." She pulled another pistol out of her—what was it? Belt? Bandolier? Backpack?—and handed her own to me.

I nodded—and even that hurt—and followed her out. Then I doubled back.

"Amy, we need to move. Now!"

I shook my head. "I need...I need to..." Speaking was too hard, and the smoke and racket in the building wasn't helping. I doubled back into the room, found what I was hoping for, and pulled. The mess rolled over. My fear and revulsion came back, but focusing on getting what I wanted helped.

"Amy—!" The bass and authority in her voice were compelling. But...

I held up Michelle's bloody scarf. I wasn't going to leave without it. "Which way?"

She paused, confused. For the first time since I met Nicole, she seemed unsure of herself: The smoke was thicker, and she looked pretty banged up to me. Her left arm was hanging, a bloody bandage crusted near her shoulder, her hand still bleeding. She was limping. Then she stared at the door and closed her eyes. This scared me.

"It opened in, hinged on the left," she said. "That's the way I came in. I think our girl finally made her entrance."

I nodded. Anything to be out of here.

"Keep as low to the ground as you can," she said, hugging the wall and practically running at a stoop.

I couldn't follow. My head was still woozy from whatever had been in that syringe and what had nearly happened in the other room. Had *not* happened, I told myself fiercely. I was alive still, and I hurt enough to prove it.

I stumbled forward, coughing. I saw a movement ahead and croaked a warning.

Nicole shouted. "Rogers!"

"Raven, here!" She handed Nicole a chain with a thumb drive on it.

"We gotta find Heath," Jayne said, "and we gotta initiate Taps. He knows I'm here, and he'll be waiting."

278 *Exit Interview*

I nodded. "I'll help."

"No!" she and Nicole said at the same time. "You're getting out of here. Can you find your way out?"

I tilted my head toward where we were heading.

"Right. Leave. I'm going back to look for Heath."

"You can't! This whole place is about to go up!" I said.

"He's here. He's here because I told him I was coming. We need to find him."

"We can't stay here," I said. "Let's leave! All of us!"

Down the alley, a container door blew open. The concussion shoved us against the wall, which was now positively warm. I picked myself up and coughed. The air, acrid with God knows what, burned in my nose and throat.

"Get out of here, Amy." Jayne was using the voice of command. "Tell the cops to haul ass to your families' homes. Mrs. Kola threatened them. I assume she meant Maryelizabeth but call them all. I left her in the trunk of my car. Make sure she didn't leave orders for her guys."

I hesitated, just a second.

"We'll be two minutes, Amy. Get out of here."

"Two minutes," I repeated, doubtful, looking at the two of them.

"I promise." Jayne smiled. She grabbed the two of us in a brief hug.

"You did good, Blondie," Nicole said. "Y'know, apart from pointing a gun at me." Grim smile. "Now you go finish, and we will too."

"Make sure to tell them outside that if Heath gets away from us, he doesn't make it to any airports," Jayne said, checking her clip. "You ready, Raven?"

"So ready, Cave Girl."

I watched them take off, instantly obscured by the smoke. They'd made promises before and kept them, too, after a fashion. I was reluctant to leave, but I didn't want to suffocate here if I didn't have to. And I had to warn my family.

A rush of cold air told me I was outside before my eyes finally adjusted to the different lighting. Not fire, but portable lamps illuminating the night. Men with guns shouted for me to get down on the ground. I almost didn't care, the distant nasty airport smell of diesel and tar was so sweet.

More shouting, until everyone was satisfied I was who I was. That I was no danger. Then two EMTs took over, asking questions, taking my vitals, giving me oxygen, which made it complicated to answer the questions from another set of folks who seemed to be reporting to a big guy sweating in a wrinkled suit. Typical career politico.

I managed to tell them about Mrs. Kola's last threat and heard them call the Fairfax County police.

Finally, sending someone off to run another errand, he deigned to glance at me. "This the reporter?" he asked an underling.

"Yes, sir. Amy Lindstrom."

He stuck out his hand. "I'm Matthew Dickens, from the Office of the Inspector General, NSA. Ms. Bradley says you've got a lot to tell us about all of this."

Ms. Bradley? Ah, Nicole. I shoved the oxygen mask aside. "Can't you do anything? To help them?"

"I'm not going to risk any more of my personnel."

"You need to get them—Jayne Rogers, *Dr.* Bradley—out of there!"

"I've already called them back." He looked around. "Someone, get her out of here. Keep an eye on her."

I slumped, and Dickens patted my hand. "They're smart enough to get out when they need to."

Patronizing son of a bitch.

There was nothing else I could do. Outnumbered and outgunned, I let an EMT lead me away. He stopped and turned. I followed his gaze.

There was a creak, like the ice on a pond before a thaw, then an explosion I felt before I heard.

The warehouse roof collapsed.

A series of explosions followed, each worse than the last.

The EMT turned and ducked, instinctively covering his head with his arms. I would have followed suit, but Nicole appeared suddenly at my side, looking exactly like she'd barely escaped a firefight and explosion. She grabbed my arm and nodded to the car. "Get in. You're driving."

"Jayne?" As I got in, I recognized that it was Dicken's car.

She shook her head. "We gotta get Mrs. Kola, make sure she doesn't vanish. Cave Girl told me where she's stashed, but I don't trust that woman, even drugged, cuffed, and locked in a trunk."

"Okay." I nodded. It was better than thinking. And between Mrs. K and Speitzer, I suddenly understood Jayne's consuming obsession with killing someone who really needed it.

Chapter Fifty-One: Jayne Rogers

After sending Amy out, we dive back into the smoke of the main part of the warehouse. I realize how hard it is to breathe. Heath will be breathing it, too. He'll be cleaning up. Looking for me.

The door is locked. Time to stack up, one last time…

Gotta find yourself a better way of thinking, girl.

This time, it's the truth. It's the last time, now or never.

Then make it a good one.

I nod to Raven, and she nods back. It's nice to have someone on my side. For a change.

No point in taking deep breaths. There's nothing to breathe, even with the mask.

The door opens before I can get the first card near the reader.

Heath is holding a Glock.

"Jayne Rogers," he says, like I've shown up at his office door in time for drinks. "Come in."

As if we never parted ways, as if he never betrayed me, never gave me a family, only to take it away with a lie. I know he's under pressure. There's less emotion, less of *him*. Less of the charisma that makes you want to believe whatever he says.

I'm tired, thinking too much. I hesitate.

Raven does not. She steps out of the shadows, shoots him twice, once in the shin, once in the shoulder. That wakes me up, and we bundle him into the office. We cuff him, pat him down: Apart from the Glock, there's another pistol and two flick knives. He likes knives.

"We haven't got a lot of time," I point out. I go in, closing the door behind us. Might as well keep the smoke out a little longer. "He's bleeding too much."

Raven frowns—like, who cares?—then a look of amusement flashes across her face. She reaches into her bag and pulls out something white. "This is gonna hurt. Hold him."

Heath stifles a scream as she applies a minimum amount of first aid: a tampon to stanch the bleeding in his shoulder.

But he's still acting like he's in charge, though. "Gnnnnn! Ah—wait, is that Bradley? Working with Rogers? I'll be a sonofabitch."

"Don't talk about your mother like that." Raven's setting up her notebook, plugging the keys from Chase and Rodriguez, and getting ready to scan his retina and initiate Taps. I concentrate on holding him down.

"How much time do you need?" I ask.

"Once I get the scan, I have to get to my server on the dark net, give the net bots my password, and have them execute. It's ready to go, but it's gonna take some time to get to the server."

"Hurrying would be good," I suggest.

She responds with a high-level stink-eye, but types faster. The pain in her hand and arm are no longer evident: She's running on a high-test combination of pure enthusiasm and outrage with a dash of panic.

"Okay, we're ready to scan. Get his head."

I hold him by the chin, keeping him steady with two fingers hooked under his eyebrows. She scans him, then types again, furiously.

I push him back on the chair, watch his hands without seeming to, getting the whole picture, just as he watches me.

"Look, without me, you're dead, both of you. But we all walk out of here together...I'm betting they'll believe me that this was a deep-cover op to nail Philomena Kola. You'll need work; I have unbelievable opportunities for your skills—if we leave now."

He talks as if I'm no more than a tool, not capable of seeing the big picture, that he'd already ruled us out as employees. I was blind not to see it before,

Dana Cameron 283

conditioned by military training. Conditioned by Heath himself. It gave me a way to deal with the world when I needed it most, gave me a community and purpose when I was at the end of my rope.

I know his offer is bullshit; Raven snorts. Things are happening on her screen now, and she's holding her breath.

I need to give her a few more seconds. I hold up my hand. "Mr. Heath, all due respect. You sent men to kill me."

He shakes his head. "Find you. They were only supposed to find you and Kola's files."

I was such a fool, believing him. But anyone would believe him.

"What about the rest of the Department, sir? Why not let them go their own ways? Killing them, blaming me and fake 'foreign operatives' for their deaths? Forgive me, but that seems way above your paygrade."

"Jayne." His quiet voice is shocked. He sees the look on my face. "Oh, Jayne—you didn't think I was doing this on my own, did you? My idea, but with the full backing of the Executive."

It takes every bit of my training to not freeze up at the thought. It's exactly as bad as I feared. Too many responses rush into my head, but we don't have the time for logic, because smoke is filling up the room. I glance at Nicole, see her smile, then flinch: Her jaw is hurting.

She hits three more keys, then shuts down the notebook. "Well, no need to worry about that now. They've all been dismissed, officially retired with full government perks and some very lovely bonuses."

I want to give her a hug, scream, to celebrate saving all our colleagues, but we're not done yet. "Okay. What next?"

"We get out of here, all of us. Let's go, shall we?"

We hoist up Heath. I can tell he's not ready to give up, but none of us can stay in here much longer. I'm losing my focus; Nicole is beat to shit and so am I.

We frog-march him out of the office, an uneven cadence as we're all limping, down a smoke-filled corridor of containers.

A slight hitch in his step; Raven and I exchange a glance. She nods, barely.

He stomps the foot of Raven's wounded leg, swings his head at me. I see stars as he makes contact. We'd like to keep him alive, and he's not working with that disadvantage. Even wounded and cuffed, he's formidable. He's the one who taught us everything we know about escape and evasion.

He swings an elbow at Raven, who's hanging onto her computer and her pistol and trying to hang onto him.

He runs back in the direction we just came from, away from the front door. "Wait," I say, holding up a hand. "You get out of here. Here's the encryption key to Kola's files."

"You're a mess! He's not going to escape."

"I'm not going to take that chance. Get out of here."

"Stubborn. Bonehead."

"Get your smartass self out of here. I'll be right behind. With Heath."

"If you're not out in—"

"If I'm not out in three minutes, go to my car, get Mrs. Kola. You need to make sure she doesn't run."

She doesn't argue. I'm making sense, and I give her the location of Kola and my car. There's a crash not too far away, and that decides us.

She nods and is gone.

I follow Heath's trail; there's blood here and there, shiny in the emergency lights and fire. I find the crate of Glocks and the fragments of the cuffs. He's free and rearmed.

Just at the door to the empty room, the one that gave me pause before, I see him. I fire. He stumbles. He drops to his back and fires. I'm ready for it. I judge his aim will be a little off to the left. I dive through the doorway to the room on my right. There has to be a reason he chose this spot. Probably going to make a bid for the back exit. Or does he have another escape hatch?

I return fire, enough to keep his head down. He's worried I might actually hit him. I'm younger, faster, but more beat up. He's got age working for and against him, and he's suffered considerable blood loss. He's rested, hasn't been fighting in the smoke for as long as I have.

I don't hear anything. I snap off a few more rounds, change weapons, fire twice. I see him. He's moved. Faster than I thought. He shoots, misses, readjusts—

He's hit me. There's blood every-damn-where.

The impact is like nothing I've ever felt—but I say that every time I get shot. My shirt soaking is through. My arm is pouring red. My chest hurts unbelievably. I didn't expect it to go this way. Not really, not ever. The pain is more than I'd imagined. It's even harder to breathe. I can't make my right arm work at all. For a few scary seconds, all I can do is stare at the pistol, covered in my blood, hanging uselessly in my hand.

I'm not used to feeling like this. With all my experience, this is new to me. *Snap out of it, Rogers. Finish the job.*

I get down behind the wall in a hurry and take up the pistol in my left hand, fumbling. It's slick with my blood. I readjust my grip. There are more shots, too close. There's a scary sound like the warehouse giving up the ghost. That fire is starting to cause whatever's in the containers to...react badly.

I focus. I aim for his hand. It's a wide miss, no surprise. I can't aim anywhere where I might hit something vital.

I have to make Heath leave here under his own steam.

I'm not going to make it out with him.

It narrows my options. I'd love to stitch Heath up, but my goal is to get him out the door. I have to be careful. I keep aiming, a little closer. I nick his hand. He starts to panic. He needs to get out, *now*.

I get lucky. The shots I'm using for cover keep him from getting nearer to me. I nail him and hold my breath. Again, I luck out. It's his wounded shoulder, not his neck or his lungs. That slows him down long enough for him to register what's going on. I take that moment to check my clip.

It's my last. There are two rounds in there. One in the chamber.

I'd like to keep one in case things get very bad, the last option. That's a luxury I have to buy by making the other two count.

The first is a shot at his feet to get him to the back door. It hits—another indication I'm not doing as well as I'd hoped. He staggers forward, uncertain. He can't see me in the smoke and obstructions. He's bleeding lots more now.

He's worried. Good.

I pick my next target with every bit of care and focus I can bring to bear. I'm going to make him pay for what he did to me, to my ideals. If nothing else, he'll have this moment of fear and doubt and then he'll be out of everyone's hair forever.

There it is. I can just about manage it. I squeeze the trigger.

I miss.

It's time.

I drop the gun, reach into my pocket, and press the button. The charges I've set begin to go off. The warehouse is about to collapse, with us in it. Animal instinct for self-preservation kicks in and Heath automatically flees for the door.

The last thing I see is the back of my former boss as he stumbles out to the loading dock.

The job is done. I win.

I crawl deeper into the room. This is where he was heading when he made his play, the room with the cheap wooden door. Movement is awkward. Maybe I'm delaying the inevitable, but I can't give up. It's hard to imagine I've ever smelled anything but bitter smoke, felt anything but this terrible heat. This pain. Even the concrete feels warm. Every movement is harder because of the blood that's everywhere.

I pull the door closed behind me, for all the good it'll do. The room is already hazy with smoke. The barred window is broken, acting like a chimney. Worse luck for me.

I'm dizzy, the kind of dizzy that headshaking doesn't help.

You know, it's not so bad.

It was a good day. I worked to save the lives of my colleagues. Killed a few traitors. Worked and played well with Bradley...

It hurts to laugh.

Amy, hang in there. Testify—

Nicole—

I drag myself to the far wall, near the filing cabinet. It feels oddly cool. I cough and close my eyes for the last time.

Chapter Fifty-Two: Nicole Bradley

I give Blondie the directions, stopping just outside the parking lot where Cave Girl stashed Mrs. K. She was right; the woman is a terror. Somehow, she managed to escape. Three cars surround the one that had been her prison, full of bodyguards. She's castigating two of the men or telling them their next step. The others wait for their orders inside the cars.

"Why aren't we—?" Lindstrom is wound up, beat up, angry, and looking for someone to take it out on.

"Hang on a second. All that time, hanging with Cave Girl has you thinking like her. I have something smart in mind that'll maximize damage, minimize our exposure, and will...well, I think it'll be fun. Be patient. Sit quietly."

She looks at me like I'm crazy, but I don't have time for that. I turn back to my keyboard. I'm delighted to see that the cars driven by the bodyguards are the same ones I saw on the accounts I was looking into.

I spoof the tracking system into believing I'm the monitoring service, and go in through the entertainment centers of the cars. Once I'm there, I...take over the vehicles.

A few more lines of code, and suddenly, I'm the brain inside the cars. It's almost like being a giant mecha, controlling this much steel and circuitry, but I can't afford to have too much fun.

"Here's what we're going to do. I'm about to lock all of the doors and add a little confusion to the mix. I need you to drive over there quickly, so I can take out the ones outside the cars. You just stay put after that; I've sent a text to Dickens telling him where we are and that we'll need help. With any luck, we can contain them until we get backup."

"Just sit here?"

"Yes, when we get there. Quietly. But now, drive!"

Before we can be seen, I lock all the doors to all of their vehicles.

I turn on the satellite radios, pick a tune, full volume. "Bitches Brew." Go get'em, Miles.

Then I deploy the airbags. All of them. I've just told the ACM computers in the cars that they've all been in a massive, multisided collision.

Now, this won't have the same effect as an actual collision, but with any luck, some of the men will have been caught too close to the exploding airbags, maybe some broken noses, some burns. Glasses smashed into faces, if I'm lucky. Organs will be rattled, and there may even be concussions, perhaps. Even if I'm not lucky, chaos will ensue and they'll be temporarily blinded, confused as to what's going on outside and outside the cars. They may be smart enough to break out—assuming they have life hammers in the cars—or dumb enough to try shooting their way out.

"Okay, stop here."

Lindstrom is learning. She does what I say without asking. Even folds her hands over the wheel.

I get out, kneel next to the open door. It takes three shots to dispose of the first guy. The other comes at me.

I use too much ammo taking him down and I have to close on him. I'm really near the edge of being able to manage anything at all. My foot and leg hurt like sin and my back is killing me. I try not to think about my left arm.

Kola takes off.

Before I can say anything, Lindstrom backs up the car and goes after her.

I don't have time to think about that. I finally manage to kill the bastard, and lean against their car, trying to catch my breath. I can't help a giggle as I enjoy the jazz and what I'm watching.

Lindstrom is like a rescued greyhound taking off after a rabbit. Poor kid; I wouldn't have been able to resist chasing Philomena Kola, either.

She's chased Kola to a culvert. Stops the car and goes after her.

This job is indeed rewarding, and I'm sorry to be leaving it shortly. And this—this is the best show ever.

I settle back to watch Blondie drag the other woman out by her hair.

Chapter Fifty-Three: Amy Lindstrom

I got more inches, more ink, more hype than I ever had in my life on the day the first of my articles about Kola ran. I was never so disappointed by anything I'd written. It wasn't my fault: After much wrangling and resistance on my part, I'd signed so many nondisclosure agreements my hand ached and my lawyer could comfortably retire to Monaco for six hundred years. The government's interviewing techniques were less circumspect and calculating than mine, but the sheer repetition of it all was almost like torture. It was terribly effective.

The pieces were vetted by so many three-letter agencies it made all my editors look as though they'd been afraid to use red pencil, flags, comment boxes, and Post-it notes. I missed Jacob's touch. Where once I'd thought of him as a butcher, a vampire capable of draining every bit of blood and life out of a story, now I recalled his slashes of red ink across my copy as gentle hints, nurturing and supportive.

And the other part was: I'd promised Burke he'd get a byline out of it. I do not like working with other people, but he actually...wasn't bad. He had ideas of how to get angles on something I wouldn't have thought of.

As far as the story went, I was in a double bind. Most of what I could write was about my personal experiences, highly expurgated. When I couldn't write about the secret things I knew, the editors told me to put more of my own feelings into it. I hated that so much I realized I had to use it. I stared at a blank screen for a long time, the cursor winking slyly, surrounded by piles of notes and sketches and timelines, and wrote nothing. My dedication was to the truth and accountability; I wanted nothing to do with pouring out my messy feelings into the world.

Jimmy Breslin said something about rage fueling every reporter he'd ever met. He was right about that, if nothing else. If I couldn't write what I wanted, I could write about the insanity of the paltry oversight and checks on intelligence. I could write about the collective psychosis of our present notions of gun control. The need to get behind the international efforts to put teeth into the UN's embargoes. I could renew my interest in Senator Bowen's close connections with Kola. I could write about how a bureaucracy tacked together with the Patriot Act ensured one hand never knew the other even existed. I could write about how I wasn't the story, and yet had to do my part, and challenge the readers to do something, anything, to correct how government worked with business. I could write about the way arms dealers walked the invisible line between legalities and fueling global warfare for personal profit, for so many things.

Finally, I realized that if I didn't completely condone what Jayne and Nicole had done, taking matters into their own hands, I had to do my legally sanctioned job.

When I thought of both officers, I shivered while I smiled.

Jayne was completely missing. Not just lost in that inferno of a warehouse, but from my articles as well. She was the one thing I absolutely could not discuss, exonerated though she was, and it drove me crazy to use elliptical phrases like "intelligence officers uncovered" when I should have been writing things like "and then an operative called Jayne Rogers, straining every interpretation of Executive powers and generally trampling the Constitution all to hell, while violating several local firearms ordinances and all common sense, saved my ass."

Jayne Rogers was dead, and so was Marie Tremblay/Cara Jones and all the lives and lies she lived.

Dr. Nicole Bradley—her I saw once or twice, mostly when I was being interviewed by Dickens, though she ignored me. It kinda hurt my feelings, after all we'd been through. She was doing her job, digging out the truth, probably

Dana Cameron 293

hacking into CERN to check the physicists' math, or crank-calling Putin's cell-phone on her breaks.

I understood that Dr. Bradley stayed long enough to brief Dickens, confirm my testimonies, and then she...vanished. Completely, utterly. Her protective custody detail woke up with sore heads, carefully strapped to the bed of her safe house. Good; she'd done so much to save the lives of her fellow operatives that she deserved her own retirement. I hope it's someplace warm, with good shopping.

When Dickens asked if I had any idea of where Bradley had gone, all I could do was laugh. I realized she'd intentionally kept her distance, so I couldn't be accused of being in on her disappearing act.

Finally, I was able to talk my government minders into letting me go to Jayne's funeral at Arlington National Cemetery. They were going to bury the idea of Jayne right along with her file, but I protested and had gotten her that much.

An honor guard, three guys I assumed were NSA muckity-mucks, and I showed up on a muggy, steamy, rainy day in June to watch a chaplain speak over flag-draped casket. I had a hard time concentrating on the words. My eyes wandered over the rows and rows of headstones, stark white against the grass, the Washington Monument visible off in the distance. I had no idea what would be on her stone, or even if they would erect one. Taps played and the flag was folded. A young Black woman in Army dress greens inspected the flag critically, adjusted one of the folds with white-gloved hands, and then presented it to the potbellied gent in a nondescript raincoat.

"Ms. Lindstrom." The heavyset man called to me after the service. The one from the warehouse and the so-many interviews, Mr. Dickens. "It was nice of you to come. She had no next of kin—"

It was like he couldn't say Jayne's name. Security reasons? Guilt? It offended me to the core.

"— and her colleague..."

"I know. All undercover. Scattered." Good for Raven and Cave Girl, I thought.

"I found your series of articles...provocative."

I smirked. "Nice choice of words. In what sense?"

"Provoking. And...thought provoking. I can't say I agree with you one hundred percent—"

I snorted.

"—but it was fair enough. You did a good job of avoiding what needed to be...kept under wraps."

I shrugged. "Thanks. Wait until you see the book."

He looked up sharply. "Book? You know, that will be subject to the same—"

"Don't worry, I know. But I do think a book's in order. This has all given me a great deal to think about."

Until that moment, I hadn't even considered a book, but it made perfect sense as soon as I uttered the idea. As Jayne had said, not everyone can do what we do. So yeah, I'd tell my side of the story, my feelings, my involvement, everything. It wouldn't have worked for the paper. It would be hard, talking about my own experiences like that, but fuck it: I had a voice. I had to use it. Maybe writing would make me feel less lonely. And watching Dickens flinch was worth every moment I'd struggle with a book.

He fiddled with his watch band. "I'm sure you'll remember all the agreements you signed for us."

"Of course."

Dickens continued. "It will still take a while to root out everyone else Heath had corrupted and to figure out how to implement the oversight to make sure it never, ever happens again."

"And Heath?"

Dickens only smiled. "Quite safe. Ready to stand trial, as soon as he's healed."

"And Philomena Kola, her men?"

"Ms. Bradley had been very helpful; she gave us the files and the encryption. We've been...very busy."

Almost every day, they found another shockingly large hoard. I knew there were close to 875 million guns and light weapons on the planet, 378 million in civilian hands. Kola's inventory was only a drop in the bucket—but an important drop, I kept telling myself. Yet every find of land mines or machine guns or biologicals or hardware or Sidewinders depressed me.

"Too bad Ms. Bradley didn't consider staying with us to help with the mainframes we've been finding."

I looked him in the eye. "I think you should be glad *Doctor* Bradley didn't take it all for herself. I mean, we both know that's not really a stretch of imagination."

He straightened up. "If you ever consider changing careers, come talk to me first."

He handed me a card. I took it automatically. I could feel my mouth open and close, and the bastard had the gall to be amused. All behind the eyes of course.

"Maybe you can find more ways to serve your country than through the press. Technically, we've eschewed use of journalism as a cover, but in your case...your own words would make the best cover ever."

I haven't been absolutely speechless since I was ten, but the audacity of offering me a job in the very field I'd just finished excoriating, that had endangered and killed so many people, some near and dear to me... It simply took my breath away.

"Ms. Lindstrom. Good day." With a tip of his hat, he left me there in the drizzle. He nodded to someone behind me and got into a waiting car. I noticed this time that he had left the driver in the car, just in case I got any ideas about stealing it again.

Burke was suddenly behind me, his carroty hair uncovered against the rain, the only thing that stood out. The rest of him was grayish, forgettable. The glasses gave his face definition.

"I'm surprised you took that," he said.

"I'm not in the habit of refusing cards from important intelligence directors." I stuck it in my bag. "I may need him when I write the book."

"How's the stitches? Your ear?"

I raised my hand to my head. "Still itches. I guess the plastic surgeon did a good job, though. Some hearing loss, tinnitus for miles. I'll live. Burke, why are you here?"

"I'm here for you. Amy, if not a friendly face, then an understanding one. I mean, we've argued over word counts and phrasing. Let me get you a coffee."

I backed away, hands up. "Don't. I don't want...I...can't."

He thought about that for a moment. "I suppose it's easier to keep distance between you and everyone else in the world to keep doing what you do."

I looked away; he was right. He was sopping wet and had hair plastered against his pale, freckled skin. His raincoat was new, but there was a button already missing and his shined shoes were mud-spattered with blades of grass stuck to them. "I can't...because I have therapy. I keep my promises, too."

He brightened. "Good, good! Well, okay, maybe another time, then."

We were at my car now.

I reached out for the door handle and heard the car automatically unlock. "Okay. We'll see. Just...just don't push it too fast, okay?"

"Okay. Great. Good, no problem." He was smiling.

I opened the door, just as he was going in for the hug. "Don't hug the reporter," I said.

"You're right; that means you can't hug me either. How about a handshake? That trample any boundaries?"

"A handshake is okay," I said, and held out my hand.

We shook.

Epilogue: Amy Lindstrom

Maybe it was because she was so completely absent from my story, so thoroughly erased from any record, that I got curious about Jayne and what had happened at the warehouse.

Nothing could have survived that explosion. No one could have, but there should have been some trace of her remains in the warehouse.

So, as a distraction, as a way to warm up in the morning before I started writing my pieces, I went looking for her. When someone doesn't want to be found, it makes me want to find them all the more. It seemed a futile exercise. Everyone else believed she was dead, but that was okay. I'd hunted down dead people before.

If nothing else, maybe I'd be able to flesh out the mystery that was her life. I had some information from her file, the one George had sent me. The file no one else knew I had.

I asked the authorities who knew the story but couldn't pry anything from Dickens or anyone else. They wouldn't let me see Heath's testimony, which I understood, but then they wouldn't even confirm or deny there was a body in the casket I'd seen buried at Arlington. In fact, the more I asked, the more they clammed up, and the more I began to wonder if they knew anything at all about what had actually happened.

I did the other obvious things, too. Dickens had referred to Jayne as an "officer." So had she, back in the cabin. She must have left some bureaucratic trail. I checked the Army, called VA hospitals, approached the Association of Former Intelligence Officers, all with no luck. I called everyone I ever knew who had anything to do with foreign or domestic intelligence, I even called the fake numbers on the resume Jayne had given Jean-Yves the caterer. You never overlook the obvious, just because it's obvious or you might feel dumb asking.

Finally, running out of leads, I tracked down AP, the minivan arms dealer. She remembered me and agreed to call me back on another line, but she needn't have bothered.

"If she's gone, I'm sorry," she'd said. "If she isn't, and I knew, I sure as hell wouldn't tell. I gotta go. My kid hacked the school system computer, 'in protest against the impractical nature of public education.' Little smartass. I'll 'protest' him. I have to convince his principal and the cops he still deserves his shitty public education."

"Hack" and "computer" got me thinking about Kola, his computer, and the encryption key. And that gave me an idea that would either be the solution or mark the unsuccessful end of my search.

The next morning, I went back to Tommy's bench.

The bench was empty. But Kola's mark had been renewed, in what looked like permanent marker.

I drove to the Excelsior Hotel in Pentagon City, and, as calmly if I got encoded messages from beyond the grave every day, found the bartender.

I swallowed, then said, "I think my employer, Mr. Pastorelli, might have left his wallet here."

He nodded and passed me an envelope. I slid a bill across the bar. He made it vanish with a pass of his hand. "I'm sorry Mr. Pastorelli had such a difficult time. He informed me personally he wouldn't be back here again."

"He does have a temper," I said, nodding. I got the message. This was the last time anyone would use this drop.

I drove a ways, making sure as best I could that I wasn't being followed. I pulled over and opened the envelope.

Inside was a cheap postcard of flimsy cardboard. The picture was of a family restaurant outside Annapolis. The back was blank.

My heart soared. Then I was immediately filled with a paranoid dread: Maybe it was from her, maybe it wasn't. But if anyone could have survived the explosion at the warehouse...

Was this anonymous message was like her colorful choice of T-shirt, the night we first met, her way of ascertaining whether anyone was looking for her by making herself obvious? Maybe it was a government trap for anyone who knew too much about the Department or the Kolas. I had no idea what might be waiting for me at the other end. There was no way I wasn't going to check it out.

The next day, I changed into sensible shoes and out of my new favorite T-shirt, the one that said, "Go ahead, I dare you: Plead the Fifth." I found something marginally smarter. With a high neckline. Leaving plenty of time to check for tails—the defensive driving course I'd taken since the night at the warehouse had been very thorough—I hit Route 50 and headed northeast to Annapolis.

I pulled off a small artery and down a secondary road, so beat up it might as well not have been paved. It was rural here, the houses few and far between, set well off the road, backing onto woods or river. The ideal spot for feeding someone to the fish. There couldn't be a restaurant down here. It was too wooded and residential. But sure enough, at the end of the street, jutting out over the river, was the ramshackle joint in the postcard. It looked like it had been kept in repair by a weekend carpenter since the 1970s. The smell of the river, boats and diesel fuel, stale beer and hot cooking oil reached me. Suddenly, I was ravenous.

I locked the car then went up the worn stairs. Brightly colored flowers filled the boxes under the windows. It all seemed overdone, but homey. A local joint, if ever there was one.

The inside matched the outside: neon bar signs, red checked plastic tablecloths, rusticated beams, and "buoys" and "gulls" spelled out in nautical rope letters on signs on the restroom doors. A community bulletin board kept the

Dana Cameron 301

place at "casual family dining by the river" rather than "sleazy joint at the end of the road."

Inside the bar fryolators hissed and a pinball machine pinged. A young woman with short spiky red hair and heavy black-rimmed glasses was playing; one arm in a cast. I took in the green cargo pants, purple tank top, and expensively beaded flip-flops, and almost walked past.

I looked again and saw it was Jayne.

I watched her play. She wasn't very good and lost all three balls within a few minutes.

"If you let the ball hit a little lower on the paddle, you'll get more momentum," I said finally. I couldn't think of anything else appropriate to the occasion.

She shrugged, unsurprised, apparently, to see me. "Of all the things I need to excel at in my life, pinball isn't one of them."

"Yeah, I suppose so."

My eyes filled, and my breath hitched, and without thinking, I hugged her. Surprised, she said, "Hey, there, it's okay," and hugged me back. Her cast whacked me in the shoulder, and I laughed.

"You're looking well," I said. *Not dead,* I thought. *Not blown up, not buried.* "Besides the cast, I can only see stitches by your hairline."

"Yeah, little patch job, a new 'do," she said. "It was a time for a change. Nicole had thoughts on the color."

A young Black woman with block braids, a ball cap, and sunglasses came in through the dock door. She was dressed for a day on the river in shorts and a long-sleeved tee; nearly the same outfit I had. She looked like she was ready for a photo shoot; I looked like I'd been rolling around in the dust kittens under the bed, and her silent appraisal gave me a generous C+ for effort.

"Yeah, but they weren't good thoughts," Nicole said. "Jayne, I filled up my tank and I'm heading out. Blondie. Good to see you."

"Ah, you too." I wasn't sure how to greet Nicole, either. I mean, a hug didn't seem right, and a handshake seemed...cold and weird. We'd been through a lot together, and I still had questions.

"Nic, your food will be up in a minute."

Before I could ask either of them what had happened in the past months, and how Jayne escaped, something gigantic, straight out of Norse mythology came tearing across the floor. I plastered myself against the wall, but Jayne knelt and welcomed the beast. The dog's greeting was ebullient and earnest and quite wet.

It was mutual. I'd never seen her so unguarded as she kissed the dog back—less wetly—and rumpled its fur.

"Who's my good girl? Who's my booful? Look at you, good dog!" Then she spoke in Russian, and the dog sat suddenly, alert, happy to be near her. "Go see Auntie Nic."

The dog greeted Nicole with similar enthusiasm, then back to Jayne. "Meet, Vera."

The dog trotted over, stopping within three feet of me.

"Friend of yours?" I eyed the dog nervously. All of her friendliness seemed to have evaporated. She was very well trained.

"I found her in the warehouse. I don't know what she was doing there, but she sure needed a friend. We needed each other. She alerted me to the filing cabinet that concealed Heath's secret exit."

The dog's fur was shorter and curled in some places than others. It had been singed. One of her ears looked shorter than the other. I noticed shorter patches in her fur and could see faint traces of stitches in her side. She'd been though the wars.

She turned to the dog. "Vera, this is Amy. Amy, Vera. Vera, say hello."

The dog turned and barked once. Jayne gave her a nod, and Vera came over to me. I put my hand out for her to sniff, fingers closed. After that, she trotted back to Jayne's side, and sat, watching us intently.

I'd passed some kind of test.

Jayne crossed to the bar, found glasses, and pulled two beers. "I'm having a beer—want one?"

"No, Blondie's a wine drinker," Nicole said. "Give her something from my personal stock. She doesn't need to drink that boxed swill you keep for the locals."

"That boxed swill pairs nicely with the crab cakes, you snob." Nonetheless, Jayne pulled a bottle with an aged label in French and poured me a glass. She poured one for Nicole without asking.

I took a sip. "Holy shit."

"Yeah, holy shit. It's possible I liberated it from one of the Kolas' warehouses." Nicole looked smug and pleased with herself.

I stared at the glass and took another reverent sip.

"Just the one for her, Jayne," Nicole said. "She's got that book she's gotta write."

"Oh, yeah. Heard about that."

The thousand other questions I had fled, and I looked back and forth between them. They had to be fucking with me—hadn't they? "How do you two know about the book!"

"I know lots of things." Jayne picked up a large bag from the pass-through and handed it to Nicole.

"And I know more than she does." Nicole finished her glass. "I'm outta here, Bam-Bam. Later, Blondie."

"Yeah, we all gotta get back to work," Jayne said. "Vera, come!"
She walked briskly across the bar to the tables, followed by the dog, and left me to scramble after her, if I would. ✳

Acknowledgements

I had a lot of help and encouragement writing this book, and I'm very grateful for all of it. The initial idea came from James Goodwin coming home and announcing that he had wrapped up everything at his old job, and only had the "exit interview" left to complete. Which made me immediately wonder what such an interview would look like for a covert operative...

James Goodwin, Charlaine Harris, Toni Kelner, and Steve Kelner gave me awesome feedback from the start, and read many drafts of this book. John Goodrich, Bracken MacLeod, and Errick Nunnally offered excellent criticism; thanks also to Errick for designing another super cover for DCLE. Thanks, friends.

Many of the "Teabuds" chat group offered advice and assistance: Big thanks in particular to Donna Andrews, Jan Burke, Eileen Dreyer, and Laura Lippman. Cheers as well to Ellen Byerrum, Laura Weatherly, and Ellen Crosby. I may have taken some liberties with what they told me, but as it says on the tin, this is a work of fiction.

I couldn't have written this without some advice from some professional folks who inspired some of Jayne's best lines and badass behavior. They preferred not to be named individually, but have my thanks nonetheless, and the beer's on me, next time we meet.

Clarence Haynes is my amazing development and copy editor, and I always learn something from him. Josh Getzler is my fantastic agent; he and the wonderful Jon Cobb helped enormously with critique, advice, and strategy. Thanks to them and everyone at HG Literary.

Thanks always and especially to James Goodwin, Muse in Residence at DCLE Publishing LLC.

Dana Cameron writes across many genres, but especially crime and speculative fiction. Her work, inspired by her career in archaeology, has won multiple Anthony, Agatha, and Macavity Awards, and her short story "Femme Sole" was short-listed for the Edgar Award. Dana is best known for the Emma Fielding archaeology mysteries (now on Hallmark Movies & Mysteries) and the Fangborn urban fantasy novels. Since she hasn't been doing much traveling or visiting museums, she's been weaving, spinning, or yelling at the TV about historical inaccuracies. You can find out more about Dana and her writing on her author website and blog at danacameron.com.

Printed in the USA
CPSIA information can be obtained
at www.ICGtesting.com
LVHW031546260923
758843LV00005B/16